UNDONE

UNDONE

LESLIE McADAM

HeartEyes
Press

This book was inspired by the True North Series written by Sarina Bowen. It is an original work that is published by Heart Eyes Press LLC.

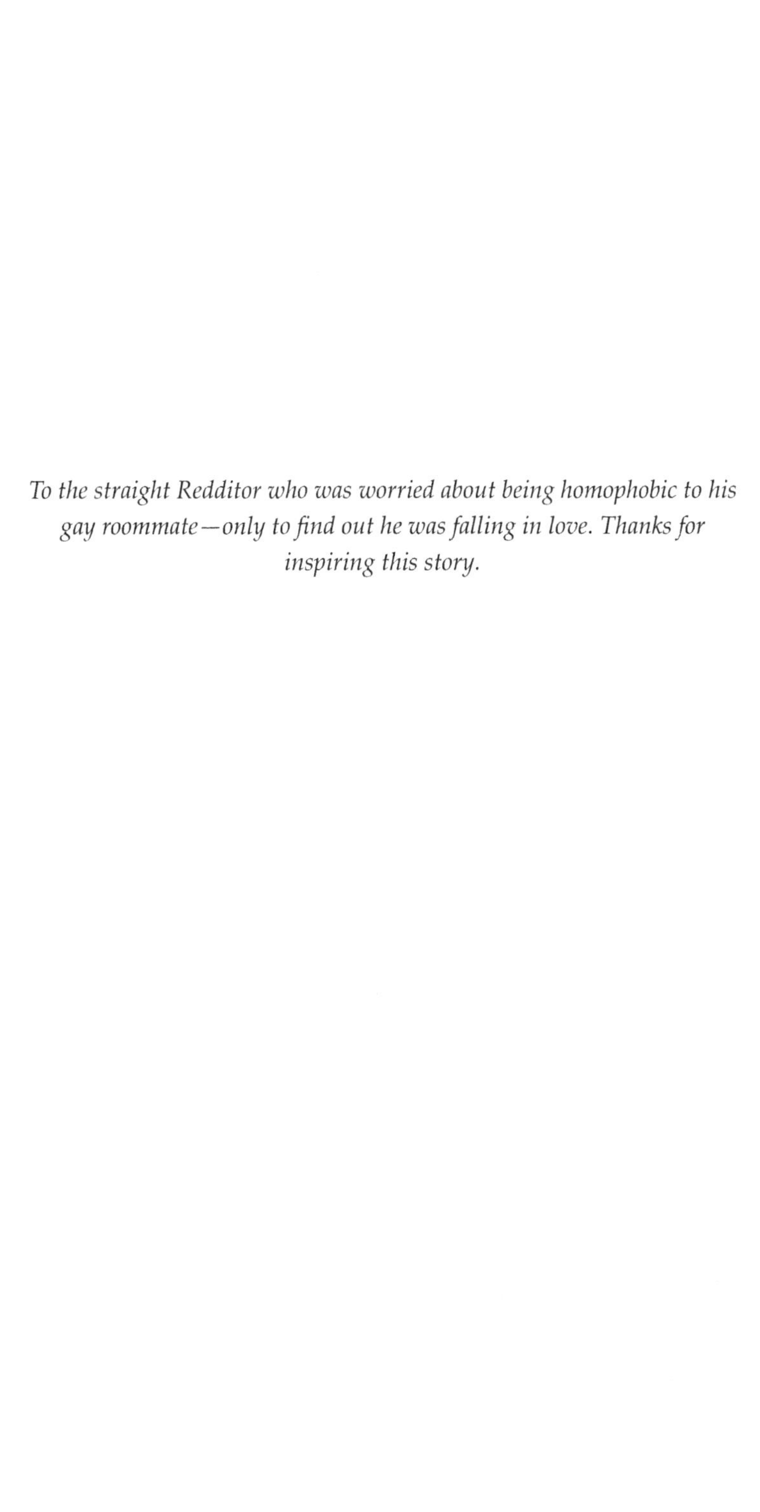

To the straight Redditor who was worried about being homophobic to his gay roommate—only to find out he was falling in love. Thanks for inspiring this story.

JASON

"That was fun," Marnie murmurs. Her naked ass presses against my bare hip. Reaching away from me, she yawns and picks up her phone to check her texts.

Or TikTok.

Or I have no idea what.

I don't know what she's doing, and I'm not really curious. She can scroll on her phone all she likes, because we're done with today's activities.

Activity, singular—a Friday nooner.

I grin at the ceiling, relaxed and content, an idle hand grazing up and down my belly. It's groomed. I'm no Sasquatch.

Drowsy, I smile wider at the randomness of my thoughts—the state of my body hair has to be among the stranger ones—but whatever. I like this postorgasmic mind-wander time. Sex makes me forget about my crappy workweek.

All the crappy workweeks.

And for that I'm eternally grateful.

"Yeah. It was fun," I say.

What do normal people do after sex? Run their fingers through each other's hair? Trace circles on each other's skin? Whisper sweet nothings?

What's a sweet nothing, anyway?

In all the time that Marnie and I have been getting together—a few years now—I've never had a lot to say to her. Or she to me. Between our high sexual appetites and nonexistent need for a relationship, we don't talk much outside of the bedroom. (Kitchen table. Couch. Hallway.)

Don't get me wrong. I'm not unfeeling. I care that she's happy and healthy, and if she needed something, I'd give it to her. She's also very beautiful, so banging her is no hardship.

At all.

I don't, however, envision myself spending the rest of my life with her, nor she with me. I don't feel any spark with her beyond a simple and straightforward fondness. At most, we're friends.

"I'm getting a new roommate," I say to Marnie's spine. Her skin's a rich, dark umber, and I run a finger down her warm back. Not sure why I'm feeling talky.

A long moment passes, so I nudge her.

"What?" Marnie says absently. She stops scrolling and looks over her shoulder at me, only she can't quite see me, so now she's talking to the ceiling.

I repeat myself. "My new roommate moves in today."

That's why I took off work early. But I skipped lunch to sneak in sex with Marnie before I have to go meet the guy and give him the keys. It's convenient hooking up with someone who works from home.

"Greg moved out? I didn't even know."

Maybe I mentioned it. Maybe I didn't.

"Yeah, he's moving in with his girlfriend. Becky found me a replacement. Some guy she met at a bar. He paid first and last and the deposit. Sounded nice enough."

Sounded flamboyantly gay on the phone, but whatever. There was a gay guy in high school I had a lot of classes with, so I got to know him. We'd do homework together. There were plenty around at my superliberal college, too. No biggie.

My sister vetted New Guy, and I trust her judgment. Plus,

she's a realtor who does property management. If she thinks this guy would be a good roommate for me, she's probably right.

"Cool." Marnie's voice sounds distant—even though we're sharing a bed.

"Greg was hardly ever there, you know? The perfect roommate. New Guy will have big pants to fill." I don't know why I can't shut up. Maybe it's dawning on me that I'm going to be living with a guy I've never met. I should perhaps rethink having my sister do everything for me.

"I think the expression is 'big shoes to fill.'"

"Greg was the size of a small elephant, so it's both big pants *and* big shoes."

She giggles. "What kind of elephant big are we talking about here?"

"Man, we get random after we fuck."

"Yeah." She finally sets her phone down and flops over, the tight brown spirals of her long, curly hair bouncing as she moves. Her half-lidded brown eyes widen to catch mine, and she squeezes my hand.

I knife up, breaking the contact, and head to the bathroom to ditch the condom. When I get back, I hunt around for my boxer briefs while she watches me from the bed, legs bent in a zigzag. Perky breasts exposed and vulnerable.

She's so sexy.

Too bad I'm not in love with her. But she's not in love with me, either.

I check my phone. "*Fuck.* I'm running late. How'd it get to be two?"

After I tug on my underwear, I hike my jeans up and lean over Marnie's reclined form, giving her a quick kiss while simultaneously doing my best to pull on my T-shirt. The move doesn't work that well. After I'm all done up, I pause, sitting on the side of the bed to slide on my socks and boots. She wraps her arms around me from behind, resting her chin on my shoulder.

I interrupt my shoe-tying to tug her into my lap. I give her a big hug, my arms wrapping the whole way around her body, then kiss her gently, once. I embrace her again and lay her back on the bed as she smiles.

"You're the best," I whisper in her ear, not knowing if that sentiment goes too far toward the girlfriend scale rather than the land of friends with bennies. But it's the truth.

"See ya later," she whispers back, her eyes closed and her button nose tilted up. And then she fumbles around for her phone again.

I'm dismissed.

After tying my other boot, I skedaddle, closing the door to her bedroom and the door to her house behind me, and climb in my car to go home.

It's a warm August day full of leafy trees and that feeling that school's about to begin. Kids run around, some on bikes and some on skateboards. Or they huddle over their phones.

I pull up in front of my Victorian house and park behind a U-Haul van. I own the whole place, which has been divided into apartments I rent out. I'll be sharing the two-bedroom top floor with my new roommate.

A slim, pale, dark-haired guy hops out of the van. He's wearing skinny jeans, a tight, light-blue T-shirt, and red Chucks.

Must be my new roommate.

Before opening the car door, I study my reflection in the rearview mirror. God, I have sex hair. I do my best to comb it with my fingers, but it's hopeless. Oh well.

I get out and walk toward him.

The precise cut of the guy's hair makes me want to get mine trimmed, although I keep it on the longer side. He's got very blue eyes that gleam from several paces away. And there's a manner about him that's graceful. A dancer, almost. At six-one, I have to have four or five inches on him, at least.

"Hey," I say when I near him. "It's Dave, right? David Murphy?" I extend my hand.

Is he wearing lipstick? Lip *gloss*? I don't know. His cheeks are sparkly with some glitter shit, too.

Not sure I've met a guy who wears makeup before. But his sexuality isn't a problem. I'm not a homophobe.

I care more about whether my roommate has a criminal record and if they can pay the rent, but my sister's skip tracing—fancy background search—takes care of that. I don't want anyone stealing my shit. Other than that, my tenants can do just about anything.

He pauses and grimaces before he shakes my hand, his hand narrow but strong, and I wonder what I've done wrong already. Did he not want to touch me after I messed with my hair? Did he see that?

Then he starts to explain, and I realize that the reaction was for the name, not the handshake. His words all come out in a rush. Like he speaks at one-and-a-half speed.

"My mother named me David, and my last name is really common, so I have quite possibly the most boring name on the planet. Try googling it. There's a million of us Murphys out there. That's the real Murphy's Law. Can you do me a favor and do what most people do? Call me Murph. I'll answer to Davey, too. But only if you're good."

A laugh bubbles out of me at the end of this speech. "Got it, Murph. I'm Jason Falkner. Welcome." I fish out a set of keys from my pocket and hand them to him. "Well, this is it."

"Thanks." The guy hits me with a mischievous smile as he looks up at me and accepts the keys. Then he pulls a key chain from his pocket and threads them on the ring. The plastic rectangle adorning the chain says, *I'm gay, and since we're getting to know each other, I also like nachos.* When he's done, his eyes trace my body from head to toe. "It comes with a built-in handsome man, I see."

I snort, trying to hide a blush. "Right. Only good-looking people live here," I say. Then, realizing he might take my sarcasm as hitting on him, I clarify, "I mean, I'm kidding. Well, you're plenty good looking. But I don't exclude people based on what they look like. Or choose people based on their looks." I let out a laugh. This is hopeless. Murph's eyes are all kinds of delighted at my misery, a hand cupping his mouth to hide his smile, so I change the subject as fast as I can. "You know what? Let me help you with your stuff."

Murph opens his mouth like he's going to protest, then shrugs. "Glad you think I'm hot. And I'm not gonna say no to a kind offer of assistance." He turns and opens the van door, which has a mattress, bed frame, boxes, and suitcases stacked inside.

It's not weird to think he's adorable, right? I mean, anyone would. You could put him in your pocket.

"What is all this, anyway?" I gesture at the open van door.

"Clothes. And more books than I can carry. Don't worry, it'll stay in my room." His eyes twinkle. "What happens in my room stays in my room."

I chuckle and hoist a retro-modern lamp in one hand, in addition to slinging a bag over my shoulder and grabbing a dark gray duffel. "This is Vermont, not Vegas."

"You can take the boy out of Vegas, but you can't take the Vegas out of the boy," he says airily. He picks up another two bags and walks with me up to the front door. I swear he sashays as he moves.

"You're from Las Vegas?"

"Yes, cutie. Mom's a showgirl. Dad's a gambler. Got out of that one-horse town as fast as I could."

"So you came to Vermont." I can barely keep the incredulity out of my voice. While there are gay people in Vermont, I'm trying to remember if I've ever met one as, I don't even know the word—feminine?—as him before. I'm coming up short.

I look over at him, and his grin widens. "Yep."

"From Nevada." My tone remains flat.

"Yep."

I shake my head. "You know there's only one area code,

right?" I gesture with my elbow to indicate all of my home state. "And the most cows per capita in the country."

Now I get a full-on hearty laugh from the little guy, and it's a good one, full of mirth. "I know. I've lived here for a while. I like it a lot."

Furrowing my brows, I try to place him. Burlington isn't that big, and he's the kind of guy who stands out. "My sister says you tend bar?"

"Yes. At V and V." That's Vino and Veritas, the new LGBTQ bar and bookstore. Well, it's not so new anymore. But it's made a splash in Burlington. "I love it there. All the gossip, all the time. Plus the bookstore side is where my heart lies." I keep my eyes ahead and aim for the door, but I can picture his eyes shining, and I can see how the owners would love him. He's effervescent.

He'd talk to each and every customer, remember all their favorites, and know all the goings-on in this part of the world. You can just tell he's a people person.

That's great for everyone *except* someone who keeps to himself, like me.

I exhale and dig out my own keys.

Oh, man. What have I gotten myself into?

2

MURPH

I have a case of the vapors. Watch me hyperventilate before I even make it inside.

It's official. I'm going to be living with the most handsome guy I've ever met.

And because of him, I'm gonna be one horny puppy for the foreseeable future.

I struggle with my bags and follow him up to the large porch of his stately old place. It's painted white with gray accents and very well maintained. He explains which key to use on the outside door, but all I can think while Handsome McHandsomer talks is that he's got striking green eyes and summer-golden skin and his hair is that sort of darkish blondish brownish reddish that can't decide what color it is, so it's all the colors at once.

Jason and the Amazing Technicolor Dream Hair.

And it's long enough to curl behind his ears and at his nape. Like he needs a haircut and can't be bothered to get one, but it's now at the point where it's *fabulous*. Sing that last word with me, darlings.

What does it feel like? Is it soft?

Sheesh, Murph. Of course it is.

I'm so distracted by the beauty that is his hair that I've got no idea what he said, so I guess I'll have to figure out which key to use on my own through trial and error. Apparently there's some trick to it. I'm not gonna learn it today, children.

Plus, I'm out of breath. I packed heavy. Clothes are my weakness—or one of them, along with sangria, fantasy novels, and burly Vermont men.

But I'm not panting because of my luggage. I'm in great shape.

I'm panting because of him.

He apparently assumes that I listened, so he picks up the duffel he set down and continues up an interior flight of stairs.

There's one apartment on the bottom floor, rented to Moo U graduate students, and another on the second, leased to a pilot. We're on the third and have this grand oak staircase to go up to get there.

This place is so cool! I'm giddy, now for more reasons than one.

Last week, after meeting his sister, I'd talked with Jason on the phone, but he'd sent her over to show me the place, because *apparently* he had to work and couldn't get away to give me the tour. *Apparently* he was too busy to bother interviewing someone who was going to live in his own damn home.

I personally like to know who I'm sharing my toothbrush cup with, but I liked his sister and fell in love with this place—the building's beautiful—so I went with the mystery.

And oh man, have I scored.

I do have a minor complaint already, though.

When his sister and I went through the place last week, she showed me the nice-sized bedroom with a surprisingly big closet, the vintage kitchen, and the gorgeous view of the woods. She was sweet. Becca, was it? Becky?

Anyway, she's now lost all credibility, because she didn't mention during the walk-through—I'm serious, not one single word—that her brother's a total snack.

Who I will be living with.

Sharing a bathroom with. Sharing a shower with. Sleeping with. *Correction.* Not sleeping *with.* Sleeping next door *to.*

Stop it, Murph. Stop it.

But he's grade A steak, and I want a bite.

We keep going upstairs, and I almost groan thinking of all my precious belongings that I've got to drag up here. I could downsize, but you never know when you'll need vintage Pucci. So I'll suffer a harder move today for all the joy my wardrobe will bring me tomorrow and in the days to come.

Tra-la.

In my head, I sound like I'm living in some historical novel with a dashing hero, looking forward to getting my "and they lived happily ever after." That would be fun.

Too bad it's not happening. Especially not with a heterosexual male. Because with the way Jason reacted to my flirting—stuttering rather than playing along and sassing me right back—he's straight. Or on the ace spectrum, I suppose.

"How long have you lived here?" I ask Jason's behind instead, following it up the second flight of stairs.

I'm quite happy to be having a conversation with his taut, juicy ass. It's cradled in dark denim and exposed when his T-shirt rides up as he climbs the steps. I'd like to be on a first-name basis with that ass. Hey, a boy can dream.

"Two years," he rumbles. I don't think the growly tone is directed at me in particular. It's just the way he talks.

Yummy.

I want to pepper him with questions just to hear that voice. Or tease him until he babbles.

Flustered Jason has immediately become my new favorite thing.

I follow manly man up the last flight of stairs to our (yes, in my head it's ours—*squee*!) apartment. When he gets up to the top floor, he opens the door, and as I remember, it's *delightful.* Sing that, too.

Not as delightful as Jason. But close.

Even though I'm breathless, you can't shut me up. "I like old houses. Not too many of those in Vegas growing up. More likely to see a fake indoor Parisian street than a house that's over thirty years old. I like that a lot of people have lived here before. The house has gotten accustomed to people and knows how to behave. Unlike me." I wink.

He laughs and heads into the room that's my new home. It's empty, so now it's up to me to turn it into something. "I like old houses, too. Grew up in one. Bought one. People say they've got character. But I don't think of character as crooked floorboards and lots of molding. To me, character is the house taking on the personality of its owners. If they were nice or cool people, then it's a nice or cool house. Reasonably happy people must have lived here before, so it's a reasonably happy house."

"I've never heard anyone else phrase it that way. Most people are just scared of ghosts."

Jason shrugs. "Guess it's been my experience."

This is something I like about meeting new people—learning the way they look at the world. Jason gives me the impression that he listens more than he talks, and when he says something, it matters.

He carefully sets down my bags and lamp at the far end of the room and stands there, larger than life—really, he seems to take up more space than he occupies—with his hands crossed over his chest.

That's a broad, meaty chest. I like.

"Thanks," I wheeze. "I can take it from here."

"Nah. I'm here to help. I'll go get some more of your stuff."

I watch his back disappear out of my bedroom and then, after catching my breath, chase him down the stairs.

This is going to be a *lonnng* year.

In the most delicious way possible.

A few hours later, all my things are in the room. We centered the rug on the floor, and it lies under a bed that we're almost done assembling.

Currently, Jason's sprawled on my floor mechanic-style as he screws the sideboards to the headboard. I'm holding the two pieces together for him like I'm at a perfume counter handing out samples.

While all I want to do is straddle him. I mean, he's just lying there on his back, waiting to be ridden.

Down, boy, I scold myself, and adjust my jeans.

In addition to a library's worth of books, Jason helped haul up the mattress and the dresser. Navigating the stairs with the box spring turned out to be tricky, but we managed not to punch a hole in it or the walls, so I count that as a win.

Plus, I got to see his biceps flex. Bonus.

"I'm normally not this much of a wuss," I say, as I hold the pieces together while he uses the drill. "I, you know, lift weights and stuff."

That's a lie.

"You do?"

"No," I admit instantly. "But I like to run. And if you take me out, I'll dance with you."

I expect him to tell me he doesn't take men out, but instead he asks, "How were you going to move all this in without me?" With a big hand, he gestures to everything piled in my new room.

My first thought is that I never want to do anything without him ever again. But that might be coming on a tad strong, especially since he's my landlord.

Like that's the only reason not to flirt with him. I might as well flirt with a mirror—then at least I'd know I was talking to a gay boy.

I shrug. "I suppose I'm like Blanche DuBois in *A Streetcar Named Desire*. 'I've always depended on the kindness of strangers.'"

His voice drops an octave and gets even gruffer. I had no idea that was possible. "My pleasure. I'm happy to help." He sits up and dusts his hands off. "All done. Now you've got a place to sleep."

"Or do other things."

Shit. I said that out loud. In a singsong voice.

Change the subject, Murph.

Jason only smiles and gazes at me like I'm some fascinating specimen. Like he doesn't know what to do with me.

It's an almost indulgent look, and it makes me really happy.

"Am I keeping you from something? Work?" *A girlfriend?* Yeah, I'm fishing and deflecting. Two of my many talents that involve my tongue.

But I don't want the confirmation about women. Not yet. Let me have at least one day of fantasy.

"No." He starts tugging the box spring onto the bed frame. I guess I should help instead of standing here watching his back muscles tango under his shirt. Together we maneuver the box spring into place and set the mattress on top. "Took the afternoon off to help my new roommate move in."

"I'm gonna tell your sister you played hooky. She said you work too much."

He closes his eyes and smiles like he's going to throttle her the next time he sees her. "She's always on me about that. I'm fine. But no, I'm not working for the rest of the day."

"And you've spent your day off helping me move. Thank you."

"My pleasure."

I like the way he says that. So many people say, "No problem," but that implies that whatever you thanked them for could be a problem.

Being Jason's *pleasure*, though?

That's *tempting*.

After we've set up my furniture and double-checked that everything is out of the van, Jason doesn't stop being awesome.

He helps return the U-Haul and then takes me to my old place to pick up my car. I swear he's the perfect man.

Perfect except that he likes girls.

Most likely.

I mean, he could still be perfect if he likes girls. If he's bi or pan, that would be … *happy sigh*.

Of course, this is the All About Murph perspective. In general terms, he's perfect whether he's straight, ace, or anything else.

All I mean is I don't think he will like *me* that way. And I wish he would.

Goddess, sometimes I can spin in circles inside my head. Jason's not the only one who gets flustered.

When we're all done, he stands in my doorway and surveys the clutter I have to go through. "Need any more help?"

I'm bent over, ass up, as I dig out my sheets and pillows to make the bed. "Nah. Now I just need to figure out where everything goes."

"Well, let me know if there's anything else I can do." He gestures to the room across from us. "Need the bathroom? I'm gonna take a shower."

I grab a purple pillow and hold my breath to suppress a groan.

Having Jason's nakedness right behind a door—even a heavy oak door with charming, reasonably happy Victorian character—is gonna be agony. I tell you, I'm a horny puppy over here.

"Nope," I say primly. "I'm good." I go to grab more pillows, but his voice stops me.

"Have you got anything to put away in the kitchen?" He glances over my things.

"No. I'm not that great of a cook, but I was going to go shopping later and pick something up. Or I could order pizza for us, to thank you."

He nods, like he's making a decision for me. "Don't bother. I'll make dinner."

My eyes widen. "You cook?"

"Yeah, I really enjoy it."

"Did you do this for your old roommate?"

He pauses. "Sometimes, yeah. Grew up cooking for my sister, when my mom left. Just kinda got used to being in charge of feeding everyone. Pasta okay? Are you allergic to anything?"

His mom left? I'll have to ask him about that when we know each other better.

"I'm only allergic to mean people," I say. "And you're not one."

He laughs. "Okay, I'm gonna get cleaned up and start dinner. Let me know if I can help with anything else."

I watch his fine posterior as he pivots and heads into the bathroom, then sit back on my heels and try to figure out which box to open next to find my duvet.

I'm buzzing with excitement from the move, and I'm also worn out. I can't wait to get started unpacking, and I really need a nap. I want to hurry up and hang out with my new roommate and also close my door and figure out the answer to the following equation: cute, straight Jason plus cute, gay me equals what, exactly?

Can't figure it all out today, children.

My back's sore from all the hoisting and lifting, and my hands ache from packing and moving all my worldly possessions.

Or maybe they hurt in some sort of psychosomatic anticipation of how much I'm going to be jacking off, dreaming about my hot housemate. I should invest in tissues and lotion now, because the market forecast calls for supply to go down and demand to skyrocket up.

That's not all that's gonna be up.

I sigh and open another box.

This is going to be torture.

3

JASON

I wrap a white towel around my waist and rub my fist in a circle on the fogged-up bathroom mirror to study my face.

At least I don't have sex hair anymore. My scruff will need to be trimmed soon, but I can let that go a little longer. I look good enough, I guess.

Although it's only Murph out there. Not like I have to impress him. He'll have to get used to me being, well, me.

Opening the bathroom door, I exit to go to my bedroom to get dressed.

Murph is sitting cross-legged on his floor across the hall, surrounded by piles of neatly folded clothes. His legs look bony in his jeans, and his lean arms are fussing with fabric. His dark head tilts up as he hears me, and I don't miss the slow sweep of his eyes from my head to my feet, lingering on my torso and my towel.

A missed drop of water trails down my chest, and I wipe it away.

Murph licks his lips. I can almost see the resolve on his face as he swivels his head, picking up a stack of shirts and setting them to the side.

It takes all my acting ability to maintain a poker face until I get to my room.

I'm going to have to get used to that. I don't usually mind being ogled—not that there's that much to ogle, though I stay in decent shape by running and keeping active.

Dropping my towel, I step into navy blue sweats.

Does it bother me that Murph looked at me that way? Like he wanted to have me for dinner instead of the baked ziti I'm planning to make?

I tug a battered old gray T-shirt over my head while I consider the question. Because now that I'm living with a guy who's into guys, I have to sort out my thoughts on the matter.

If my roommate were a woman and she checked me out, would it bother me?

No. I'd be flattered.

So I guess I'm flattered by him as well. This doesn't have to be complicated.

I take my towel into the bathroom and hang it up. Murph's still on his floor sorting clothes, either absorbed in what he's doing or ignoring me.

I'm not scared he's going to put the moves on me or anything. *Obviously*. Since he knows I'm straight.

At least, I assume he knows that.

Shit, maybe I should be clear with him. So he doesn't think there's any chance—

Jesus, Jason. Not everyone wants to bang you.

I don't know why my brain is getting all weird like this. And I'm not sure how to bring it up in conversation. *Hey, Murph, I know you're gay, but don't try anything.*

Yeah, that sounds like an utterly arrogant thing to say. It assumes he wants me and, moreover, that he'd act on it.

Neither of those assumptions is accurate, I'm sure.

Well, if it comes up, I'll tell him. Otherwise, no need to make things awkward.

I pad out to the kitchen. It's dinnertime, and I'm hungry. Between Marnie and Murph, I've been busy all afternoon—both activities fun in their own way—and I haven't eaten since breakfast.

Soon I've got sauce simmering on the stove, browned meat soaking up the tomatoes and spices. The kitchen smells delicious, and my stomach rumbles. I pinch some cheese from the pile I grated and pop it into my mouth.

Murph walks into the kitchen to help, but I shoo him out, handing him a beer and snacks. I opened the bottle for him—I swear he almost gets misty-eyed when he notices—and he goes to sprawl on the couch, feet on the beat-up coffee table, selecting one kernel of kettle corn at a time to munch on and scrolling through suggested movies on Netflix.

While I watch him.

"I had no idea this room came with board," he mumbles. He's changed into a cream kimono with large flowers on it. Maybe peonies? Sunflowers? Big flowers, at any rate. Under it, he's wearing a loose white T-shirt with one of those necklines that slips down the shoulder and a pair of blue satin pajama pants. With matching slippers.

Murph's kinda lovable in an over-the-top way. I can see how him being in your face with his gayness would spook straight guys who aren't secure in their sexuality. But I find him entertaining and am watching to see what he'll do next.

He's just so … *him*. I don't know if I'd ever be brave enough to wear anything other than, well, jeans and T-shirts. Or suits.

Murph was born to stand out, though.

"Don't get used to me feeding you," I grumble, not meaning it.

Actually, I love to cook, and I particularly love having someone besides myself to prepare food for. So in all probability, Murph will be getting used to my cooking, which alternates between old standbys like tonight's dinner and experiments I find on recipe sites. For a first night, I'm not doing anything weird. That'll come later, when we know each other better.

By doing anything weird, I mean *cooking* anything weird.

God, my brain's gone all kinds of haywire.

"Jason, I wouldn't dream of taking advantage of you." His voice is low, a kind of thrum.

Wait, what? I have to remember what I said, since I'd gotten lost in my thoughts.

He's watching the television screen, which gives me an opportunity to look at him without getting caught.

I like his face. Whatever the opposite of RBF is, Murph's got it. It's like he radiates joy.

If only I could tap into some of that joy. But spending all day studying actuarial tables and telling people they're going to die, so they should buy life insurance from me, isn't conducive to happiness.

Not for the first time, I wonder if I should look for a new line of work. But then what would I do?

My new roommate stifles a yawn.

"Are you beat from today?" I ask.

"What?" He tilts his head to the side, finally catching my gaze, and sucks his lips in as if he's stopping himself from grinning.

"Are you tired? From the move?" I turn my back to him and check the pasta water.

"I am." He sighs dramatically. "I may never leave this couch. I'm stuck. Like an iron-on patch on a pair of jeans."

I snort and look at him. "If you're gonna use the couch as your bedroom, that'll be extra rent."

"Ha ha. No. I can make it to my bedroom by the end of the night." His eyes dance, and he takes a pull of beer from the bottle. "I think my muscles found muscles they didn't know existed and had a fight."

God, this guy. I return to the stove and grin into the sauce I'm stirring. He makes me laugh, and I don't have a lot of people in my life who make me laugh. I crouch down and pull out a pan to assemble everything for the pasta.

"Also, in case I pass out?" Murph continues.

"Yeah?"

"Dinner smells amazing, this place is gorgeous, the rent's fair, and you're the nicest roommate I've ever met."

Something inside me bubbles up at his kind words, and I get this warm feeling all over my skin. I like how genuine he seems to be under the sparkle. But all I say is, "I appreciate that."

He gestures at the plates we're using. "Those are really unusual. I like them."

"Thank you."

"I bet there's a story to them."

"There is." I grin. I wait to see what else he says about them, but he moves on to another subject.

"I loved my last place—I lived with my best friend Reeve—but he went and fell in love with his boyfriend, so ..." He shrugs. "I'm just glad you had space."

"My roommate needed to move, too. Everything seemed to work out."

Murph gazes at me. "Yeah. Something like that." He sits up straighter. "Tell me about yourself, Jason Falkner. Like, where do you work?"

"New England Life and Casualty," I rattle off absently, now paying attention to dumping pasta in the boiling water and setting the timer for it to cook.

He's quiet, so I glance over at him, wondering why. He blinks at me. "Isn't that, like, insurance?"

"Yep." I turn the knob on the oven so it will preheat.

"So you're an insurance salesman?"

"Yep."

He makes a show of looking around. "Is this 1950?" Lowering his voice, he stage-whispers, "Are you the man in the gray flannel suit?"

I snort. "That's ... Cary Grant? Or, no, Gregory Peck? Not quite. Though I do usually wear suits to work. I only wore jeans today because I figured I'd be helping you move." Making my way through the kitchen, I stir the sauce, add more salt to the pasta water, and pull out salad fixings from the fridge. In some ways, cooking is choreography. "And the firm has been around since the fifties. It's where my dad works. And my granddad used to."

"Do you like your job?"

The question knocks me back. "I'm not sure. I kind of think it's slowly killing my soul, if you must know."

Saying the words out loud gives me a sour feeling in my stomach.

"I'm sorry," Murph says simply.

"But I know how to do it—it's familiar, I mean—and it pays well. Money matters."

"Tell me about it," he groans. "I love Vino and Veritas, but right now I don't have enough hours to bring in enough moola to keep a girl in sequins and nail polish. So, like everyone, I've got a side hustle. Multiple, actually. Web design is the biggest. But don't worry about the others," he says, sotto voce. "I almost never have to resort to harvesting people's organs to make rent. And when I do, I always clean the tub afterward."

I can't help my laughter. He joins me, and I think this arrangement is going to work out. At least, it's a good first day with a new roommate.

When I'm finally composed again, it's time for the pasta to be drained, and I assemble the baked ziti.

After I slip our dinner in the oven and toss a salad, I plop on the chair across from him with my own beer and put my feet up on the coffee table. I go to reach for popcorn, but my phone buzzes. I pull it out of my pocket, and Marnie's name flashes on the screen.

"Girlfriend?" Murph asks. He crosses his arms.

"More like friends with benefits," I mutter. Or fuck buddies. But friends with bennies is more polite. "Her name's Marnie."

She wants to know if I'm available tomorrow afternoon.

Am I?

Jason: Not this time

Jason: Still moving in my roommate

Marnie: K

I'm not sure why I turned her down. Guess I don't feel like fucking her tomorrow.

Marnie: Next Friday?

Jason: Ok

"Ah," he says and turns back to the television screen.

I can't help but think confirming I've got a girl I'm intimate with disappoints him. But his flirting with me will go nowhere, so it's good that he knows about her.

Now that's over with, I relax into the chair. I hadn't realized how tense I'd been, thinking I had to explain my sexuality to him.

Although he doesn't have to explain his to me.

I've been overthinking this.

Still, I'm glad he's here, and I hope we can be friends. He amuses me, and I can use some levity in my life.

"What's your schedule like?" I ask, and he launches into telling me his hours at V and V and the time he spends on web design.

"Sounds like you're a busy guy," I say, impressed.

"Never too busy for you, sugar." He winks.

His winks don't make me feel uncomfortable. If anything, they make me happy. Like, aww, that's Murph.

He's certainly the most chipper person I've ever hung out with, and his energy's contagious. Time slips away as we talk, until the buzzer goes off and it's time to eat. I fill the plates with food, then serve him one.

"Did you grow up around here?" he asks as we sit at the table across from each other.

"Yeah. My mom's parents are French Canadian, but they moved to Burlington before she was born. My dad's family already was from here—like I said, insurance has been the family business for generations. They're separated, though. My mom took off when I was young."

"I'm sorry to hear that. My parents don't get along that great, either."

"No?"

"A gambler's hard to live with," is all he says. "Did you go to school here?"

Clearly, he wants to change the subject. "No. I went to Brown. Studied philosophy."

"Oh, fancy-pants."

I chuckle. "You're the one with the fancy pants," I say, leaning over to eye his satin pajama pants under the table.

His eyes widen, and I can tell he's biting his tongue to keep from making some flirty comment. "Did you like school?" he asks instead.

I nod. "I did. I took some pretty esoteric classes, and I was friends with a diverse group of people. It was just so beautiful, and the classes challenged me. I liked being somewhere where what you thought mattered. You know?"

"Yeah." He takes a bite of the pasta. "This is so good. Seriously."

"Thanks. Did you go to college?"

"Two years at UNLV before I dropped out."

I frown. "Why'd you drop out?"

He rolls his eyes. "School wasn't really for me. I get it, you know? I get that part of going to a four-year college is about stick-to-itiveness. But I've always been easily distractible, and sitting in classrooms didn't work for me."

"I understand that."

"So I quit and got a job in a casino, because Vegas. I bartended for a while. But then I thought I needed to figure out something about myself and get away from that place while I could. A friend of mine from college had moved to Vermont for law school, so I followed her. When she went back to Vegas, I stayed."

"A female friend, huh?"

He nods. Then he visibly steels himself to share the next part. "Actually, there was a guy, too. Her brother. My friendship with her covered up the fact that I was dating her brother, who went to the same school. And it got ugly."

"Why?" My fingers form fists. I force myself to relax them.

"Because he was so far in the closet, no organizer would've found him even if they'd tossed everything out. He was stuck in the back. Like in a panic room *above* the closet."

I don't laugh. "He wasn't public with you?"

"He was barely private with me. And it sucked, because I liked him. A lot. But he was ashamed." Murph gives me a brave grin. "How could you be ashamed of all this?" He gestures down his body.

"I wouldn't be," I say seriously. "And he has shit for brains if he didn't treat you the way you needed to be treated. The way you deserved to be treated."

"Well aren't you all Sir Jason the Gallant? So *chivalrous*." He pretends to swoon, falling back in his chair with his hand on his forehead.

"No," I scoff. "Only a human being with some morals. I hate that shit. When someone likes something but denies it because they're scared they're going to get teased. A girl 'too old' for dolls who wants to play with them anyway, or a guy who prefers poetry over sports. Then, when they're older, the habit of pretending they don't like it stays, and it sucks. They should be proud of who they are. If we were all the same and liked the same things, imagine how boring the world would be."

"Preach it, knight in shining armor," Murph says and lifts up his hand for a high five, which I dutifully give him, trying not to crack up. The high five turns into a quick hand squeeze, and then he lets go. "You're an upstanding guy, Jason."

"Thanks. I try. You're not so bad yourself."

"Oh, no. I'm *extraordinary.*"

"Yeah," I admit. "You are." But I wonder how much damage it did to Murph to date someone, even follow him across the country, when he wouldn't admit publicly that he liked Murph. Whoever dates Murph needs to accept him fully. That's basic human decency.

I frown, and Murph notices. "What's wrong?"

"Just thinking about your asshole ex."

"Oh, don't bother. I've totally forgotten about him. Tra-la. He's gone. Poof!"

But Murph's light words don't fool me. I think he's scared of being hurt again.

I may know something about that, too.

After dinner, which he describes as "the best thing I've ever put in my mouth, and that's saying a lot," he tries to kick me out of the kitchen to do the dishes. I'm not used to anyone doing things for me, so I butt in. He washes, and I dry. There aren't enough dirties to put in the dishwasher, so we do everything by hand.

I package up the leftovers for my lunch and make him one, too, showing him where I put the container in the fridge.

"Well, this is cozy," he says, nudged up beside me as we peer into the refrigerator together. I'm aware of how much smaller he is than me. And my hip accidentally grazes his butt as I close the door. "You're so thoughtful, looking out for me like that."

His blue eyes catch mine, and heat gathers in my cheeks. "Pshaw. It's nothing. Just leftovers." But Murph's reaction makes me think that for him it means something more.

It's the first night with a new guy in my space. And strangely enough, while I'm aware of him, it's no big deal. He's quiet, and we go to bed around the same time.

I want to go knock on his door and check on him, but that's a weird move, right?

Just as I'm about to get up and see if he's got everything he needs, my phone lights up on the bedside table.

Marnie: I have to cancel Friday. Gotta go see my sister in Syracuse. She's having a baby and the doctor told her she needs to have bedrest

Jason: Oh shit. I'm sorry. Is she going to be okay?

Marnie: I think so. She's at 36 weeks, so not that much more to go

Jason: Wait, isn't that like nine months? Is she about to pop?

Marnie: Silly boy. Babies come out at 40 weeks

Jason: I knew that

Jason: Actually, I didn't

Jason: And you knew that

Jason: I mean you know that I didn't know that

Marnie: LOL

Marnie: Anyway, sorry, I'm going to be scarce on week-ends for the next month or two. That gonna be okay?

Jason: No problem

Huh. No fuck buddy for a while. I feel … nothing about that. I wonder if I should start looking for an actual girlfriend instead of a sex partner.

Or if I should be by myself for a while.

That thought sobers me, and I fall into a restless sleep.

4

MURPH

It's the morning, and I'm perplexed about where I am. Who I am. Why someone is bothering me.

Then I remember I'm in a new home. A new bedroom. New light pouring through new-to-me windows.

Every part of my body aches from moving.

I groan. I think a knock on the door woke me up, but I can't be sure.

Not until after I've had coffee.

"Murph? You awake?"

Oh my sweet heavens. Is it my beautiful roommate-slash-man-of-my-dreams Jason Falkner? Hovering at the door to my bedroom?

And why the hell is he doing it this early in the morning? I mean, if he'd been at my bedroom door last night, this would be an entirely different conversation. But now, in the light of day? A girl needs rest.

"No," I mutter into my pillow.

A low, already-familiar chuckle reaches my ears. "I heard that. Come with me," Jason coaxes from behind the door. "It's a gorgeous morning. Let's go somewhere. Get out of Burlington. Can I come in?"

"Mumph," I say from under my covers, curling up like a pill bug.

"I'll take that as a yes."

It's certainly not a no.

I hear the door open but make no move to emerge from my duvet cocoon. "Is it daylight? I'm only fully operational in the dark."

He chuckles again, and the warmth of his tone reaches somewhere deep inside me. I shiver, but I am very very far from cold.

"Is this normal roommate behavior?" I grumble. "To wake me at no-way thirty in the morning?"

But before I can get too grouchy, I push the comforter off my head and open my crusty eyes to see him stretched out in the doorway of my room. His hands hold either side of the doorjamb, and I don't know if I've ever seen anything prettier on a Saturday morning.

What right does he have to be all glowy and standing in my door? My gaze travels up his tight black T-shirt to his scruffy face and down to his dark jeans, and good gracious I have a hard-on. I grunt and roll onto my stomach, closing my eyes again.

His voice is cajoling. I can hear the grin, even if I can't see it. "Mur-rph."

"Don't know anyone by that name, sorry."

"There's a great farmers market today in Norwich. C'mon. You know you want to come. What else are you doing today?"

"Why do you want to drive that far? Isn't there a closer place to buy food? Isn't there a farmers market in Burlington? Like, today?"

"Sometimes I just like to go for a drive. Get out of town. And it's the mother ship of farmers markets. We can stop off in Colebury for breakfast at this great place I've heard of. I'll buy you coffee."

I open one eye. "You speak of the nectar of the gods?"

Jason laughs, a full-on laugh, and it's the most beautiful thing

I've heard in the morning. Like, ever. "I do. Come on. I don't feel like going alone today. And it'll be fun."

I heave a heavy sigh, but honestly, I'm excited. By the time we go and come back, it will be hours and hours with Jason.

If my charming roommate wanted to take me to get elective surgery and then file a few tax returns, I'd still probably love hanging out with him. "Okay. Give me a few."

He turns to go but then looks back at me, a hand on the top of the doorway. Exposing a sliver of his toned stomach.

Goddess, does he know how sexy he is? It's like he's posing, only I know he's not.

He gives me a hard stare.

"What?" I ask, trying to not sound defensive and failing miserably.

"You'll just take 'a *few*'?"

Yawning into the mattress, I snort-laugh, and it's kind of embarrassing, because princesses don't snort. "Okay, yes. True. I'm a little high-maintenance. You love me anyway. I can be ready in under an hour."

"I'll be waiting."

Forty-seven minutes later, I'm sitting in the front seat of Jason's car as he deftly navigates us through the leafy Vermont-ness. I'm surprised by his choice of music—*Hamilton*.

"You like musicals?"

He reddens. "A little."

Huh.

We drive on Vermont's main highway until we get to a bakery, the Busy Bean. We step inside to the good smells of fresh bread and hot dirty bean water.

"My treat," Jason says. "What do you want?"

"Will you marry me?" I ask as I yawn, rubbing my eyes.

Jason laughs. Then he turns to the cashier, who I recognize. "We're together. I'd like coffee, black, and a sourdough bagel, toasted, with cream cheese." With his chin, he indicates that I should order.

"Hey, Roderick," I say. "Can I have the same?"

Jason stares at me.

"What?" I ask.

"No latte or something fancy?"

"Nope." I chose the same thing as him partially to not be rude by ordering something more expensive. But it's also because I genuinely don't like things that are all that sweet.

Except for my landlord, of course.

Don't get me wrong. I'm happy with an occasional umbrella in my drink. But I don't need everything to be filled with sugar all the time.

"Coming right up," Roderick says. He glances between us, and his tone goes all flirty and kind of accusing. "Where are you two going? Is this your new man, Murph?"

Before I can open my mouth, Jason lets out an embarrassed noise. "No, we're only roommates. He moved in last night."

"Too bad."

"Thought we'd go for a drive. We're headed to the farmers market in Norwich." Jason glances between us and turns to me. "I didn't realize you knew people in Colebury."

"This guy?" says Roderick, giving me a wink that means nothing, because I know how devoted he is to his other half. "Murph and I go way back."

"I've been your bartender, what, twice?" I deadpan.

It's been a couple more times than that. Besides, while not every gay guy in Vermont knows every other one, Roderick's partner, Kieran Shipley, is in a well-known family. His … cousin, I think, sells prize-winning cider. Wouldn't surprise me if there was a Shipley contingent at the farmers market today.

Roderick says something back, but I tune him out. Then he and Jason start chatting.

But I'm still staring at Roderick. Because ... he thought I was with Jason? That's *amazing*. It makes me want to twirl.

Now I'm lost in a world where I could walk down the street holding hands with Jason. Where I'd wake up with him in my bed, not my doorway. Where—*goddess*—he'd kiss me.

Or much more.

But no. I can't let myself feel things for Jason. Sweet Jason who buys me breakfast.

Because loving someone who's unavailable is the quickest way to heartache.

I should know.

"Hey there, space cadet," Roderick says. "Here's your coffee."

I blink again and remember that I'm standing in the coffee shop next to this bearded hottie who dragged me out of bed. I need to wake up. I need to stop this fantasy.

I focus on Roderick. "Thanks, cutie," I say.

"Taken," he responds, shrugging. Then he gets this dreamy, faraway smile on his face.

"Shame." I sniff.

But I'm only kidding around. I follow Jason back to the car, each of us carrying our coffee and bagel.

Jason turns to me before he starts the engine. "Funny that your friend thought we were together."

"Yeah," I say. "Funny."

But it's really not.

It's kind of a bummer, actually.

The enormous farmers market is so full that people are parked in places that aren't meant for cars. Patrons of all types—families, ag types, hippies, foodies—swarm everywhere.

We're in the heart of late summer, speeding into fall, so apples and all kinds of gorgeous fruits and gourds are starting to show up. I resist making some kind of phallic gourd joke to Jason, because I'm above such humor.

Instead, I try sophistication.

"You know," I say, "In Vegas you can get a lobster or oysters or whatever the hell you want, but it has to be trucked in or flown in. But here in Vermont, it seems pretty special to get tomatoes from up the road."

Jason gives me a big grin. "Exactly. I figured you'd been to a farmers market before, but this one's unique, and it's ending for the season soon. I wanted you to come."

I want to come, too, but I keep that to myself.

We wander past stalls where woodworkers sell toys, people hawk quilts and old-lady-style crocheted toilet paper holders, and tables showcase stacks and rows of all the lotions and potions a guy could want.

"What are we shopping for?" I ask.

"Food, mostly. Do you want to cook together? We could do meal planning. Cooking for one sucks."

Again, the man of my dreams is, in fact, the man of my dreams. Not even my mother cooked for me. I had to scrounge around for boxes of cereal and mac and cheese as a child.

"I would love to," I say. "But I don't know the first thing about it. I've never been that great at planning."

"Let's start with your schedule this week." Jason eyes a box of heirloom tomatoes. "You're working in the afternoons and evenings, right?"

"Pretty much. Sometimes I go in early, though."

"Then let's get stuff for breakfast and lunch, and I'll make soups or things that keep. You could pack them up to have for dinner on your break."

If I thought my heart couldn't get any meltier, I was so wrong. I stare at him. "Jason. You don't have to do this for me. I can fend for myself. You're under no obligation to feed me."

His cheeks pink under that beard. "I know. I just. I'd like to. If that's okay."

"Oh, shmoopie, I'll let you," I say. "But let me split the bill."

"Sure." He sounds distracted as he looks at the produce on display.

I really need to stop mooning over him, or this is going to get out of hand.

But maybe I'm allowed to wallow in him for one more day. A second day of enjoying him just as he is.

And then we can go about our lives, and we won't see each other since I work most evenings. For right now, though, I love wandering through a farmers market full of people with this big guy at my side.

Jason buys salad ingredients, as well as a few loaves of bread and some cheese. I pick up ingredients for sangria, because hello, is there a better drink? It'll be amazing with white peaches and raspberries. I also get artisanal sausages, because I can't help myself. Jason stifles a snicker.

We wander past a stall staffed by a woman who gives off every impression of being a soccer mom. I say this because she's wearing one of those sweatshirts that has a kid's soccer team on it and the name of her kid. So I'm not being *that* judgy.

But she is.

My T-shirt reads, *Sounds gay … I'm in.* A little on the nose, but I like it. When she sees me picking up a cucumber and inspecting it, she pulls down her glasses and gives me a flat gaze over the rims. I can't resist hamming it up.

"I have a lot of ideas for what we could do with this," I say, licking my lips and cocking my hip.

"Shh," Jason says, laughing. "No. Murph!"

The soccer mom makes a choked noise, and her face blanches. Then she gets an ugly twist to her mouth.

I turn to her, wide-eyed. "What? I meant salads. Pickles. Gazpacho. Cucumbers are very versatile." *So am I.* "What were *you* thinking of?" I set it back down.

She starts laughing, her face red. "Oh, my goodness. I'm sorry. I'm just not used to … Never mind."

"Not used to queers like me? Oh, honey, I know. No worries." I whisper, "There are lots of uses for the cucumber."

Jason shuffles his feet, pressing a fist to his lips, trying not to laugh.

Soccer mom's hands drop to her sides, and she leans toward me, her head tilted to one side and her face softening to a smile. I can see the moment she decides that I'm her new friend. She's gonna tell all the other soccer moms about me.

I count that as a win.

"Tell you what," she says. "For that laugh, the cucumber is on me. You and your partner have a good day, now."

My head swivels fast to my dangerous hunk of a roommate, to see him staring at me, mouth parted in … amazement?

Turning back to soccer mom, I hold my hands to my heart. "You sweet thing, you." She picks up the cucumber and hands it to me. I accept it like it's a bouquet of flowers, and Jason and I move on to the next stall.

Jason turns to me, shaking his head in disbelief. "How did you do that?"

"Do what?"

"Turn a moment that could have been awkward into something hilarious."

"Look, Jay Jay. This isn't my first time being the main exhibit at the zoo. I get looks all the time. You have to learn to roll with it, you know? I can't take offense that easily. Otherwise I'd be taking offense all the time. I'd rather be someone's safe and chummy first gay friend than someone they fear."

"You shouldn't have to be anything but you," he says.

I shrug. "That's correct. And that's exactly what I do."

JASON

When we return home, Murph heads to his room, probably to unpack some more, and I head to the kitchen with our farmers market haul. I like to do meal prep for a few days at a time, but it's always felt like a waste because I had no one to share it with. I like being able to share with Murph.

Once I have a roast in the oven, chili on the stove, and veggies cut and portioned out for lunches, I settle on the sofa with a beer and turn on my favorite show.

I hear a gasp. "No way!"

Turning around, I see Murph hovering behind me, his hand over his mouth. He's wearing another kimono, this one with a peacock-feather design, with pajamas underneath.

He looks elegant. The blue background makes his eyes pop.

I furrow my brows. "What? You have a problem with *Forged in Fire*?"

A grin takes over his face. "Quite the opposite. All those burly guys with tattoos, banging on metal? Sign me up." He scoots around the couch and settles at the other end, eyes rapt on the weapon-making competition show.

I cough to hide my laugh. "I never thought of it that way. I only thought it was cool to learn about all the different kinds of weapons."

"Oh, that, too, Jay Jay. The eye candy's extra credit."

"I never really noticed the contestants, to be honest. Although the judges have fun personalities."

As the same time, we quote Doug—the *Forged in Fire* judge who violently tests swords against tactical dummies with a very kind smile—saying, "It will keel," in his distinctive accent. Then we both laugh.

We watch until a commercial, when he asks, "What else do you watch?"

My mind's gone blank. I'm not very good at being put on the spot. After a moment, I come up with, "Um, *How It's Made*?"

He wiggles in his seat, rearranging his legs so they're under him. "Oh my goddess, you are such a classic nerd. Don't tell me you play D&D?"

"Okay, I won't." I look away, trying not to smile.

"You do?"

"Maybe." I grin. "Nothing wrong with being a nerd."

He sits up straight. "Seriously? Because for five years I was the dungeon master of an online group."

"No kidding?" A surprised noise bursts out of me.

"You think queers don't like to go fight trolls?"

I sputter. "I never thought about it, actually. I mean, usually I play a paladin or whatever, not a queer."

He holds his flat belly as he laughs, and he reaches over and touches my thigh. "I'm giving you a hard time. But see? We're a match made in heaven."

The news that my roommate and I won't be fighting over the remote puts me in a great mood. Like something's lifted inside me. And I was already happy from spending the day with him. "What else do you watch?"

"*Rick and Morty*. That's what my blog's about, actually."

I turn fully to him. "Seriously?"

"Not to brag, but I'm considered a world expert on Rick

Sanchez, the semi-improvised, burping cartoon scientist grandpa."

"No shit?"

"No shit." He pulls out his phone to show me. "I've been interviewed on *BuzzFeed, HuffPost, The Onion* ..." He holds up a finger as he recites each name.

When I process what he said, I raise an eyebrow. "You're kidding about *The Onion*."

"You caught me." He bites his lip as he scrolls on his phone, then hands it to me.

A complete *Rick and Morty* fan site is displayed, with GIFs and giveaways and places for people to interact with each other. It's really easy to navigate and chock-full of information about the TV show. "This is amazing. All these analyses. Each episode. You write all this? Wow." Then a text pops up, and I blink.

"What?"

I stroke my chin and try not to laugh. "Uh, I think your, um, guy wants you to come over."

"Shit." He reaches out his hand, and I give him back his phone.

Murph clicks on the thumbnail photo and expands it so we can both see that it's of some dude's hard dick. The text came from "London." His hand flies to his mouth. "Oh, goddess, I'm so sorry."

"Don't worry about it. It's not like I haven't seen a dick before."

"To be honest, it's a nice dick." He tilts his head to the side. "I'd give him a six on the lighting, four on the angle, eight on the manscaping, and seven point five on the size."

I burst out laughing. "No comment." I sip my beer and gesture at the phone. "You can go see him, you know, if you want. You don't have to hang out with me."

"Nah. He's trying too hard." He puts his phone down and gazes at the television expectantly. Like it's going to give him the answers to everything.

"So, it's funny. I guess I wouldn't think a guy like you was into *Rick and Morty*," I say, to change the subject. "I had to stop watching it. I thought it was one of the worst for being sexist, racist, homophobic—"

Murph raises his hand like he's in class. "Am I only supposed to like Judy Garland?"

My cheeks heat up. "No, of course not."

"I'm just giving you crap. Although who doesn't love Judy? But you're absolutely right, *Rick and Morty* is an extremely crass show and a lot of people take offense to it, with good reason. I use my blog to talk about that very topic. I call myself a critical fanboy. When the show goes too far, I point out why and analyze it."

"Interesting."

"Like here." Murph taps at his phone and shows me an article about how the show expects people to find gay sex disgusting and uses "gay" as a pejorative. He continues, "As you may have already guessed, I do not find gay sex disgusting, nor do I think 'gay' is a put-down. I happen to think both are *fabulous*." That mischievous Murph smile is in full force, and his voice turns to a purr. "And so do a lot of other people."

"I caught a few episodes and felt embarrassed about watching it. Like OMG this is so bad, and I shouldn't laugh. I'm amazed you can look past the offensive shit."

Murph gives me a cheeky grin and shrugs, putting his phone down. "I'm complicated."

"You're using it as a platform, then."

"In part. I can be critical of something and still find redeeming qualities in it. The things I really love about it are all the Easter eggs and references and that it's existential."

"Existential?"

"I told you, puddin'. I do read, you know. A lot."

"But you're into existentialism?" The philosophy major in me perks up.

Murph quiets for a moment, and I think I lost him. But then he opens his mouth. "Aren't we all into figuring out why we're here?"

"Yeah, I guess so. I think most of us are seeking the reason for our lives."

"I've always thought that the reason to be alive is to *be alive*. Like, it is its own reason. So maybe we just need to *feel* alive, and we're good."

"Now, who's the philosopher?" I grin at him. "Joseph Campbell said something like that."

"Huh. But isn't that what you want, too, Mr. Insurance Salesman? To feel alive?"

I lose my smile, and his expression immediately morphs.

He reaches out and touches my hand. "Hey. I'm sorry. I didn't mean to tease you."

"Don't worry about it," I mutter. "We don't always love what we do. Or love it every day. Even if we're good at it."

"True."

"I'm fully aware that I'm in charge of my own life, and I can do whatever I want. Still, it's hard to get out of old patterns. What people expect of you. You know?" I look up, and Murph's eyes are soft and friendly. "Sorry. Didn't mean to get maudlin on you."

"I'd love it if you got anything on me," Murph says.

I laugh and don't take it to heart. Murph disappears into the kitchen to make a pitcher of sangria, which he apparently has a secret recipe for.

And we spend the evening drinking and watching *Forged in Fire* together. I go to bed very happy.

I stretch out on my bed and yawn.

Monday morning. Another day to spend telling people they're gonna die, so they should spend money on insurance.

Great. I've been awake for approximately three milliseconds, and I've already depressed myself.

But I'd better get up.

I sleep in boxers, and I don't know if I should put more clothes on to go across the hall to the bathroom for a shower. I don't need to, right?

I scratch my belly, and I hear the water running. Murph must be in the shower.

Getting out of bed, I decide fuck it, I'm not putting anything else on, and go into the kitchen to make coffee. Murph can get used to me in whatever I wear around the house.

Right?

Murph didn't add anything to his coffee when we went out Saturday morning, and I didn't see what he had yesterday, but I can't believe that's the way he likes it. Or am I being prejudiced? Like, just because he wears pink doesn't mean he can't drink his coffee black.

Why am I so concerned about how he takes his coffee? He's a roommate. He can figure out his own damn coffee.

I put down a few pieces of toast and get out Greek yogurt and berries, figuring I'll make breakfast while I'm waiting for him to be done in the bathroom. I'm surprised when I hear the door open just a minute or two later.

He said he's high-maintenance, but he really isn't.

Murph exits, hair wet, a dark purple towel tied round his waist.

"Hey," I call. "Want some coffee?"

He startles and looks over at me. I can see his eyes trace my torso. But I've got nothing to hide. He shakes himself and then walks toward me, a drop of water sliding down his forehead.

"Oh my goddess, yes," he says. "I have to get going early today to help with inventory."

He steps into the kitchen. He's got a more defined body than I thought. His biceps, while small, are certainly rounded. Lean muscles run all the way down his torso.

I clear my throat. "Here," I say gruffly, handing him a cup. "You seriously don't want sugar or cream?"

"Not in my coffee, no. But thank you." He wiggles one hip. "Sorry I'm overdressed." Then he flips a hand in the air as he saunters away.

I stare after him.

And blink.

Shaking myself, I pop up my toast, which has burned, and swear under my breath. I sigh and start over again with new bread.

When I'm dressed in a suit and ready to go, I head to the door. Before I leave, I stop and call out, "See you, Murph." I straighten my tie in the mirror.

"Bye, toots," he says from his room, the door still closed.

I have a lighter feeling in my chest than I did when I woke up.

But the good mood evaporates by the time I've hung up the phone for the tenth time this morning. It's the tenth rejection. I sigh, regroup, and pick up the handset to call again.

"Jason. Got a minute?" My dad barges into the room.

Forrest Falkner's tall and imposing, with strong opinions. If you didn't know him, you'd be scared of him. Mostly I try to tune him out. "What can I do for you?"

"When I retire, I want to make sure we transition our best clients to you. I'm going to start scheduling lunches and meet-and-greets with them for you. I want them to know I've personally blessed the transfer." He says this in his booming voice, like he's bestowing something on me. I didn't know he was retiring anytime soon, but part of this business is planning for the future.

Oookay. "Thanks, Dad."

"My clients will be thrilled to know that you're keeping the family tradition going—you're no longer just my son but their trusted advisor. They're going to want to know more about you. Some of them have daughters your age."

Oh, god. I know where this is going. But all I say is, "Uh-huh."

"Are you dating anyone?"

"No one serious." Marnie'd be the first to agree that we're not dating.

Marnie gets shit for having a fuck buddy instead of a boyfriend. No one's said the kind of things about me that they say about her, so the comments are just because of her gender. I don't know what to do about it, though, other than defend her if it happens when I'm around.

"Our clients love to know their accounts are being handled by a family man. It gives them comfort."

I want to stare at him and call him on his bullshit—hypocritical much?—but the problem is, it's true. Our whole business is based on giving people comfort. We get smaller mugs for the office so our elderly lady customers' petite hands aren't overtaxed. Our carpet is inoffensive blue and our walls are painted inoffensive tan and our art is barely one step up from hotel art (because a lot of that shit can be offensive) in an effort to be inconspicuous. We don't want to be noticed. We want to be part of the background.

Murph wasn't kidding about me being the man in the gray flannel suit. That's how Dad sees this place.

That's why he pretends Mom's still around. That she's just on a business trip. Still.

"Thanks for the offer. I'm glad to meet with clients." And I won't be talking about anything personal.

"Mrs. Riley really enjoyed meeting you at the company picnic in May. She mentioned you specifically."

Oh my god. Mrs. Riley is a widow and certified cougar. "Dad, I'm not—"

"I'm stating facts, Jason. You're at the age where you should be settling down."

"I am settled down. I own a house. I work. I eat right and exercise properly," *and I don't have to explain myself to my father.* "What more do you want?"

"It's not about what I want. It's about what you want. And I think you really want a wife, you just haven't found the right one."

"I don't even know how to respond to that," I mutter.

"Well, in any case, you're going to start coming with me when I meet with clients. Even if you don't have a girlfriend yet, at least we can move your career along in the right direction." He turns and leaves the room.

After my dad is gone, I come up with all the things I should have said in the moment. To tell him to get the hell out of my personal life. Or, more politely, that I'm thankful he wants to help, but it isn't needed.

I don't need to be reminded that I don't have anyone. I have a girl I fuck and don't talk to, my sister who orders me around, and a brand-new roommate who happens to be homosexual. That's it. All my friends have left town.

I text Becky.

Jason: Dad wants me to find a wife

Becky: Did you tell him about Marnie?

Jason: No

Becky: You don't have to do what he says

Jason: Yes

Becky: But you're texting me because you want me to remind you of this fact?

Jason: Yes

Becky: Consider yourself reminded

My phone rings, and I pick up. Becky starts talking without

saying hi. "I get it, okay? I really do. I still want his approval. And so do you. I still wear clothes I think Dad will like when I go over there. Even though I should wear whatever the fuck I want."

I force out a laugh. "You do it, too, then? Censor yourself around him, to please him?"

"Yeah. I wish he'd like us just the way we are."

"Me, too."

"So what are we afraid of?"

I make sure Dad isn't listening. "The Look. You know the one."

"Don't scare me, big bro! I'm gonna go hide."

"You can't tell me I'm wrong." Dad can take us down with a single glare.

"You're not." She sighs. "Dad's a diva. It's always about him."

I cock my head. "Diva? I've never thought of him that way. I picture a diva as someone who wears sequins." Unbidden, an image of Murph comes to me, but I can't see him as a diva—at least not one who puts himself over other people. He's just too sweet.

WTF? When have I ever thought of a guy as sweet*?*

"You know it's true."

"Yeah." I pause. "Thanks."

Becky adopts a serious tone. "That will be twenty bucks. You can pay the next time you see me."

"Har har."

"Listen. When you get stellar advice, it's worth something."

"What's your advice?"

"Do whatever you want. It's your life, no one else's."

I look down at my desk. "Yeah. I might start taking you up on that."

MURPH

"How's your new place?" Tanner asks as he pours glasses of merlot for a table of customers. The din of the wine bar surrounds us: tables full of couples, groups, single people reading books. It's afternoon, and since I came in early, I'll be off soon. We finished the inventory an hour ago, so now I'm tidying up before the evening rush.

While Vino and Veritas isn't technically a gay bar, it's also not *not* a gay bar. It's an inclusive place that serves wine, with rainbow flags in the windows, owned by a gay man—who wants to make sure there's no bi erasure. And it's connected to an outstanding bookstore. I lucked out when I got hired here.

I look up from where I'm wiping glasses and nod. "It's great." I think about my farmers market excursion with my generous roommate. Actually, the part I'm obsessed with is how I'm pretty sure he's straight, but everyone thought we were together.

Okay, by *everyone,* I mean two people: Roderick and soccer mom. But that's enough.

I'll note Jason didn't deny that second one, but maybe he was distracted by all the cucumber talk.

Are they seeing something in him that I'm not? Because my gaydar didn't ping when I met him.

What also confuses me is, well, the whole day felt like a date. An odd, very early, coffee and shopping date, but a date, nonetheless. He made me feel so special. But then I wonder if he cares for everyone that way, and my face falls.

So does the glass I'm holding. It smashes into pieces on the floor, making an embarrassing racket. Lucky me missed the part of the floor with the rubber padding.

The room goes quiet as every single person searches for who broke whatever it was that broke.

"Fuck." I reach for a broom to clean up the shards. "Shit, I swore. Sorry."

Tanner nods at a customer walking in, then turns to me, noticing my shaking hands. "You all right?"

"Yes, absolutely."

"Ohh-kay. You're acting like Molly." She's our resident klutz, not working today. He eyes me distrustfully and takes the tray of drinks over to a table.

Is Jason just being friendly? Or does he *like* me, like me?

I pick up another glass to dry and fumble it, too, but I catch it in time—and luckily Tanner doesn't see me.

Get it together, Murph.

When Tanner brings a tray of dirty glasses back, I reach for one and knock them all over.

And I get a repeat of the whole room looking at me. At least this time the glasses didn't break, they just made a racket.

"Shit. Sorry, I swore again. *Fuckbuckets.*"

The owner, Harrison, passes by on his way to the office, looking amused. While this really is the best place to work on the entire planet, I need to stop fucking up. I already give both Harrison and Tanner enough heartburn with my adventures in pushing the "dark clothes" dress code by adding sparkle wherever I can. They don't need me adding property damage to my list of issues.

So I take a big, cleansing breath.

Just because I live with an unselfish and giving man doesn't mean anything. Maybe I don't have enough experience with healthy relationships to separate kindness from attraction.

I do my best to carefully take each glass and set it in the dishwashing tray. Mission accomplished. I let out the breath I was holding.

Then I whirl around and send a stack of menus flying across the bar.

I give up.

"Murph?" Tanner gives me a hard stare from the other side of the bar as he picks up another order. "What the fuck is wrong?"

"Why do you think something's wrong?"

"Because normally, as you flit around here, you off-gas glitter."

I stick my nose up and sniff. "That sounds disgusting. I don't have gas."

"You know what I mean. Normally you're … floating."

Gathering up the menus, I take one and very carefully wipe it down. Then another. "It's nothing."

"Bullshit."

I let out a breath, debating what to say.

He narrows his eyes. "Out with it."

"I'm already out."

"Your rainbow nail polish gives you away." Tanner scans my outfit, which today contains no trace of Murph-ness except the lavender socks. "At least you're otherwise following the dress code." He sighs. "Look, you don't have to tell me."

I blink at him, warm fuzzy feelings blooming in my chest.

It's not a question of whether I'd share my personal life with my manager. I already know Tanner is safe to confide in. Something about him—how he's inked and tough but doesn't gossip—makes him a vault for other people's stories. He's the perfect bartender, ready to lend an ear but slow to judge.

And even if I didn't trust him, I'm not the kind of guy who keeps my heart secret. If my life were on stage, I'd gather all the players and sing the story of my unrequited love while they danced around with ribbons and did their utmost to console me through verse. The stage decor would be outstanding, of course. And I'd change clothes midsong like Elsa from *Frozen*. How they did that shit live, I'll never know.

I maybe am getting a tad bit far afield from the here and now. No wonder my fourth-grade teacher told me not to daydream in class.

But if I say out loud what I'm thinking and feeling, will it make it real? Worse, will it make it come true?

Fuck it.

"Alas, my dear, sweet Tanner"—no one else calls him sweet, but I think he is, underneath it all—"I've broken rule number one. The only rule, really."

No one appears to be ready to start singing while I relate my tale of woe. Still, I prepare to tell it as tragically as I can, batting my eyes like a fair maiden. I open my mouth to explain, but Tanner puts both hands on the counter and leans toward me. "Who is he?"

"Who is what?" I straighten the menus, not looking at him.

"The straight guy you have a crush on."

The *probably* straight guy I have a crush on.

Ugh. Tanner's as perceptive as a bird of prey. "How did you guess?"

A sympathetic smile stretches across his rugged face. "Because that's rule number one, Murph."

Dammit. I kick at the floor.

Tanner tilts his head. "You're talking about Jason Falkner?"

"You dare say his name!" I hiss. "His name has power!" I pick up two empty wine bottles and toss them in the recycle bin. At least, with those, it's okay if the glass breaks. "I will neither confirm nor deny that he's the object of my affection."

And I can't make Jason confirm or deny his sexual orientation. Because reasons. Reasons like, if I know for sure he's not into men, my heart will hurt. And if he *is* into men, but not into me, my heart will hurt in an entirely different way.

Tanner comes around the bar and hip-checks me good-naturedly. "You goof. We all know where you moved. Jason's a great guy. I can see why you have a crush on him. Almost everyone has had a crush on him. He's younger than me, but I remember him from high school."

"You went to school with him?"

He nods. "He's gorgeous. Rough around the edges. I'd bet he's hiding a gooey center inside."

It's funny. Tanner could be describing himself. I'm sure his partner, Jax, would say the exact same thing about him.

"I knooowwww," I moan. "He's so perfect, he's like Audrey Hepburn. The only thing keeping him from being perfect is that he's perfect." And his *niceness* confounds me.

"No one's perfect. But I'm pretty sure your instincts are right. Jason's not gay. I think he has a long-term hookup. The gossip mill sees him coming out of Marnie Madison's house all the time. And I'm pretty sure they aren't there to play UNO."

"I'd play UNO with him," I mutter. And Tanner goes to the storeroom to retrieve another case from the back.

When he returns, he sets down the box and says, "Hey. Come here." Then he gives me a big bear hug.

See? Best place to work ever.

It's soothing, but it's the wrong guy.

For the remainder of the afternoon, I manage to not drop anything else, but my thoughts are on a one-track Jason station, playing all his greatest hits, all day long. Even though I've only known him a few days.

The first night, when he made me ziti.

How he looks wearing a white towel ... and nothing else. Good goddess, he deserves a warning label.

How he's neat and conscientious.

And how I want to kiss that scruffy face of his more than I want caffeine, which is saying something.

Somehow, I make it through the rest of my shift.

When I get home in the early evening, Jason isn't here—he must still be at work. There's a bowl in the fridge with a note on it in Jason's all-uppercase writing.

"Chili if you want it. Just heat it up."

How on earth did I win the roommate lottery? Seriously.

It would be a lot less complicated if he were a jerk, because that would override how attractive he is. But if he were a jerk, I'd probably want to move out ASAP.

I pick up my phone and call Reeve. While I adored living with Reeve, since he found a Viking to snuggle for the rest of his life, I had to move. But he's still my best friend.

"Tell me if I'm asleep or awake," I say without preamble.

He laughs. "Do you usually call me when you're asleep?"

"But I must be sleeping," I protest, "since I'm living in a dream world."

"I take it you're doing okay in your new place."

"More than okay." I tell him all about moving in and Jason taking me to the farmers market.

"You're feeling things, aren't you, Showgirl?"

"Yes," I confess. "I haven't felt this way about someone ever. This infatuation. Whatever Jason does is immediately my favorite thing. I know it's dangerous to let myself feel something, since I have no idea how he feels—or if he's even queer—but I can't help it. I like him."

"I understand."

"I should just forget about him. But I can't. It's impossible, because I'm living with him, and he's my ideal man. Not simply physically ideal—although you should see him. I'm not at all sure he knows how sexy he is. Because it's a lot. Jason is *all* the sexy." Reeve chuckles. "But it's more than that. When I lived in Vegas, the people I knew were as fake as the architecture. They only cared how much money you had or what they could get out of you. No one was real. Jason's real." My voice drops to a whisper. "So real it aches."

Reeve's tone gets serious, and I can picture the frown on his face. "Are you setting yourself up to get hurt?"

I sigh. "He has a female fuck buddy. Although this morning I thought for a second he was checking me out. But that's wishful thinking."

I can hear Reeve's smile over the phone. "Well, who wouldn't check you out? You're beautiful."

"Thanks, babe."

Reeve *is* a babe, all dark-haired and dashing, like men in that sexy romance show with dukes and viscounts in breeches. But he and I have never been more than really good friends.

"You positive he's not, like, in the closet?"

"Well, that would almost be worse than him being straight. Because then he'd just be a tease." I sit on the edge of my bed, pull out my glitter nail polish, and touch up my pinkie. "Part of me wants to push him. And the other part wants to forget about him and go find someone else." I pause, thinking. "Even if he's straight, I'm sure he wouldn't say no to a blow job."

Then I wonder. Maybe he would. Most guys don't care whose mouth they stick their dick in—at least if their inhibitions are down. Not that I'm into creepy shit like getting guys drunk to have my wicked way with them. But does Jason care how he gets his rocks off?

As if Reeve can hear my thoughts, he says, "Murph, nothing you can do can force him to like you. You probably need to go find someone else."

"I could see if he responds—"

"Let me ask you something. Does Jason respect the fact that you're gay?"

I sigh. "Yes."

"Are you respecting the fact that he might not be?"

I kick the ground. "Not so much."

"If you flirt with him, and it goes too far and he rejects you, how will you feel?"

"Like crap."

"And what are the chances of him rejecting you because he's straight?"

"High."

"Then I vote for finding someone who will actually respond to you."

"I hate that idea." I also hate saying my next words. "But you're right. I'm going to do my best to try and forget about Jason. Because it isn't going to work."

"You know ..." He pauses. "If you go out with someone else and Jason objects, that could be your answer. It's a twofold solution. You'll find out how Jason feels, and it might get you laid."

A wee bit of happiness warms my heart. "You're brilliant. Operation Get Murph Laid and/or Jason Out of the Closet is now officially beginning. And I know how to start."

"Oh? How?"

"London texted me the other day." I smirk. "His equipment."

Reeve chuckles, then sobers. "Are you gonna send him something back?"

"I'm not that kind of guy."

"Uh-huh," he says, not convinced. Because he knows me. "Good luck."

I'm not sure whether Reeve is wishing me good luck with London or with Jason. Or both. "But enough about me. Tell me everything about you, Hotcakes."

After I talk with Reeve about how he and Oz are the best thing ever, I text London back and we arrange to go out on Friday.

And now I wait.

JASON

"How's it going with your new roommate?" Becky asks. She shoves a chip into her mouth and washes it down with a sip of Coke.

We're hanging out at my place on Wednesday. Murph's working tonight, and I'm done for the day. I sent him to work with a container of soup for dinner along with some crackers. He looked at me like I'd given him a whole house.

It's only soup.

"Good," I say, thinking of the way his eyes seemed to almost tear up when I gave him the meal and wondering if anyone has ever fed him before. "How did you meet him?"

"I went to V and V with some girlfriends for a bachelorette party. He was our server. He cracked me up. And he complimented me on my shoes. Then I heard him asking Tanner if he knew of anyone with a room to rent, and I was like, I know the perfect place for you. The owner of V and V vouched for him."

I swear Becky knows everyone. Guess that's part of being a realtor.

"You didn't think he would be too, you know."

"Gay?" She gives me a look I can't interpret. "I didn't take you for having a problem with that."

"I don't," I say quickly. "Not at all."

"That's right you don't."

Truthfully, I don't know what I feel about Murph. Massively protective, for one thing. He's so small, and I think he deserves an easier life than he's had so far.

He's fierce, though. Ergo, I don't think he's fragile.

While there's nothing wrong with tending bar, and V and V is apparently great—I haven't been in there yet—I think Murph could shine if he got into commenting on pop culture. He seems to like it, and with how articulate and witty he is? No wonder his blog is blowing up.

I sip my drink. "After a few days of living with a gay guy, it's not the big deal I was worried it would be. We have more things in common than differences. We both like all the same things. In fact, if he were a woman, he'd be a great person to date."

"Is that right?" Becky asks.

I smile. "But since he's not, he can be my friend. And he's giving me insight into this different world."

"What world is that?"

"Ever since that wine bar opened, I'm seeing a lot more gay and lesbian and whoever people holding hands in town. And not only on Church Street. I kind of like it. The world's changing. People are able to be more themselves."

"Hmm," she says.

"Never something I paid much attention to. But I guess with a roommate who is out and proud, I'm getting my horizons expanded even more. Everything that's been going on the past few years has made me realize how privileged I am. And how I don't really want to be—or, at least, don't want to coast on that privilege. How I want to help other people. If I can help the ones closest to me, like Murph, or help Marnie with the misogynistic crap and racist microaggressions she gets in town, then I'm going to do it."

She sighs. "I hate how Marnie gets treated. Vermont thinks it's progressive, but it isn't always."

We both go quiet for a moment.

"Tell me what Murph's like. He seemed entertaining."

"He's cool." I bite into a chip. "He's funny, actually. Like 'ha ha' funny, not weirdo funny. He's a good guy to be around. I guess I thought he'd be all stereotypical and like *My Little Pony* or something, and while he does do some of that stuff, that's not all there is to him. He likes a lot of the same things I do."

"Oh, god. He watches *Forged in Fire*?"

"He plays Dungeons & Dragons, too."

"No. He's that much of a geek? Oh no."

I chuckle. "Hey, geeks make the world go round."

"He's your perfect roommate, then."

"He's actually becoming a friend."

She bites a nail. "So tell me. Did I do good? It sounds like I did good, but I need positive reinforcement."

"You did," I assure her.

"You should, you know, go somewhere fun together. Take him to a beer festival. Or a movie."

"He's not my date. And he likes sangria, not beer."

She stares at me. "You're hanging out with him. I'm just suggesting you go do something fun."

"We hang out and watch movies," I say. "And I'm glad to have someone to cook for. I wasn't in the market for a new best friend, but he's a candidate."

"Uh-huh. Interesting."

The look on her face is strange, so I change the subject. "Have you heard from Mom lately?"

"Nope. You told me she was off in New Mexico." And now she changes the subject fast. "Can I ask you something?"

"Sure."

"You and Marnie." She sighs. "I think Marnie likes you more than you like her."

Becky and Marnie have been best friends since high school. It's a little weird, perhaps, that Marnie and I are fucking, but Becky never seemed to have a problem with it. Over the years, she's kept introducing me to women, but they never seem to do it for me. For now, Marnie's good for me, and I'm good for her.

At least I think so.

But this news? I don't like it.

"Don't tell me that," I say. "She and I have talked about what we're doing. More than once. She's the one who came up with most of our rules."

"Oh, she thinks she's a big girl and can handle it. And yes, she's perfectly mature. But when emotions get in the way, we're all more vulnerable than we'd admit. I just get this sense …"

My gut sinks. Marnie's the last person I want to hurt.

"Are you and Marnie ever going to be more than what you are?" she continues.

"No," I say. "I don't think so. We talked about this from the very beginning. I don't think it's going to change."

Or, if it changes, it'll be from me calling things off with her.

"But people do change, Jason. If they're lucky, over time they become who they really are meant to be."

I can't help but think of Murph. Who's always expressing who he really is.

If only I could do that, too.

I'm kicking back on the couch late Thursday night watching TV when I hear the key in the door and Murph comes in. I can tell he's tired by the way he's a little grayer than usual—but he perks right up when he sees me.

"What are you doing up?" he asks.

"Couldn't sleep."

"Aww, poor Jay Jay."

No one else calls me Jay Jay. It'd make me feel like a kid from anyone else, but I don't mind it when Murph says it. From him, it's just the way he is.

"Want me to make you some warm milk and crackers?" Murph continues.

I stare at him. "You're kidding."

"Yes, I'm kidding, but I would if you wanted me to. Or I can mix you a drink."

"That sounds better."

Murph sets down his man purse and goes into the kitchen. He washes his hands and then gets out two dark purple glasses and a bottle of rum. He makes some sort of drink and brings one over to me, then crashes at the opposite end of the couch. "I really like these glasses," he says, inspecting his.

"Thanks. How was work?"

"Well, wifey-poo, that place was hopping. We have some new varietals in, and Tanner made a production out of it. It was a big night."

"Sorry I missed it." I sip my drink. It's delicious. "Also, *wifey-poo*?"

"What would you rather have me call you?"

"Jason is fine."

His shoulders slump, and it's like I took all of the life out of him, goddammit. "Sure. If that's what you want."

Murph's voice has gone quiet, and I turn to face him, holding up a hand. "No."

"What do you mean, no?"

"I don't want to be the one to dull your shine. If you want to call me anything, please do it." My voice lowers, and I say, "Don't ever stop using nicknames."

He studies me and takes a sip of his drink. "If you're sure."

"I'm sure." I sigh. "It's been a long day."

But seeing him has made me happier than I ever expected.

He gives me a smile. "Yeah, it has, wifey-poo."

And I burst out laughing.

As we chill in the living room, he tells me more about his evening. "I should visit you at work sometime," I say, when he's done.

"You'd class up the joint." He smirks. "Kidding, kidding. Don't let Harrison hear me say that. V and V is a nice place, not some dive bar. Although you don't have to go there to get me to make you a drink."

"You make good ones." I drain my glass. "What is this?"

"A dark 'n' stormy. Rum, ginger beer—the good stuff—and lime juice. Want another?"

"Sure."

Murph goes into the kitchen and comes back with two fresh drinks and a bag of pretzels.

"Can I ask you something?" He toys with his glass. When he glances up at me, his eyes tell me he's serious.

"Anything." I sit up straighter.

"You started cooking for your family because your mom left, right?"

"Yeah. When I was in elementary school."

"Why did she leave?"

My chest tightens. I think what he's asking is, what did I feel about her leaving? I haven't really ever talked about this with anyone other than Becky. But the alcohol's making me not hold back, and I'm starting to think of Murph as a real friend.

"Becky and I used to hear our parents fight all the time. I tried to always do everything they asked. Like, if I was perfect, they wouldn't fight. It never worked. One day, Mom just stormed out. She came back a few days later, took her things, and left for good. I was too young to know exactly what was going on, other than it scared me. When she said goodbye, Mom swore up and down that she wasn't leaving because of anything Becky or I did, she only needed to go take advantage of some 'opportunities.' But ..." I shrug.

The look on Murph's face is so compassionate, I almost tear up. I focus on my drink.

"I'm sorry," he says when it's evident I'm not going to volunteer more. "Did you see her much after that?"

"Not really. She moved out of state. She started working for this company that puts on conventions, so she's always traveling. At first, Becky and I would go see her for a month during our summer vacations, but we missed a few summers because she had to work." I heave out a breath, and my voice cracks. "She couldn't put aside her own life to see her kids. Dad spouts some bullshit about her having this great career opportunity, but the truth is, she couldn't stand to be tied down by him or by us."

"That sucks, Jason." He offers me the open bag of pretzels, and I take one. I focus on the salt and the crunch, because it's easier than thinking about my mom.

"With an adult perspective, I think I can sorta see what happened. She was really young when they got together. He was older, and she was in college. I get the impression her parents pressured her to get married and have kids right away. She must've felt trapped. I guess she'd had enough." That tightness in my chest hasn't loosened, so I force myself to shrug. "Becky barely speaks to her. I guess I've gotten over it. Mostly."

"Parents can really fuck you up."

I study him. "Are you speaking from experience?"

Murph nods. "My mom is great. She just wasn't around, because she worked nights. But my dad's an addict. He abandoned us, too, even though we still lived in the same house. Anyone who'd pick cards or slot machines over his family has got problems."

A rueful laugh escapes me. "Jesus, Murph. What did you put in these drinks? Truth serum? It's depressing the hell out of us."

"Sorry. My fault. I asked the questions." He looks at me, and I get the idea he's seeing deep into me. That could be the booze talking, though. "It's funny how kids react when they can't rely on their parents."

"What do you mean?"

"You were all Mr. Perfect. I went the opposite direction. I was so desperate for someone to pay attention to me that the first chance I could, I fell into a relationship without realizing how toxic it was."

"Your ex?" I've been curious but didn't know how to bring it up with him.

"Yeah. Dirk. More than two years of my life being jerked around."

I'm trying to picture the kind of man Murph would be with. "What was he like?"

"He's a few years older, and I'd been friends with his sister for a while." He gives me an ironic smile. "If you haven't noticed, I can be a bit of a flirt, so I used to tease him all the time. I liked him—he seemed sophisticated, and he paid attention to me. One night we were out, he had a drink or two and told me he'd liked me for years, and we hooked up. Then he froze me out for a week. Then he apologized, told me he'd freaked out because he'd never been with a man before but that I was special, and took me to a suite at the Wynn. And … rinse and repeat." Murph's eyes are overbright. "I wanted someone to love me, and he could be so dashing, make these romantic gestures. Send me dozens of roses with the card signed 'from your one and only,' stuff like that. He reminded me of Clark Gable or some movie star." Murph holds up his drink. "Except when he was drunk. Then he was just a piece of shit. But foolish me thought it was *soo* special when he took me to these exclusive places where we knew no one. I was impressed because he was rich and he thought I was worth the best. In reality, we went to private suites because he had to keep me a secret."

I echo his comment to me. "That sucks."

"So much suckage. He'd tell me he loved me and we'd be together in the end—that if I waited a little bit longer, he'd come out. First it was going to be when we moved to Vermont, because it was a new place, new school, all that. But then he met all these new people and had to impress them, so he said he'd come out at the end of the semester, after he finished taking his exams. Or the summer. I believed him—I wanted to believe him—but it just never happened."

"What happened to change that? I'm assuming you left him?"

He nods. "V and V helped. I looked around at the friends I was making and saw their healthy, loving, *visible* relationships and started wondering why I couldn't have that, too. I woke up one day with the power of a Gloria Gaynor song in my heart and told him we were done. I swore I was never going to be with a closeted man again."

"Sounds like you've come a long way."

"I have," he says. "I learned to set healthy boundaries." He grabs the remote. "Enough of the heavy stuff. Feel like watching something set in outer space?"

I grin. "Anything you want."

As we watch the movie, I feel like a weight's been taken off my shoulders that I didn't know I was carrying.

8

MURPH

By Friday evening, after a week of living with Jason, I've learned a few things.

First, he works hard. He often leaves before I would normally even get up and remains at the office well after regular office hours. Since I work most evenings, if I'm going to see him during the week, either he needs to stay up late or I need to make him breakfast.

So I do. That way I get to see him headed out the door, smelling scrumptious, in a trim suit that makes him look serious and sober and professional.

And edible.

I tried cooking for him the first night I had off, but he got home so late, it was cold. Still, he gave me a look of such genuine appreciation that it was worth it, even if I was disappointed.

The past couple of nights, he's stayed up and hung out with me when I get home. I like it.

Neither one of us is getting much sleep, though. I guess that's what the weekend's for.

Second, the thing with Marnie may be more serious than I thought. Because it seems like every time his phone's on a surface, it lights up with a text. They must be from her, which means flirting is a no-go. I knew it would be, but part of me couldn't help poking at him a bit just to be sure. But the boundaries are drawn. I know my place. That's fine.

Okay, it's really not, but what choice do I have?

I'm lounging on the couch, about to get ready for my date with London, when Jason walks in.

Goddess, he looks amazing. His nicely tailored dark gray suit hugs his biceps and curves along his behind. He's undone his tie, and his heavy scruff darkens his jaw.

"Hi, honey!" I call. "You're home!"

He chuckles. "Hey, Murph. Have a good day?" He shrugs out of his jacket, placing it on the back of a chair, and slides off his tie.

There's something yummy about a guy taking off a tie. Then he unbuttons his top button and rolls up his sleeves, and all the blood rushes from my face down south. "Yes," I squeak. Then I clear my throat. *Tamp down your Jason kink, Murph.* "Busy at work, and some new marketing ideas coming up that I might get to help design."

"You designing for the wine bar?" His green eyes catch mine, and he smiles.

This is not good. Jason has a force field that catches me in its tractor beam. Maybe he's in some other alternate reality that draws me in. I must resist his luscious face.

So I focus on my phone and nod fiercely. "Yeah. It'll soon be fall, and that's time for mulled wine. Hot grape juice."

He snorts. "Is that what you call it?"

"Only when I'm disrespecting it. But it's there for me in the morning."

Again, he laughs, and it makes me so happy to make him happy.

He settles down in the chair opposite mine, then throws his head back in relaxation. I watch him for a second.

"Want to go to the farmers market tomorrow?" he asks.

"I don't know. I might be out late tonight."

"Working?"

"No. I have a date."

Jason lowers his head to face me. "Ah. I see."

It's my imagination that he looks disappointed, right? It has to be. My mind's playing tricks on me. "London. The guy who sent me the … nude art earlier this week."

"Where are you going?" Jason asks. Then his face falls. "Sorry. That sounded like a dad or something. I just wanted to make sure …" He fidgets in his seat. Then he tries again. "Just always wanna make sure you're okay."

"Aww, buddy," I coo, fluttering my eyelashes. "You care about what happens to me?"

Jason's frown deepens, if that were possible. Which, I guess it is possible, since I'm looking at it. "Yeah, I do. Where are you going?"

"Speakeasy. I have to leave in less than an hour. Time to go spruce up."

I glide out of the room as Jason sits back and stares at me.

Murph 1, Jason 0.

When I get to Speakeasy, all the way in Colebury, it's packed. I love crowds. Drinks of any kind. Dancing. I adore the energy and feed off it like I'm a new kind of zombie. I can have fun even if I don't know anyone, and this place is perfect—good vibes, not too pretentious, not too dingy. Just right.

It's going to be a fun night. I'm glad I took an Uber.

I see Reeve and wave energetically. He's snuggled up to Oz, his beau. He waves but gets caught in a kiss. Darn beau, taking my friend away from me.

Speaking of which, where's *my* beau?

In the dim light, I scour the room for a guy I've hooked up with a few times, and then I spot him. His hair's light brown, and he has a nice smile. He was good for a quick blow job in a bathroom. And I guess he's back for another round.

So maybe this isn't a date. It's a date-*ish.*

Truth be told, I'm a personality whore, so looks really aren't everything, but this guy's a poor man's Jason.

That's not a very nice thought, Murph.

Jesus, I'm pathetic. I straighten my spine and beeline over to him. When I get to his table, I muster up a smile and hold out my hand as if he's gonna kiss it. "Hey," I draw out the word. "How's the amateur porn?"

London laughs, and I'll agree it's a nice laugh. He looks me up and down. And, darn it, I know I look good in my white jeans and my red sweater that exposes a shoulder. "Wanna stay here? Or get going?" He licks his lips.

Something about his blatant once-over makes me hold back. "Let's stay here." I'm not opposed to moving fast, and I'm not sure why I don't want to just leave with him, but I guess I need to ease into things tonight. Apparently I've forgotten how to hook up.

"Buy you a drink?"

"I thought you'd never ask," I say. He leaves me at the table to get our beers.

When he comes back with the brewery's latest release, I take a sip. It's a bit hoppier than I like, but I can taste the quality in it. London and I chat about the menu and the brewery. He drinks the first beer fast and has another before I'm even done with half of mine.

And judging by the way he's slurring, I think he did some pregaming before he got here. So now I'm wondering if he'll be too sloppy for anything tonight.

Figures. Even my hookup doesn't seem to jibe with me.

But then the door opens and my heart does a colossal flip-flop, because Jason walks in.

Knock it off, heart.

Also, what the hell is he doing way out here?

Helpless to do anything but watch the way Jason moves, I track him across the place as he goes to the bar and orders a beer.

Quit it, Davey Murphy. You are on a goddess-damned date-ish. Pay attention to London.

I turn away from my crush and focus on my date, who natters away about hops and alcohol percentages and I have no idea what. "You really know a lot about brewing," I say.

He flushes. "I do some home brew."

"Ah." I try to think of something to say. Normally it's really easy for me to chat, flirt, make other people feel at home.

But I imagine Jason's eyes boring into the side of my head, and it's distracting. Even if he is doing no such thing, he's still distracting.

I chance a look.

Jason is sitting at a table by himself, his brows furrowed, drinking a beer. He's changed into a hoodie and jeans, and he's giving off lonely vibes.

Why would Jason be lonely? He has Marnie.

I force myself to talk to London. Now he's telling me about sugar quantity in beer and something about the yeast.

Closing my eyes, I open them again and give him my best smile. "Hey, my new roommate walked in."

"Who?"

I gesture over to Jason. "Him."

"He's cute." London eyes him.

That makes me bristle. London's supposed to be my date. What the hell is he doing drooling over Jason? It's *my* job to drool over Jason. "He's nice, and not gay." I add that last bit even though I don't want to admit it.

"Too bad."

"What do you mean, 'too bad'?"

"I was wondering if he'd be interested in a threesome."

Okay, I'm no prude. I've done my fair share of ambitious sex acts. But the idea of sharing Jason with London makes me irrationally angry. "No," I say. "You're not gonna get anywhere with that."

"Babe," he says. "I'm sorry. Don't take everything so seriously."

"I'm not," I snap. "And I'm not your babe."

This was a bad idea. I'm not sure why I'm so pissy, but I think it has something to do with the fact that the guy I really want just walked in. And he'll never want me the way I want him.

JASON

Why'd I come here?

Some days I can't explain my actions even to myself. After Murph left to go on his date—hookup—*whatever*—I stayed at home for approximately a nanosecond. Enough time to change out of my suit.

I told myself I only wanted to chill. Get a beer. Relax. After all, it was a grueling week of sales calls and being turned down right and left by people not wanting to buy insurance. Plus dealing with my dad. Sometimes a guy just needs to let off some steam, and on a Friday night that means either copious consumption of alcohol or getting laid.

I have no chance of getting laid, since Marnie's out of town. So alcohol it is, although I'll admit driving this far to do it might be what the kids call a poor life choice. Now that I'm here, though, I'll take it easy.

It's worth the drive, since the brewery's a nice place. I've come here before, by myself or with friends—back when they were still around.

But in reality, I don't know why I'm at a bar in Colebury. I have beer at home, and I'm acting like an overprotective older brother. I'm not even that much older than Murph—we're about the same age, I think.

Something about Murph, though. I can't explain it. Not even to myself.

When I entered the crowded bar, my eyes landed on Murph immediately, because he lights up a room. He's unapologetically unique, and you can't help but watch him. He's so secure in who he is that he doesn't care what you say. He's gonna be himself.

I can appreciate that about a guy.

I mean about a friend. A *new* friend. I can appreciate that about *Murph*.

Not wanting to be in a bar without something in my hands, I ordered the first IPA I saw on the list and came over to a table, wanting to be alone and unwind from the week. I tried to get so I wouldn't be in Murph's sight line, but it was the only table available.

So much for trying to not be overbearing.

But I do my best to keep to myself and take in the whole room, not just my roommate. The music in this place is decent—jazzy stuff tonight. I recognize a few people from town.

I notice, though, that Murph's date is talking his ear off. Murph doesn't give off miserable vibes, but he's not the life of the party, either. I suspect that makes this a rare situation, although I've only known the guy a week. His smile seems too polite, like it's plastered on his face.

I have half a mind to go interrupt, but that would be an asshole move, and I can barely justify being here in the first place. I've already done too much by showing up without a decent explanation.

One beer, and I'll be gone. I take another sip. It's good, and I do relax. My jaw unclenches, and my shoulders loosen.

But Murph swivels his head to me, and his expression is a different one than I've seen before. This isn't his happy face, nor his flirty face. But it's not a "come rescue me" face, either. It's contemplative, almost yearning. I find myself wondering what he's thinking.

There go my shoulders, binding up again.

Murph's date orders more beers, and I see him down one after another. Murph's still on the same one, as far as I can tell.

Meanwhile, I've switched to water. And I can't explain why I went to a bar forty-five minutes from home to drink water.

I guess to make sure Murph's date doesn't hurt him. After all, this is the aggressive guy who sent Murph the dick pic. It seems my fears are justified, since he's swaying, and his cheeks have that flush some people get with alcohol.

I watch, wary, as London reaches over and takes Murph's hand.

Murph draws it back, and I know I'm not mistaking the look on his face or the way his mouth forms the word, "No." But the guy practically climbs on top of Murph—getting very handsy—and kisses him.

I want to rip the man's head off.

Murph stands up and pushes him away, and I'm on my feet in one millisecond and at their table in two.

"Hey," I say. "Back off."

But this twat knocks his chair over so he can keep his hands on Murph, even reaching around to knead Murph's ass.

Murph has the sass to be able to tell London off, but for some reason he's not. He's struggling to get away, so I tug London by his collar. He stumbles back, and I stand between him and Murph.

"Do you want this guy bugging you?" I ask Murph.

"No." He looks over my shoulder at London. "I think you've had a few too many."

The drunk guy rolls his eyes. "Don't be like that. You didn't have a problem with me the last time. Get your asshat friend here to leave us alone."

"Jason's not an asshat," Murph says, sticking out his chin. "You don't know what you're talking about."

"Seems like an asshat to me."

"Fuck off," I hiss at him.

"S'make me." And he lunges around me, toward Murph again, this time aiming for, I don't know, Murph's ear.

I grab the first thing I can find, which is the guy's own beer, and throw it at him like he's a dog and it's a hose.

Liquid drips down his face. "What the fuck, man? Why'd ya do that?"

My pulse races. "Because he said to get off him."

"No, he didn't."

"He said no. If you couldn't read that as no consent, I don't know what's wrong with you."

"Nothing the fuck's wrong with me," slurs the guy. "Just you, jackass."

"Hey," Murph says, placing a hand on my shoulder. "I can stick up for myself." But his hand trembles.

"I know you can." I turn to him and study his wide blue eyes. "I only wanted to help. Are you okay?"

"Course," he says. "Why wouldn't I be?"

Now his whole body is shaking.

Fuck.

"Murph, let me take you home."

He takes one last look at me and at the other guy and nods.

The guy's still wiping his face with napkins and swearing up a storm. Security arrives to escort him out.

Murph turns and leaves, with me following close behind.

We drive home, and for the first time, there's a tense silence between me and him.

"I didn't mean to interrupt your date," I say. "I just ..." My words trail off, because I can't think of a reason why I was there other than it's a free country and if I want to go to a bar, I can. Even to drink water.

"Oh, you didn't." He gives me the patented Murph grin,

which I can see even in the dark. Then it slips. "He wasn't doing it for me. And he was rather drunk. I think he was drunk even before I got there. So thanks for butting in."

"I think you could have handled it yourself," I say, meaning it.

"Normally, yes. I may be small, but I can be mighty. It's great to have backup, though."

My hackles immediately rise. "You've been hurt on a date before?"

"Easy, Cujo. No. But there've been a few times where the other guy was on something or had too much to drink, and I had to stop things." He glances over to me. We turn onto my street. *Our* street. "Do you even want me saying this? You probably get grossed out hearing about men touching each other."

I don't know how to answer that. I don't want detailed descriptions. But I'm also pissed off at anyone who would take advantage of Murph.

But he's telling me he isn't helpless. And maybe I should let him handle his own situations.

I glance over at him. "You can tell me anything, and I'll listen."

A long beat goes by before he says anything. "That's truly great, Jason. Most people just talk. It's nice, if you're a talker like me, to find someone who will hear you out."

"I'll do my best to keep an open mind."

"I know."

We pull up to the house and get out. I unlock the front door and follow him up the stairs. His legs are longer than I thought.

When we get up to the top floor, he opens the door, and we both go inside, shucking our shoes.

"Want something to drink?" I ask, suddenly not tired.

"Yeah."

"Sangria?" I head to the fridge and poke my nose in. Murph had made a pitcher.

"Sure, unless you want something stronger." He tucks his stockinged feet under him on the couch and drags an old blanket of mine over him, and he looks so cozy I don't want him to have to get up for anything.

"I think if we had whiskey, I'd probably end up doing something stupid."

Murph perks up. "Oooh, then we must."

I laugh. "No way. You just dealt with a guy who drank too much." Grabbing two highball glasses and the pitcher, I go into the living room. I pour, then join him on the couch.

"Cheers," I say, and we clink glasses.

"Cheers." He gives me a small smile.

"Can I ask you something?"

"Always."

"Why were you so uncomfortable with that guy? I thought you'd gotten together with him before."

Judging by the look on his face, that was the one question I shouldn't have asked.

MURPH

My crush on Jason Falkner is getting out of control. *Seriously* out of control.

What right does he have to show up at a bar that's not even in Burlington, his hair all disheveled and flopping in his eyes, his shirt exposing some lickable golden skin at his Adam's apple, his boots sturdy on the floor, drinking beer like he's in an ad?

What right does he have to outshine my date? Poor London, that drunk asshole.

What right does Jason have to be all chivalrous and not get drunk, then stick up for me and take me home and give me what I really want—sangria and time with him?

No right. He has absolutely no right. Especially when he's so completely off-limits. Especially when my thoughts about him are only going to lead to my utter heartbreak.

Then he has the audacity to ask the only question I have no intention of answering honestly.

Except I can't lie to him, either.

"Guess I didn't want to go home with him." There. That's truthful, even if it's only part of the truth. Most of the truth.

Jason nods as if I've said something profound. "How often do you go home with guys?"

"Fairly often." At least, before I got obsessed with my new roommate.

"You don't date anyone long term?" He looks down at his glass and shakes his head. "Sorry, I'm being pushy."

"Oh, my life is an open book, sweetheart," I croon. "I'll tell you anything. But I'm not sure you want to hear it."

"That may be." His fingers stroke the pale green glass, and I wonder if he knows what it looks like. If he realizes his move's kinda phallic and therefore erotic. Or maybe I'm the only one with a dirty-enough mind to think so. To ignore my thoughts, I down a big ol' swallow of the alcohol.

I catch his eyes. "It's easy to find a guy to spend an evening with. It's hard to find one to spend the rest of your life with. And I guess I assuage my desire to find the right one by finding the one right now."

He raises an eyebrow. "Assuage?"

"Hey, my vocabulary kicks ass."

Jason's grin settles somewhere deep in my soul, making me feel like all is okay. Like he accepts me for who I am … and that's way too dangerous a thought for me to indulge in. Balancing his heel on the toe of his other foot, his long legs stretched out on the coffee table, he goes back to the previous topic. "So you're playing the field, but you're actually looking for someone to stay with."

"Yeah. Are you? I mean, other than Marnie." I internally applaud my ability to hit the badminton birdie he just lobbed at me back over the net to him.

"No, I'm not looking to settle down." His words don't match the sad look on his face, and I don't believe him for a second. Rather, I believe that *he* believes this. But I don't think it's what he really wants.

"Why don't you want to settle down?"

Jason stiffens. "Because I don't."

I give him my most charming smile. "That's okay. You don't have to tell me."

But I can tell he wants to tell me. That's the thing about

Jason. While he listens well, he also shares. He's quiet, but not *that* quiet. And sure enough, within a few seconds he starts speaking again. "I guess ... the first girl I dated, I fell for her hard. And the last one. Well, all the girls I've dated, I've fallen for hard. And each of them dumped me. It was like I couldn't see that they weren't that into me. And I figured, if I was that clueless, I should just completely knock it off. I couldn't trust my feelings, because they obviously weren't reciprocated. So I quit dating. Or rather, I quit going out on dates. I hook up, but that's it."

I blink at him. "I'm very sorry."

"Don't be. I was a kid."

"Wait, your first girlfriend was in high school, no?"

"Yeah."

"And when were the others?"

"College."

"Any since then?"

"No."

"But weren't you trying to figure yourself out in college?"

"Don't get all psychological on me, Murph."

"I'm not," I protest. "Okay, I totally am. Give yourself a break. You were just a kid trying to figure things out. Maybe it took a few tries to get it right. You'll find the right person."

I'm kidding myself by not saying "woman." But still, I couldn't resist putting it out there.

I make a point of looking around the comfortable room we're in. "What are you waiting for? You're a landowner with a steady job, a wardrobe that isn't exclusively ripped jeans, and a jawline to die for. You're quite a catch."

Did I just make him blush?

I made him blush.

Awesome.

"I don't know," he says. "If I fall for someone, then it happens. But I'm not looking right now."

I'm beginning to think Jason wouldn't realize I'm romantically interested in him even if I erected a digital sign over my head with a flashing arrow pointing to me.

Maybe I should be more direct.

Hmm.

"Hungry?" I ask. "I can make snacks."

"Sure."

I get up to go find the microwave popcorn.

I'm kneeling on the floor, rummaging at the back of a lower shelf, when Jason comes into the kitchen to set down the empty sangria pitcher.

"Well, this is convenient," I say, noting the position of his zipper right in front of my face.

He laughs, but it sounds strangled.

My heart's pounding in my throat. "If you wanted me on my knees, you could have said something."

"No, Murph. I'm not that kind of guy. You're great, but I'm not into dudes."

And something about the way he says it makes me so utterly sad. Because it's final.

Fuck.

Before I say anything else, he asks, "Wanna watch something?"

I nod. He takes the popcorn from me and sets it in the microwave, then helps me to my feet.

His hand feels warm in mine.

I want to touch him. I want to slam him up against the wall and climb up him, using his body as leverage. I want to see what he tastes like.

But Jason isn't in the closet.

He's straight.

And I must get past this crush on him as fast as I can. As far as I can.

So I won't be tempted to keep knocking on a door that'll never open.

After watching *Rick and Morty*, we head off to bed. Me in my room, and him in his. We both close our doors behind us.

But I don't turn off my light.

I spend an inordinate amount of time wondering what's going on behind his door, because there's no way in hell he's wondering what's going on behind mine. (Which is a whole lot of nothing.)

It's a truth universally acknowledged that I'm never going to be able to date the straight guy. Therefore, I need to cast out a line again, hoping to reel in a real fish.

Not literally. In this case, "real fish" means "gay man, preferably very sexy and fun."

I pull out my phone and scroll. Now, what am I in the mood for?

Off-brand Jason. That's what I'm in the mood for.

No.

I'm in the mood for *Jason*.

So I need to find the exact opposite. I can't have Jason, I'll never be able to have him, therefore I have to snare someone else.

I flip through the hookup app on my phone. But I'm thinking, "No, no, *no*, NO, definitely NOT," as I sample Vermont's finest.

Sometimes it's hopeless. Sometimes all I want is so close but still impossible.

I stare at this room, full of familiar things in a new space just trying to make their home here. Like me. I stare at my hand holding the phone, and I wonder what the purpose of all of it is anyway.

A little queer boy grows up to be a very bendy gay man. He's out and proud. But secretly, underneath it all, he's scared. Scared that he's always going to be lonely.

I sigh and turn over and wish I could crawl into bed with Jason and feel his big body warm mine. Maybe he could help this loneliness go away.

Even though I know that's the wrong thing to wish.

JASON

On Saturday morning, the hanging bells on the door of a frilly women's clothing shop on Church Street announce my arrival, and I refrain from ducking for cover. My scuffed boots and flannel are as out of place here as a cactus on a massage table.

This is a terrible idea.

But brotherly duties call. Becky used to make me do this in high school, because there was no way our dad would take her shopping. He'd give us money and tell me to drive her somewhere to pick out whatever we needed. That meant she picked out school clothes for both of us while I played on my phone.

Still, somehow she persists in the notion that I have an opinion about clothing in general and hers in particular. I don't.

Becky drags me to the back dressing room area. "I'm going to try these on"—she picks up two garments that were on a hook marked "Hold for Becky Falkner"—"and you need to tell me which one you like better."

"I'm really bad at this."

"It's an emergency." Her eyes plead with me. She has some Chamber of Commerce function tonight where she needs to be all dressed up, and no friends were available at the last minute to give her a second opinion. "I made you enchiladas for lunch."

I sigh. Food bribes work. I still think of myself as the family cook, so when she does it, it's a special event. "Fine." I start wandering around the racks while she tries on the first dress.

She can't seriously want my take on whatever the hell she's going to wear. I think it's a passive-aggressive way to get me to acknowledge everything she does for me. But I'll readily admit she does a lot for me—collects rent, negotiates leases, hires maintenance people when repairs are beyond my ability. Even picks out my suits and ties.

With Becky cooking, I wonder what Murph will do for lunch, though. He's working, so maybe he brought the leftover casserole I made.

Why am I thinking about him?

The only explanation I can come up with as to why I'm preoccupied with feeding him—besides it being ingrained since childhood—is because he's so slim. He's like a hummingbird who needs to sip nectar all the time to keep up his energy.

Well, that and because, after hearing a few of his stories, I think no one's ever properly cared about him before. If I can help him out with food and shelter, I'll feel like I'm being a better person.

Maybe I'll feel better about last night, too.

I glance up. I never go into stores like this, and the person behind the counter can tell, because she watches me warily.

But my eyes snag on a row of scarves on the counter. They remind me of someone. I can see the cobalt blue one around a certain roommate's neck.

I owe him an apology. It isn't so much that I think either one of us did something wrong at the bar or back at the house. But I don't want things to be awkward. I'm not sure how to process last night—me going out of my way to the bar only to break up his date, him offering me a blow job, me turning it down. And I didn't miss the disappointment in his eyes at my rejection. He tried to play it off like me saying no didn't matter. But I think it did.

Too bad I don't like him that way.

Tell that to my dick, though. I'm embarrassed to say that seeing him down there got me aroused—at least a little bit.

But any guy'd get aroused by an offer like that from someone who knew what she—or he—was doing.

At least, I presume Murph knows what he's doing.

Moving on …

I touch the light-as-air scarf, the dark blue shot with silver strands reminding me of his eyes. So, okay, it's a women's shop, but I'm certain Murph won't care. He wears eyeliner, after all.

Before I lose my nerve, I pull out my wallet. "I wanna get this for a friend."

The woman behind the counter startles at my words but perks up at a sale.

Behind me, I hear the dressing room door open. "Jason?"

"Yeah?" I turn around. Becky's wearing some kind of dress thing. She looks nice, I guess. I couldn't tell you what it is other than a green dress. "It looks good."

She twists in the mirror, trying to see herself at all angles. "I don't know. Is the color going to wash me out?"

"No," I say, not looking at her. I sign the credit card slip, and the woman hands me the scarf in an overly decorated bag. Murph'll like it.

"Ooh, are you getting something for Marnie?" Becky pads over in bare feet, a tag hanging from her armpit.

My neck feels hot. "No. Um, actually, I thought Murph would like one of those scarves."

Her eyes register surprise, but she recovers fast. "I'm sure he would. That's nice of you."

"I was a jerk to him last night and need to make it up to him."

"I see how it is. So, story of your life?"

"Maybe. I'll tell you about it at lunch." I pick up the bag and find a chair to wait in. "Try on the other one. Let me see it, and then let's get out of here."

"So I can feed you."

"Exactly."

Becky sits across from me at her house, a demolished enchilada dish between us, as we sip beer.

"Becky, you've known me your whole life."

She raises an eyebrow. "Obviously."

"Can I ask you something?" I don't know why, but my stomach churns. It's not the enchiladas. Those were the bomb dot com.

Her green eyes match mine, but she senses my seriousness and hers widen in sympathy. Or concern. "Of course."

"Do you think I'm homophobic?"

She does a double-take, then scans the room as if we're being watched. "Why do you think that?"

I tell her about Murph's date getting handsy with him last night and me losing it. "Murph's sexual orientation shouldn't bother me. But I'm wondering if I have a subconscious antagonism toward gay men from growing up with Dad. Did I flip out just because I saw that guy touching him? I'd hate it if I did."

"That doesn't sound homophobic. If it'd been different genders—drunk girl handsy with a guy who didn't want it or vice versa—you'd still come to the rescue, no?"

"Yeah, I guess." I pause. "There's more. He's always been super flirty, but last night he made a more specific pass at me. Maybe. He could have been kidding. I'm not sure. I turned him down, obviously, but I don't want things to be strained between him and me. But they kind of are. So am I now having this reaction to him because he's gay?"

She stares at me long and hard. "Huh."

I sit back in my chair, crossing my arms over my chest. "'Huh'? That's all you're gonna say, 'Huh'?"

"Yeah. Huh." She bites her lower lip.

"You're no help."

Becky shrugs. "Are you this way about all gay guys in general? Or only the ones in your space?"

I think for a moment. "I'll see guys walk down the street, some of them holding hands, and I couldn't care less. And Murph doesn't bother me when he's on his own. I think he's"—funny, fascinating, adorable—"fine."

"Interesting." She brushes her hands together as if she's wiping off flour. "Sorry, big bro, I don't have an answer for you." She goes to stand up, and I put my hand over hers, keeping her there.

"But you know I don't wanna be a homophobe, right? I'm better than that. I hate that being around him makes me such an asshole. Shit. I just blamed him. Like it's his fault I feel a certain way. It isn't. But there's gotta be some trigger I don't know about."

Her smile goes all wonky. "At least you're self-aware enough to know it's not his fault you feel something for him."

"I don't feel anything for him," I insist. "I'm only worried because I threw a beer in his date's face."

"Sounds like his date deserved it."

"He did." I sip my beer. "I thought I was open-minded, but maybe I'm as much of a douche as Dad is. I'd hoped I'd been exposed to enough diversity in college to not be driven by the programming of our childhood. But maybe I wasn't."

"Maybe Murph moving in is a good thing. Maybe he challenges you in ways you never thought you needed to be challenged."

I nod repeatedly. "He's not anything like what I thought he would be like. I thought he'd be entertaining and sort of goofy—which he is. But he's got depth to him, too. He isn't all sparkles and 'Oh, I'm gay.'" I wave my hand limply and feel ridiculous, so I stop. "That's only one facet of his personality." I sigh. "I'm embarrassed to say I had to learn that. Serves me right for judging people by their stereotypes instead of who they actually are."

"Then it's a plus that he's moved in with you."

"Probably." I start thinking out loud. "Maybe Murph just didn't know where the boundaries are with me. I mean, my boundaries are clearly drawn when the other side has a dick."

"Didn't need to know that."

"I want to be sure he knows there's no attraction to him on my side. I'm just not built that way."

"But you don't want to hurt him."

"Right. I do, however, want to be his friend."

"Why don't you show him your art?" She picks up her plate and takes it to the kitchen. "He could try doing it with you. I mean, it's a thing you could do together to show him there are no hard feelings."

I purse my lips, considering. "That's not a bad idea."

After a while, I take off so Becky can get ready for her event. At home, I watch TV until the door opens and Murph comes home again.

"Hey, wifey," he says. "Did you have a good day?"

I study him, looking for an indication that he's upset. While he's lacking his usual Murph enthusiasm—his hair is lying flat, and there's tension in the set of his mouth—it could be because he's tired from being on his feet all day at work. "Yeah. You?"

Murph nods. "I'm gonna go change." He beelines for his room before I can say anything else.

I'm itching to give him his present, but I decide to wait. It doesn't feel right to do it now. Sighing, I get up to cook.

But everything seems mostly fine with him at dinner. Then we watch a movie until it's time for bed.

The next afternoon, after I do the meal prep for the week, I knock on Murph's door. He's sitting on his bed with his laptop, wearing reading glasses, surrounded by books.

"You wear glasses?" I blurt.

He rubs his nose and scrunches his eyes. "Yeah. Sometimes. Why?"

"I don't know why. Just hadn't seen you wear them." I shake my head, remembering what I was going to ask him. "What are you doing?"

"Working on my blog. But I can take a break. Why?"

"I was thinking about doing something. Wanna come along?"

His eyes light up behind the dark plastic rims. "So mysterious, Mr. Falkner. Are you going to tell me where we're going?"

"To go get you a year's supply of free cucumbers."

He cracks up and sets down his laptop. Taking off his glasses, he wipes his eyes. "No, seriously."

"I want to show you this thing I do."

"What is it?"

"Do you want to come or not?"

"Absolutely." He looks down at his jeans. "Is this okay? Or do I need to wear something else?"

"You're good. Wear closed-toed shoes and long sleeves."

"Most fun things I do involve less clothes."

Ah, there's Murph. I'm grateful I haven't wrung the flirt out of him.

"Let me know when you're ready," I say. I go wait for him in the living room.

A few minutes later, he's wearing sneakers and a sweater but no glasses. "Are you going to tell me what we're doing?"

"Slumping glass."

He furrows his eyebrows. "What's that?"

I walk over to the kitchen counter, pick up a fruit bowl, dump out the bananas, and hand it to him. It's shiny and purple, wide and shallow, with bits of gold glass embedded in it like terrazzo. "This."

"Cool."

I can tell he doesn't get it. "That's what I make."

Murph practically bounces. "You made this? It's gorgeous!"

"Thank you."

"Wait," he says, head whipping around to take in all of the kitchen. "Not to ask a silly question, but did you make all the dishes we use? Like, did you make these?"

He holds up one of the goblets in the drying rack.

"Yeah, I did that. Different technique. But yes."

He turns the glass around in his hand slowly. "You made this."

"That's what I said."

"It's *art*."

"More like craft."

He shakes his head vehemently. "No, it's art. You have to make decisions about what kind of glass to use and what colors and shapes. I can't believe you just nonchalantly use all this glassware you made. Are the plates yours, too?"

I smile. "Yes. I don't use leaded glass. It's safe."

"That's incredible." He keeps shaking his head. "You have all these parts to you that you don't show anyone. People here think of you as, what, this guy who sells insurance? Kinda quiet. When really, you have all this stuff going on under the surface."

"Isn't that all of us, though? I could say the same thing about you."

"You mean there's more to me than blogger bartender?"

"I do. Come on."

And he follows me down the stairs.

MURPH

We head outside to an outbuilding in a cleared area behind the house. Beyond are woods, full of the last green leaves of the year.

Jason unlocks the door and heads inside. "Um, this is where I keep my kiln," he says.

What did I say about having the vapors when I met him? Now I might incinerate. Literally.

How come I didn't know my smoldering roommate was even hotter than I thought? All this time he's been cooking for me *and* serving me food on dishes he made. Dishes made out of colored glass, some iridescent, with bits of other glass embedded inside. Complicated and colorful and interesting and unique.

He's an artist.

Goddess help me.

A friend, Murph. He's a friend.

The place is painted white inside, with several windows and a high ceiling. Shelves hold bins of broken glass organized by color and cardboard boxes marked as containing different kinds of glass.

He goes over to a large kiln at one end of the room and turns it on.

"You seriously do this?" I ask.

Jason gives me a big grin. "Yes. Take these goggles. Shoulda made you bring your glasses. Next time." He hands me a pair, and I put them on. He puts some on himself and then rolls up his sleeves.

Oh, holy forearms.

My roommate's arms are precisely the right level of hairiness —masculine, but not so hairy that I can't see his skin. And he's got a vein going down each forearm leading to long, clever fingers. I want to know what those fingers could do to a boy.

Say something, Murph. "I've never heard of slump glass," I admit.

"Instead of blowing glass, it's fusing different pieces of glass together. Basically, you take glass, put it in a mold, and let it melt into whatever shape the mold is." He grins. "I can do a tacky fish plate or fuse a bottle or whatever."

"You absolutely need to make me a tacky fish plate," I say.

He puts on gloves, handing me a pair that I slip on. They're big and very worn in, and I feel like I'm wearing a part of Jason.

"Okay." He selects a large piece of blue glass and then goes to a shelf and pulls out a mold shaped like a fish. "I'm into eighties designs." The tips of his ears pink. I remember his speech about boys liking poems. This matters to him. "You know, with lots of neon and triangles. Like a Duran Duran cover."

"That's totally radical. I'll break out my acid-washed jeans." I pause. "Actually, I have a pair of those. They're tight."

He laughs. Then he gives me a shy smile. "Wanna try making something, too?"

"Sure!"

He pulls out sheets of glass that glow in the white room, dazzling in the afternoon sunlight. Red. Yellow. Pink. Green. Blue. Clear. Like he's holding up large square jewels.

"Basically, you have to figure out what you want to do, arrange it in the mold, and we'll fire it up and see what happens."

With him standing so close to me at the table, his words are going in one ear and out the other like when he told me how to unlock the front door. Incidentally, I'm only just now getting the hang of that piece of machinery.

But I follow the basic concept of what he's saying and set to work, choosing colors.

Using the tools, I end up cutting a bunch of trapezoids in rainbow colors and arranging them in order in the shape of a triangle.

He looks at me and grins. "I never thought of doing that."

"What can I say? It seemed right." I arrange the rainbow triangle on a clear glass square and set the whole thing on a mold so it will become a concave plate.

He reaches around me to grab a hammer to chip away a piece for his own design, and I wobble from the contact. Too soon, we're both done.

"Ready for the heat?" he asks.

"Always."

I hope he doesn't catch on that I mean it in more than one way.

He opens the kiln, and a sheen of sweat beads on his brow. With his biceps, he's got some hammer-of-Thor stuff going on. Carefully, he maneuvers one mold at a time, places them in the kiln, and sets the timer.

We both let out a breath.

"So this is what you like to do in your spare time?"

"Uh-huh. I tried stained glass, too, but I'm not that much of a fan of working with the lead. I prefer melting it into molds. It feels like alchemy."

"How come you don't blow glass?"

"I could, I suppose. I just like doing this." He wipes his brow with the hem of his T-shirt, and I almost lean over to lick him. I swear he has no idea how handsome he is. Or what his effect on me is. If he did, I'm sure he'd have some sort of gleam in his eye. But he looks innocent, and I think it's for real.

I have to change the subject. "Funny to think glass is only sand, right? On the beach it's boring and doesn't look like much. But you can make it into all these colorful things."

"Lots of things don't seem like much until you take a closer look."

"Not me. I'm exceptional." I'm kidding, but Jason's face is serious.

"You are. And then, when you get a closer look?"

"What?" I say, not hiding my breathlessness.

"There's even more to you."

I only wish I could have more with him.

"While we're waiting for this," Jason says, interrupting my thoughts, "I got something for you. Hang on. Let me get it. It's in my car."

He picks up his keys and leaves, leaving me standing there wondering what the hell Jason got me. I have no clue. It could be a jar of Lyon honey or an eviction notice.

Hopefully not that last one.

Jason returns, holding one hand behind his back, and again looks shy. "I wanted to apologize for the other night. I shouldn't have gotten in your date's face. You could have handled it. It wasn't any of my business."

I blink at him. Of all the things I thought he'd say, this isn't one of them.

"It's okay," I say. "I liked having someone in my corner."

"Becky dragged me out shopping, and I saw this and thought of you. I wanted to say I'm sorry." He shoves a gift bag at me.

I clap my hands. "For me?" I feel this lightness in my chest, and my adrenaline spikes. "This is so thoughtful!"

He shrugs. I can tell by the way he's being bashful that he hopes I like it.

The gift is wrapped up in a pink bag with ribbons cascading down it, and I wish I could've seen Jason walking down Church Street carrying it. I open it up and pull out cloth wrapped in tissue paper. I unwrap it and hold up the most beautiful blue scarf I've ever seen.

Tears fill my eyes.

"I thought it—" He scrubs his face. "It reminded me of you.

And I thought you'd like it. Also, Becky took forever to try on clothes, and there was only so long I could stand the woman who owned the place staring at me."

I'm opting not to believe that last part at all. Jason Falkner bought me a present he chose himself, and he couldn't have chosen something better if he'd taken me along and let me pick. It matches my eyes, and I wear silver like this all the time. "It's perfect," I croak out.

He shoves one hand in his jeans pocket, then rubs the back of his neck with the other.

"Can I give you a hug?" I ask, my voice stronger, as I set my present on the table. Really, I want to fling myself into his arms.

Murph, friends can buy friends presents.

"Sure," he says and holds out his arms.

I step into them and snuggle against his chest. I feel at home at once. I know he's straight. I know he's just a friend. But goddess damn, he makes remembering that hard.

"Thank you," I whisper. He's genuinely shocked me. "I absolutely love it."

"My pleasure."

And again, Jason doesn't say "no problem." I love that he's like that.

We break apart. I finger the scarf and then fling it around my neck and pull out my phone to see how it looks.

"Yeah," he says, his voice husky. "I figured it'd suit you." He pauses for a moment. "We should check the glass."

He turns his back on me to fuss with the kiln, and my heart hurts even more. Because even though I think he's acting all romantic, it means nothing. I am perhaps filling the slot of BFF of Jason Falkner.

Nothing more.

The minute I get away from him, I'm finding a hookup. Someone. *Anyone.* A guy to help me forget about my crush. Because if Jason and I are going to be friends and only friends, I'm going to need a huge dick-straction to keep me from mooning over him.

"Oh, I meant to ask. Did you watch a *Rick and Morty* episode without me?"

His words bring me out of my thoughts. I can't stop stroking the scarf. "What?"

"You posted a new blog post. But I didn't watch the episode with you."

My jaw drops. "You caught that?"

"I set up an alert. Just let me watch them with you, will ya?"

My heart flutters. Operation Don't Moon Over Jason Falkner is a bust, because oh my goddess, Jason Falkner's stalking me.

Okay, he really isn't, but the fact that he's following me and supporting me? Means so much.

Often the people in your real life aren't into what you love. So you have to find people on the internet who are into the same things you are, because no one around you *gets* you on that level.

Jason's my real-life internet.

I shouldn't elevate him in my mind as much as I do, but crushes are hard.

Every day he gets more perfect for me. And every day he's more and more out of reach.

JASON

"I won't watch *Rick and Morty* without you," Murph assures me. The smile on his face seems genuine, but there's an edge to it that wasn't there before. Or maybe I didn't see it.

"Good. I need you to help me find all the Easter eggs," I say.

He nods.

Something's muted his impish enthusiasm. Or some*one*. I hope it wasn't me.

I feel like I need to go for a run. Burn off some excess energy.

I'd thought that being nice to him and showing him I want to be his friend would help us get over his proposition—er, blow job offer. *If* it was a real offer. I still don't even know if it was. He could've been teasing me.

But maybe spending more time together confuses him. Maybe I need to stay away and be an absent roommate. Not cook for him. Not show him my hobbies. Not hang out and watch movies together. Just go to work and come back.

Problem is, I don't want to stay away, because when I'm around him I feel more like myself. And what's more important, he's become my friend.

It's been a while since I've had a new friend. Is it a guy thing that once you leave school, you stop making friends? I don't know.

Watching Murph be careful around me makes me tetchy, though, because I like him to be wild and free.

And I need to stop thinking about him all the time.

The timer rings, and we pull the glass out from the kiln. Murph's square plate ends up being a riot of color.

"Not bad for an amateur. You could sell that at a pride fest," I tell him, as I unmold my fish plate. We set them both down to cool.

"Nah. I like it. I think I'll keep it." He peers up at me. "Making art with you has been fun. Thanks."

"My pleasure," I say, my voice hoarse for some reason. I clear my throat. "Shall we go back to the house? I'm thinking of going for a run."

"Can I come?"

My eyebrows shoot up. "You want to?"

He puts both hands on his hips and stares me down. "I don't know if you'll be able to keep up with me." Then I get a flash of a smile before he heads out the door.

"Tell yourself that," I yell after him as I close up behind me. "But I'm taller than you."

He calls over his shoulder, "Runners are little people with long legs. That's me."

In two strides, I catch up with him. "Fighting words, eh? Then it's on."

Once back inside and upstairs, I dress in workout clothes—loose shorts and a T-shirt—and head to the door. While the weather's starting to get cooler, I'll warm up soon enough when I get moving. Hearing Murph come out of his bedroom, I set my phone down on the entry table, but it lights up.

Marnie: Staying in Syracuse another week

Jason: How's your sister?

Marnie: Miserable

Jason: Sorry to hear that

When I look up, Murph's stretching his quadriceps, bringing one heel at a time to his butt. He's wearing red dolphin shorts and a hoodie.

I set down the phone again. "Ready?"

Murph bites his lip. Then, out of nowhere, he yells, "Race you!" He pushes past me, and before I can close the door, he's barreling down the stairs to the outside.

"You brat!" I cup my hand over my mouth and call. I leave my keys and wallet—no one's going to steal anything—and chase after him, taking the stairs two at a time.

When I get downstairs, he's jogging in place out front, laughing at me. "Come on, old man. Which way you wanna go?"

"I know a loop. This way." We take off west, headed for a route that will pass the lake and circle downtown. "And 'old man'? How old are you?"

"Twenty-four."

"I'm twenty-six. Hardly old."

"Keep telling yourself that."

We run at a comfortable pace, a little faster than a jog but not sprinting. The weather's starting to turn into fall, and there's a bite in the air.

"I love the seasons," Murph says as we start down another leafy street. "Vegas only has cold and hot."

"You don't mind the white fluffy stuff?"

"Nope. It's an excuse to cuddle up by the fire."

When we turn onto another road, he speeds up, and I struggle to keep pace with him, my breath coming in bursts and my chest tight. "You weren't kidding about being fast."

"Only when I want to be. I can take it slow, too. All night, even. If I need to."

Trying not to trip over my feet, I stare at him, and he flutters his eyelashes at me.

Why is he flirting? I told him nothing like that was going to happen between us. Still, it's better than that guarded expression from before. This is just normal Murph, I remind myself. It doesn't have to mean anything.

Then he breaks into a grin and speeds up, so I have to chase him.

We head toward Lake Champlain. "What do you think of the apartment, now that you're all moved in?"

"It couldn't be worse," he says. "I have this awful, ugly roommate who ... wait. That's someone else. I, in fact, have this amazing, gorgeous roommate who feeds me. So it's tolerable." He shrugs and bites his lips to hide a smile.

I chuckle, although I get a stitch in my side as I do. We run along Waterfront Park. "I'm glad Becky found you."

"Does she always pick out your roommates?"

"No." I flinch. But after we go another few yards, I correct myself. "Actually, yes, she picked out most of the tenants. It's my biggest flaw: I go along with what everyone else says. She says I don't think for myself. And see? Even me repeating that isn't thinking for myself."

Murph stops suddenly, and I almost bump into him. "Whoa, Jason. No. You're definitely easygoing, but you know how to think for yourself." He pauses for a second. "Maybe you just don't do it very often."

"Hmm." I start running again. Then I think about it for a few paces. "Maybe I should try doing it more."

We jog the long way around downtown and end up back at my—*our*—house, sweating and short of breath. I feel somewhat better. Or at least more tired than I was.

Murph races me upstairs, his ass shaking as he climbs the stairs faster than any guy should after running a few miles. "Claiming the first shower!"

He heads into the bathroom before I can say anything.

I laugh and go to the kitchen to get a drink of water until it's my turn to get cleaned up.

After eating dinner—I made vegetable pasta, then Murph did the dishes—and watching a movie with some exceptionally explicit sex scenes, I head to bed, and so does he.

My downstairs appendage has been weird all week. It's like it took a vacation to awkward-boner city. Right now, I'm chubbed up from the movie and the long-term effects of Marnie being out of town. Thankfully, while Murph and I shared the couch, I was sitting away from him at one end. He lay down with his head on the other arm and his feet near me, so I could hide my burgeoning erection with a blanket. Like I want to explain that one to my gay roommate.

For now, I need to focus on the task at hand—so to speak. I turn off the lights except one on a dimmer and stretch out on my bed. My dick plumps up further at the idea that it's going to get an O.

Peeling off my shirt and pants, I run my hands down my abs.

I've got half a mind to call Marnie—she might be up for some dirty talk. But for all I know she's putting cold compresses on her sister's forehead or something, and I'd be interrupting.

My fingers dip under my boxer shorts. The elastic stretches over my wrist as I stroke my lengthening cock. I give myself a few long pulls and let out a groan because, fuck, I need this.

I open up my laptop and navigate to a porn site. It immediately makes me harder, seeing all the thumbnail GIFs, and I reach down and play with my balls. The videos are grouped by genre. Jackhammer pounding or big girls or threesomes or whatever.

I'm not sure what my preferences are. Except that I like sex. In all forms. I've never been very picky.

But talking with Murph about how my sister makes my decisions for me makes me want to make some of my own.

Dunno why I'm thinking about him (or her, *god*) with my hand on my dick.

I shove my boxers down all the way for better access, and my hard dick thumps on my belly.

I click on a video, but it's only a cute girl getting banged by a hung guy, and while that will do it for me, I'm thinking it might be fun to go more unusual. Avant-garde. Okay, *kinky*.

With one hand trailing up and down my dick, teasing myself, I start navigating the site with the other. The computer's at an angle, so I move it onto a pillow and prop myself up like I'm the king of my bed or something.

Still lightly touching myself, I decide to skip the vanilla stuff. I find a gang bang link, but when I click on it, it's too violent. I just wanna see people getting off. Something sensual and scorching hot. After scrolling, I find a scene with two guys and a girl outdoors, and I click on it.

"Oh, fuck yes," I mutter. Then I realize I need to be quieter.

The country-like scene's deceptively normal—three people next to a fence in a grassy field. One guy's under the girl's skirt, kneeling behind her and fucking her on all fours with his pants still on while she sucks off the other guy—who stands, still mostly clothed. The girl's shirt is pulled down so you can see her tits, but all three actors are dressed enough that if they got caught, they could tidy up really fast.

Maybe that's what makes it so hot. There's something sexy about fucking while wearing clothes. The guys have their jeans on, unbuckled and pushed down just enough to expose their enormous dicks and the tops of their asses. The standing actor thrusts into the girl's mouth, and I wish I were getting sucked.

I reach over for some lotion and slide my slick hand over my straining cock.

Then one of the guys lies down on his back on a blanket, shucking his pants to his thighs. In a flash, the girl straddles his face, holding up her skirt, while the other guy pulls out some lube and starts riding his dick.

That gets my attention. What would that be like?

"God," I hiss.

The guy riding tries to jack himself, but the guy being ridden slaps his hand away. Not sure how he knows, since the girl's grinding on his face, but that's porn. She gasps and cries out porn-star style, but the combined noise of all of them is doing it for me.

"Fuck yeah. Come on," I groan. And then, because I feel like it, I take a lotioned-up finger and reach behind myself. I've done about everything you can with a girl—although nothing like this scene.

A finger is a good start, but a toy is what I really need. I riffle in the drawer until I find a vibrating prostate massager, lube it up, and stick it in.

Now I'm the one gasping, because *that* feels fucking good. I hear a moan, but it's not from the screen and it's not from me.

It came from Murph's room.

The porn stars groan, and Murph whimpers, and I can't help but let out a moan myself. Guess everyone's getting some right now.

I'm kind of out of my mind with pleasure.

While I'd never say it, there's something hot about my roommate jacking off at the same time I am. I wonder what porn he's watching.

The prostate massager stimulates the right place over and over (and over) again, and my hand runs up and down my dick so fast the friction could create smoke.

I hear fast breath from my neighbor and realize I'm turning him on, which makes me feel like a proud peacock. Guess I'm discovering one of my kinks—being an object of gay lust. Fine.

It's more than that, though. It feels like our breaths are intertwining, Murph in his room and me in mine. We're both heading to a crescendo, judging by how I've lost the ability to control what's coming out of my mouth. A moment later, I arch my back on the sheet and shoot all over my bare chest, my hand racing up and down my cock.

I plop back on the bed, panting, and shut the toy off.

In a moment, I hear an exhale and a long, low grunt, and at first I think it's the guy in the video, but no. It's my roommate. "Fuck, Jason," I hear him whimper, and I can tell he's coming, too.

I blink.

Oh, god.

What's it going to be like facing him tomorrow?

I take a deep breath and give myself a pep talk—that things really couldn't be more awkward than him on his knees, that we're both adults and take care of ourselves, that this was no biggie—but in reality, I don't know what to do.

I clean up and try to go to sleep. But I end up staring at the ceiling the whole night long.

MURPH

So, do I pretend it didn't happen?

Last night was one for the spank bank of the ages. I could hear Jason trying to be quiet—muffling his voice, maybe putting a fist over his mouth. And for some reason, that made it even sexier. All those "fuck yeah"s and "god"s made me stiffer than I would've been on my own. Because I could just imagine him erect and straining and tantalizing. Who needs porn? I've seen his powerful thighs—ones that went running with me yesterday. And I imagined, right before I came, how his face would look when he let go.

Now the inspiration for the hottest solo session of my life stands next to the coffee maker wearing only his suit pants, which hang low because he hasn't put his belt on yet. His hair glistens from the shower.

As I shuffle into the kitchen, I pray to the goddess for strength and wisdom—and to tame my morning wood, please. Thank you.

She ignores me.

"Morning," Jason says. He hands me a cup of coffee, and all I see are his long fingers.

"Morning."

I'm *not* thinking about what Jason's hands were doing last night. I wasn't when he poured me my coffee. I'm not when he grasps the refrigerator handle to get out the cream for his own cup.

And I'm definitely not looking at his gorgeous torso, because is he *trying* to make life hard for me? He doesn't need to. I'm already hard and doing my best to hide it with my robe.

I struggle with what to say next.

Did you sleep well after you tickled your pickle?

Can I see your pickle?

I'm never going to see his pickle. He made that abundantly clear when I was on my knees and an arm's reach away from zunipping—I mean unzipping him. Even my brain inside my brain isn't working.

Need coffee.

So I stand there staring at my mug, unable to say anything at all.

"I gotta, um, get to work," he says, bowing his head. And he heads back to his room while I watch him go.

Yeah. So. It's awkward.

That evening on break at work, I let my fingers do the swiping. While I'm nestled in Jason's blue scarf. It warms me up but also reminds me that there are limits. Hence, I need to move on.

First, I look at my contacts. London? No. Chad? Absolutely not. Scott? Hmm. Maybe. I text him to say hey, and I get a nice text back that he's out of town. Maybe another time.

Logging into my favorite hookup app for the whatever-th time this week, I scroll to see who's around. You'd think in Vermont there'd be nobody for me to play with. You'd be wrong. Vermont has plenty of gay guys (and all sorts of other people) looking to score.

My philosophy on everything is, *It can't be only me.* I can't be the only boy looking for love, and *someone's* looking for me. I'm sure of it. I'm cute and fun, and I know how to do things with my tongue. So I always assume Mr. Right or Mr. Right Now is out there. I just gotta set out a hook to catch him.

Because Mr. Perfect Who Lives With Me isn't an option.

"Twenty-seven-year-old, ten miles away." Sounds promising. I swipe.

"Heyyy," I say to my date Friday night. "I'm Murph." We're in a club in Burlington that has gay nights a few times a month.

I fluff my feathers a little bit. I mean that literally. I'm wearing a capelet with pink feathers on it.

"Ruben." He kisses me on the cheek. He seems okay, I guess. He smells good, and he's very, very clean. One of those guys who looks like he does nothing but put on moisturizer all the time. Not that I look any different.

"Nice to meet you."

"Same. Want a drink?" he asks.

"Oh, goddess yes. Cosmo, please." He nods and flags down the bartender. If I'm gonna go through with this date and hopefully get a little somethin'-somethin,' I need to lose my inhibitions. Not that I've ever had many to speak of, but those that remain need to go bye-bye.

I look around at the meat market.

It's funny to see so many guys checking their phones. Like they're trying to match up people present with their online profiles using only abs as guidance—but very few abs are showing, so it's like a bizarre game of go fish or memory. Just nothing's getting paired.

My pic is my tush, because of course it is.

I'm going to spend the next however long trying to figure out if I wanna take Ruben somewhere and blow him.

Before I moved in with Mr. Hottie McHotterson, Ruben would've been an easy way to get laid. Now, as he's paying for our drinks, I'm noticing all the ways he isn't like Jason. All the ways this feels wrong. I miss my beardy burly roomie.

Not the right mindset, Murph. Get it together.

A few couples I know walk in, and I let out a breath, watching them. I don't mind being in a place where I don't know anyone—and a gay club is about as safe as I can get—but still. It's nice to have friends around.

Ruben slides my drink over to me, and we clink glasses.

"So, how long have you lived here?" I ask, choosing to be kinda boring, because honestly, you gather a lot of gays around and often there's this competition to be more outré. Who has the biggest personality? Sometimes I want to play. Sometimes I don't. Tonight is one of those times I don't.

"I was living in Boston but got a job teaching at Burlington University, so I moved here."

"What do you teach?"

"Nursing."

Could I date a nurse?

Not dating. This is a hookup.

Maybe.

"Where do you work?" He looks at me and seems genuinely interested.

I tell him all about Vino and Veritas. He's been there, because, hello, it's a major draw for the state of Vermont. And New Hampshire. And other places. It's got a great rep.

But he sounds like he's more into the wine side of things than the books. I'm more into the books.

I down the cosmo in three swallows. I know I should be careful about mixed drinks and all that, but I'm sitting at the bar and saw the bartender make it. It makes me feel a little muzzy.

"Dance with me," I say, once Ruben finishes his Jack and Coke.

"Sure." He giggles.

Oh no, not one of those.

Bright lights punctuate the music, which is *yawn*. Standard gay-boy dance delights. Why can't it be something better than the stuff we all like?

I realize that's a strange statement, but bear with me.

I have all these issues with stereotypes. I love them and hate them. I am them, and I'm not them. I love it when I can find my people—people who understand what it's like to be me. But I hate it when it seems as if the stereotype is all there is.

Tugging Ruben to the dance floor with me, we dance to Madonna because *of course* the deejay's playing Madonna. Still, I try to lose myself in the fun, because I do like dancing. Ruben clutches my waist, and I grind up against him. But after a few songs, I'm done.

I don't know why I'm being so irritable tonight.

No, I do know why.

It's because after hanging out with Jason all week, after he gave me a present and spent time with me and hugged me, I hoped he would say or do *something*. But he didn't.

And when dreams die hard, I can get a little bitchy.

I decide to take Ruben home with me. Jason wasn't there when I left. Now, though, he's in the living room watching *Star Wars*.

"Hey," I say. "This is Ruben."

Jason stiffens his shoulders and stands up, giving Ruben a once-over.

It's not the way he looks at me. It's more like he's evaluating whether he needs to take Ruben out and punch him. I don't favor that look on Jason, but a secret part of me loves it because he's being protective of me. I don't *need* to be protected, but I kind of want it sometimes.

To continue my #rant on stereotypes, I don't like traditional gender roles—even gender roles within gay couples. Some think because I'm, well, me, I'm supposed to be the feminine one. I mean, yes, clearly I often am. But not always.

For a heterosexual male, Jason does plenty of stuff that's traditionally feminine, and I don't know if he even realizes it. He's a mother hen who cooks and cleans—not that those are exclusively female traits by any means. He's nurturing, probably from having to take care of his sister when they were teenagers. If we got together, we wouldn't be this couple where I'm the girl and he's the boy. We'd both be just … us.

Stop fantasizing, Murph.

It's me and *Ruben* tonight.

"Come sit down," I say to Ruben, claiming an end of the couch and patting the section next to me. We should probably just go to my room, but that feels weird with Jason around. Ruben sits down and tugs me into his lap.

"Hey." Jason picks up his beer and looks like he's going to head to his room.

"You don't have to leave," I say. "I don't want to kick you out of your own home."

"Right, we'd never dream of doing that," Ruben purrs, a flirty note to his voice. "You can stay."

Honestly, his voice is more eww than yum. And again, last month it would've been no big deal. Ruben's pants would've festooned the floor already. But now? I stifle a sigh.

And what's with all my dates wanting to get naked with Jason?

Jason settles in the recliner and takes a sip of his drink.

It's not like Jason has any claim over me, so I don't know why I'm giving him this much power. I shouldn't.

Jason glances from me to Ruben, then intentionally, decidedly, back to the screen.

I want to shoo Ruben out the door and curl up in a robe as close to Jason as I can get, but I don't want to be rude to Ruben. Also, it's not like Jason will ever notice me anyway.

"Want a drink?" I ask Ruben, disentangling myself. I head to the kitchen.

"Love one," he says.

I pour us each a glass of sangria and sit down close to him again. While part of me knows I'm doing this as part of Operation Push Jason Into Being Gay, I also know it's futile. He has Marnie. Ruben is Mr. Right Now. And that's good enough for me.

Except it isn't good enough for you, a little voice in my head says.

Fuck off, little voice. I'll do whatever I need to, to make sure you stay quiet.

I start chugging my drink like a frat bro.

Because I'm going to need to be a lot drunker if I'm going to handle this night in front of Jason.

JASON

I'm being a dick. A sullen, glaring bastard, silently telling the guy Murph brought home to GTFO.

I know I need to knock it off, but I can't seem to stop. Ruben bothers the fuck out of me.

He keeps touching Murph, who's mostly sitting on his lap. If Murph wanted to snuggle, well, that'd be one thing. I think I could handle seeing that.

But Murph's giving me vibes that he'd rather be elsewhere. He's trying too hard. I watch him guzzle his sangria as if he's forcing himself to touch this guy even though he doesn't seem to like him.

Murph's good looking, and he could have any guy he wants. Any *gay* guy. He doesn't need to settle for the first one he finds.

After we watch a few minutes of the movie, Ruben gets up to go to the bathroom, and Murph hisses, "What is *up* with you? Be nice."

"I *am* nice." I sound surly and not at all nice. I'm also suffocating in here. All week I've been preoccupied—haunted—by the sound of Murph when he comes (even with a wall between us). I'm sitting here pissed off, picturing a stranger sharing something so private with him. "You know what? I'm going for a run." I stand up.

"This late at night?"

"Sure." While I know Murph's sex life is none of my business, I'm still aggravated.

Murph's face falls. "Again, I'm not kicking you out of your own house."

"You're not." I head to my bedroom to change.

In the hallway, I pass Ruben, who raises a suggestive eyebrow at me.

What the hell? He's Murph's date. If I were dating Murph, I wouldn't look at another guy.

Not that I want to date Murph.

Or push this guy closer to him, because they're all wrong for each other.

"Don't do that," I mutter.

"Do what?" Ruben asks in a demure tone, reaching out a hand and laying it on my bicep.

I move so his hand falls. "Just don't."

He raises both eyebrows and lifts up his hands like he's all innocent, but the act pisses me off. It's nothing like Murph's teasing. Ruben's a lying liar who lies, and his playful voice grates on me. "I wasn't trying anything."

"Bullshit," I mutter and brush past him.

"Hey, man, what's your problem?" Ruben puts his hand on his hip and watches me head to my room.

My voice drops down low. "Pay attention to your date."

Ruben has the audacity to pretend to be insulted. "You think I was coming on to you?"

"Weren't you?"

"And people call me a drama queen." He rolls his eyes.

Beyond Ruben, I can see Murph perched on the couch, at first looking baffled—and then disappointed. "Jason," he says carefully. "What's going on?"

I've officially had enough.

Stepping toward Ruben, I get in his face. I can tell the guy's wearing lots of makeup. His face is nice looking, except a snake is hiding underneath. "Look, I don't know who you think you are, but don't fucking treat Murph like that. If you're on a date with him, don't go flirting with anyone else."

"*Christ*. You people are so touchy."

"What happened?" Murph asks, getting up from the couch. "How did something happen that fast?"

"Your date just tried to pick me up, too," I say. "No, thanks."

Murph's face flashes with anger. And maybe hurt. "Did you?" he asks Ruben.

"I was playing around. You guys are too serious for your own good."

Ruben swishes to the living room, picks up his jacket, and goes over to Murph. He gives Murph a quick kiss on the cheek and squeezes his shoulder. "Tell me when your guard dog isn't around, and we'll *really* have a fun night." He's out the door before Murph can react or I can say anything else.

Murph sits down and puts his head in his hands.

I don't know what to say. I come over to the couch and stand before him. "That guy was a bastard. He wanted to hump anything with legs."

Murph's muffled words chasten me. "I thought we talked about this. I can make decisions for myself. I'm good at it, actually. I don't need you coming in on your white horse again, saving me from threats or what you perceive as threats."

Fuck.

If I could go a week without having to apologize to my roommate, that would be outstanding.

I get down on my knees in front of him. "God, Murph. I'm sorry."

"Just. Don't." He lifts up his head. "I thought you were going for a run."

He's kicking me out.

"Yeah. All right. I am." With a gusty sigh, I go to my room, throw on sweats, and put my shoes on. Flames heat my cheeks, and I grab my armband and shove my cell phone in it, then put on my headphones. When I come out to the living room, Murph hasn't moved.

"Bye," I say, but I don't wait for his response. Racing down the steps, I start Guns N' Roses blaring "Paradise City," and I run harder and farther than I normally do.

I run and run and run until it's really late. When I get back home to a quiet house, I'm red-faced and winded. I take out my headphones and leave my phone in Murph's dish, which sits on the table by the door. There's no one in the living room, but I hear rustling in Murph's room.

And a sob.

Worried I'm going to interrupt something but scared about him crying, I tentatively knock on his door.

There's no response.

"Murph? You okay?"

"Go away."

I take a deep breath and open the door. Murph is standing in the middle of the room. I'm not sure what he's been doing, but he's dressed the same as he was when I left. He whirls and advances on me, pressing a hand to my sweaty chest, his face so close to mine that I can see he's got little freckles on his nose. His eyes, although red and puffy, are a startling blue against his creamy skin and dark hair. He's not wearing any guyliner tonight. Or he's rubbed it all off.

His voice sputters in anger as he takes a step forward, pushing me. "What the hell, Jason? Are you going to sabotage all my dates?"

Holding up my hands like I'm being accused of a crime, I step back until I'm up against the wall, and he follows me. "I'm not sabotaging anything."

"Is it because I'm gay? Do you have a problem with seeing two guys touch?"

Do I?

"No," I say quickly, although I'm not sure that's the truth.

"Whatever," he mutters.

We stare at each other, both breathing hard. I'm huffing from my run, and apparently he's gasping from being angry. We're so close, we're almost touching at the waist and chest. I notice how he lines up right below me, his head tilted up at the perfect height.

And for some reason my dick decides this is an opportune time to say hi. I try to move away before I get another poorly timed boner—this time while I'm wearing thin fabric.

Murph seems to notice our position, says "Fuck" under his breath, and shoves past me out of the room. I follow him to the kitchen, willing the awkward boner-in-training to deflate. He grabs a bottle of rum and a turquoise glass, then stops and stares at it—likely because I made it. He sighs and pours. And a tear slides down his face.

"Hey," I say softly, approaching him like he's a wild animal. "I didn't … did I do that?" I point to his tear. I want to wipe it away, but that's crossing a line.

"No."

"Don't lie. I may be a jerk, but don't lie to me."

He swallows the drink, then wipes his eyes with the back of his hand. "Well, it's only partly you. Ruben's a dickasaur for not paying enough attention to me. And I don't think I was that into him." His voice gets stronger. "But I didn't get a chance to see if I was, because he's the second date you've chased off."

"But did you see that guy? He was a total tool."

"That's for me to decide, not you."

My stomach sinks. "Yeah. Okay. You're right." I give him a weak smile. "I'm sorry. I don't know what I'm thinking. It's your business, not mine. And I shouldn't make your decisions for you. I promise I won't interfere with any more of your, uh, dates."

Hookups. *Whatever.*

"If I didn't know you better, I'd think you cared, Jay Jay." He's poised in the middle of the kitchen, looking forlorn, and he takes another sip of the drink. He blinks away the remnants of his tears.

"Guess I do," I admit, leaning against the counter. "I want to watch out for you."

"Again, dude, don't need you to do that."

"Murph. You're strong and very capable, but you're vulnerable." He opens his mouth to protest, but I hold up a hand. "Let me finish. I believe there's great strength in vulnerability. Most of us put up walls and defenses. You don't hide, and that takes a lot of courage. But by definition, it leaves you open to being taken advantage of. Since you don't seal yourself off, you could get hurt, you know?"

He nods. "Yeah. Thanks ... I think. I don't like hiding from anyone about anything. I don't like fake. Except for fake lashes, of course. Those are amazing."

And even after all that, Murph makes me laugh. "You don't wear those, do you?"

After refilling his glass—with water, this time—he downs it and shakes his head no. "A lighter touch goes a long way on me. Other people need the whole contouring thing." A smile perks up his expression. "I could do that for you sometime."

"You're not getting me to wear makeup."

"No, silly rabbit. *I* would. I could show you what I look like when I do drag. Full makeup and a dress. A wig. All that."

I stare at him, trying to picture him in a dress. It might be very confusing, because I think he'd be, well, pretty. "I dunno. I kinda like you like this."

"So you *do* like me, saucy minx?"

"Of course," I say. "You're great. And again, I'm sorry." I go to head to my room, but he puts a hand to my sweaty chest for the second time tonight.

Those blue eyes look up at me. "Will you stop apologizing."

"I wish I could."

He pauses, inspecting my expression. "I believe you. And Jason?"

"Yeah?"

"I'm glad nothing happened with Ruben. He wasn't doing it for me."

I don't know why, but that makes me feel better.

And I keep my word. Two days later, Murph brings over some other guy when I'm in the kitchen cooking dinner. While I can't muster a welcoming smile, at least I don't yell at him. I can't say I'm particularly nice to him, either, but it's a start.

"Oh, that's just Jason," Murph says. "He's my roommate and a massive bore."

"Hey!" I yelp. "Am not."

"Only kidding, wifey-poo."

His date looks at him, puzzled. "I thought you said your roommate was straight."

"I like to mess with him," Murph says in a stage whisper.

I hold my hands out like *What can you say*. "Murph is Murph."

"This is Reeve," Murph says, indicating the guy.

I know I should come over and shake hands, but goddammit, I don't like seeing Murph with anyone, so I keep chopping vegetables with my head down so I don't slice a finger. I manage a "Hey."

Murph snort-laughs. "Reeve's my best friend, not a date. I used to live with him, and I work with his partner. He fills in at V and V sometimes, too. You don't have to do the guard dog routine again."

A tightness in my gut loosens, and I look up and smile for real at Reeve.

But the next time a stranger's in my living room, I don't think he's only Murph's friend. He looks like a lumberjack. Murph says his name is Finn.

Honestly, he looks straight, but what do I know? Just, when I've seen guys with Murph before—thankfully only two—they were always his size. This one looks like he could squash Murph.

Okay, he looks like he's a gentle giant. But that doesn't mean he couldn't turn on Murph.

The same thought arises as before: this guy doesn't seem good enough for Murph. Although they're sitting on opposite ends of the couch, so maybe …

Stop it. You don't have the right to say who Murph can date. Let it be.

I need to get out of here. Murph can take care of himself.

After a few deep breaths, I leave and feel virtuous for not saying anything.

I also feel on edge, and I can't say why.

JASON

On Saturday, Murph comes into the living room and claps his hands. "Ready?"

I look up from my phone. Marnie texted me that her sister had a baby girl and she's going to stay another few weeks to help. Benefit of being able to work from her laptop wherever she is.

While I thought I'd miss her more, I'm weirdly okay with her staying away.

"What are we doing?" I ask. We hadn't discussed going anywhere.

"I have the day off work. So do you. There's a Renaissance faire in Stowe. Normally they're in spring or winter, but this is a special fall one. Extra Vikings."

I stare at him. This is the first I've heard of it. "No."

"Yes! Come on. There's mead, fairies, knights, jesters, pirates, and a joust. Come cosplay with me. We'll go and be knights. Actually, you can be a knight. I'll be a princess."

"No."

"I'll buy you a sword."

"I don't want a sword."

He puts his hands on his hips and glares at me. "You want a sword."

"No," I protest, laughing. "I'm not going to a nerd fest."

An hour later, we're in my car headed to the Ren faire. We listen to *Cats* on the way there and argue over whether there's any story at all to it.

But it feels good to spend time with him. We've been so busy with work that we haven't seen much of each other, and I've missed him.

When we arrive and step out of the car, I look down at what I'm wearing. Murph put some kind of poncho on me and made me wear some Carhartt pants I have, saying that I'm Aragorn from *Lord of the Rings*.

Meanwhile, he's got on a light-blue, glittery cape and a pointy pink princess hat with rainbow ribbons falling from the top, which makes people stop and stare.

He's not the only one people are staring at, though. There's a dude dressed as a unicorn.

Murph pays the entrance fee for me before I can whip out my wallet.

"I can pay."

His jaw gets a determined set to it. "I know. But I invited you. We're friends hanging out."

"Okay," I agree easily enough, because it seems important to him.

Murph marches us into the first smithy shop he sees and starts looking around at the weaponry. Polished metal on the walls greets us.

Outside, a troupe of bards passes, playing minstrel music. The proprietor calls out something to them while Murph inspects the swords.

His big eyes seek mine. "Please let me buy you one. Then you could be my knight in shining armor for real."

"No. They're expensive, and I don't need a sword."

"Honey, I buy shoes that cost more than most of these. And maybe I need you to defend my honor."

I scoff. "I thought you didn't want me defending your honor. Besides," I say, pointing at a really long one, "I'm not Braveheart."

"So I won't buy you a four-foot sword." He appraises me. "I think you could wield something that big, though."

"Ha ha." We walk slowly around the tent, and a sword does catch my eye. It's simple and seems nicely balanced.

Murph catches me staring at it, so I pretend I'm not.

But he calls to the proprietor, "Can my knight—I mean, my friend—hold that one?"

"Of course, jolly sir," says the smith. Then he gets a better look at Murph. "Or madam."

Murph shimmies and puts a hand on his hip. "Just call me princess."

"As you wish, princess." The smith carefully takes the sword off its holder and hands it to me.

I don't know if I've ever held a real sword before. The heft of the metal in my hand feels different than I imagined—heavier and more elegant. I don't want to, like, start swinging it around in this tight space. But I like it.

Murph claps his hands. "Oh, this is so much yes. We need to get you leathers to wear, too."

"I'm not doing *Lord of the Rings* cosplay."

"Of course you are." He turns to the smith. "We'll take it."

"Murph," I protest, "no. It's too much."

He holds up a hand. "Please, let me get you something nice. You do so much for me, cooking and buying food, it's the least I can do."

He looks so earnest that I'm about to relent and just secretly undercharge him for utilities or something.

"What if we split it?" he asks. "Two-thirds me, one-third you?"

"Deal," I say. I can feel comfortable with that. And it's not one of the more expensive ones in the shop, so I don't feel like he's going to do without by buying it. "Thank you. It's—" I'm about to say something formal like *It's very kind of you,* but instead I smile and tell the truth. "I love it."

Tapping his fingers on the table in delight while the smith rings up the purchase, he grins back. "Perfect. See? I knew you needed one."

I don't want to argue with him that no one—absolutely no one—needs a sword, because I really do like it.

We leave with the sword in a scabbard on my belt. This is probably the one place in the universe I don't feel like a fool dressed this way.

But it's fun. I seem to always have fun with Murph.

We're about to head into another tent when I get a prickly feeling at the back of my neck. I turn around and see a group of five or six big guys eyeing some women who are showing a ton of cleavage.

Ugh. I recognize them from high school. Travis Finch. Leo Johnson. Jeremy Wilds. A few others. They're the type to call people gay like it's an insult.

I hear ugly sniggers, and I know they're directed at Murph. One of them says, "Oh my god, check out this princess. Bet he takes it up the ass."

"With relish," Murph flings over his shoulder before stepping inside the tent. I follow him and breathe a sigh of relief when the mob passes us.

"Murph," I caution. "I know those guys. They don't need encouragement."

"I can stick up for myself."

I gaze at him. "I hate that you have to. Just because someone's different than they are doesn't mean they have to look down on that person."

His eyes study the floor. "I don't want people to look down on me. I want us to look in the same direction."

"I know," I say quietly.

But we perk up at the displays of leather goods and forget about the squad of bullies.

After meandering around the faire, we buy lunch—huge turkey legs, corn on the cob, and mead served in horns. We watch a bawdy Shakespeare performance where all the characters—male and female—are played by men, while women stand on the sides making fun of them. I'm confronted with more breasts and cleavage than I've seen in a long time.

But Murph is the best entertainment of all, because he knows all the lingo. I guess his years of playing Dungeons & Dragons have taught him all the types of weapons and heraldry, and he points out all these details I would've missed if I went by myself.

When the play's over, we walk over to another market area.

"What do you want to see next?" I ask, pulling the brochure out of my pocket.

"I dunno. What else is on the schedule?" He looks up and claps his hands. "Ooh!"

Murph's distracted by a mannequin sporting a battle-ready chainmail coif—the headdress knights wear—in an artisan's booth across the way and heads over to it like it's a magnet and he's an iron filing. I smile and study the afternoon's offerings.

When I look up, though, Murph's surrounded by that loud group, who are giving off vibes like they're drunk and even more belligerent than before. Murph tilts his chin up and stands tall.

"Hey, faggot," Jeremy jeers, acting like the grade-school bully he was.

Shit. Murph's strong. But he isn't invulnerable. He's simply not big enough to handle a bunch of guys at once.

"If you're referring to me, I think the word you were looking for is 'fabulous,'" Murph says, his voice even.

I make a quick decision.

Coming up next to him, I wrap my arm around his neck and draw him in. "Hey," I say. "There you are."

Murph tenses in surprise but gets the idea pretty quickly. Taking off the princess hat and dangling it from his wrist, he snuggles close. I lean my head against his and hug him to me, glaring at the bullies. His arm goes around my waist—hesitantly at first, and then he holds me securely. Thankfully my sword's on the other side. He fits well under my arm. He smells good, too.

So I'm touching a guy. No big deal. I'll do any kind of camouflage as long as it means Murph's safe.

"You got something to say?" I growl. All my nerves are taut and vibrating, and I feel sparks between me and Murph from the energy of the confrontation.

Travis glares back at me. I remember him from track and field. "Falkner? What the hell? You're a cocksucker now?" Adrenaline zips through me, but I'm not letting them hurt him. They're so drunk they're barely standing up straight.

"Would it matter if I was? Don't be jerks. If you treat him like that, you're gonna have to answer to me." I tug Murph even closer and start walking away.

"Whatever, Falkner. Fag."

The bullies get distracted by a group of women walking by, whistle at them, and leave us, but I don't remove my arm from Murph's shoulders. I'm not letting him go until I know it's safe. I don't care who sees me.

We need to go home. Back to our cocoon where we don't have to deal with this shit.

And then I wonder—does Murph face situations like this all the time?

God, I'm so entitled.

"What?" Murph asks. We separate, and it feels lonely not to have him next to me.

I look down at him. "Here I am all worried about getting somewhere safe. But do you ever feel safe?"

"Most of the time. Some places are sketchy. I avoid them. Normally I go where I'm going to meet other queers." He gives me a rueful smile. "My friends aren't that diverse—other than being LGBTQ. You're one of my few hetero friends."

"I'm lucky, then."

"You are." He glances up. "But yes, most of the time I feel safe enough to be me."

"Good." That makes me feel a lot better.

He cocks his head. "Why did you do it? Pretend to be with me, I mean."

"I couldn't stand the thought of them hurting you. I don't care what they think. I care that you're safe."

He looks at me thoughtfully but is uncharacteristically quiet.

So I keep talking. "Did I fuck up? Should I have let you fight your battle without my help?"

"Honestly, it was one of the hottest and nicest things anyone's ever done for me. No one's ever stuck up for me when shit like that happens. Not even my 'friends' in school. When things got rough, they were nowhere to be found. I never, ever felt like anyone had my back."

"I have it," I say. "Always."

MURPH

When Jason threw his arm around me, I stumbled into him not only because I was scared, but also because of how good it felt to have him hold me up.

Since junior high, I've had slurs and physical objects thrown at me, and I've been beaten up more than once. To some degree, I expect comments as the price of wearing clothing that some people think only women can wear. I mean, hello, I'm Arwen today, to Jason's Aragorn.

Not that I'd tell him that's what I intended with our costumes. If he had a clue, though, he'd figure it out.

But I wasn't expecting Jason to hold me. I bet he didn't think twice about it. All he thought, likely, was that he gave zero fucks about playing gay—at least for a second—to protect someone else.

Jason considering he's anything other than straight for real? As established, that's only in my fantasies.

Still, it felt scrumptious to be pancaked to his side, even for a fleeting moment, because he's an incredible man. Especially with a sword strapped to his hip.

But it's made everything worse, because now I know how his body feels against mine.

I felt cradled. Protected.

For the first time in a very long time—maybe ever—I felt at home.

I've always wanted someone who wouldn't hesitate to stick up for me. Who'd be proud to say they know me. While I've never had that in a boyfriend, at least now I have it with a friend.

To distract me from running my mouth about how I want to stay in his arms forever, I say instead, "Let's go watch the joust."

He blows out a long breath and smiles. "Sounds good."

We make our way through the crowds to the arena, where horses with flags draped on them prance around amidst pageantry.

Along with an assortment of posturing hot men.

Hey, if I can't have the hot man I'm with, I'm gonna go window shopping. "This is amazing," I whisper five minutes into the show. Because it is. I'm so easily distracted from reality when there are swords and muscled men with bare chests.

He hums and leans over to whisper in my ear, which makes his beardy stubble tickle my skin. A shudder runs through me at the contact. "Glad you like it."

We sit and watch the show, and I do the self-analysis he can't or won't.

Bottom line: I don't think he's as straight as he insists he is. We'll ignore the fact that it's in my best interest to so conclude. Maybe I'm wrong. Maybe the way he looks at me is the way he looks at everyone. But there's cleavage aplenty here, and Jason's ignored it to talk to me about the finer points of *Forged in Fire*.

Seeing Jason hold that sword in the store made every part of my body cheer. Like, holy hell, he was about to rally hundreds of people and dwarves and hobbits to go fight Sauron so Frodo had a chance.

He looked like the hero he is, with that messy hair and big build.

And note, I've been good. Since purchasing the weapon, I've only made four or five sword innuendos.

But better than him sticking up for me and better than the

sword was seeing Jason really relax. When he showed me how to make glass, while it was creative and interesting, he was focused. This? This is just him laughing and looking at all the spectacles.

It's him being my friend, and it's a blast to spend the day with him.

"Thanks for taking me," Jason says, when we get back home. "I didn't want to go, but I'm glad you talked me into it. It was really fun."

If this were a date, we'd be awkwardly standing on a stoop waiting for one or the other to make a move.

Instead, we go inside, Jason starts dinner, and I set the table. He puts his sword in a place of honor above the mantel.

I wish he'd let himself do fun things like this on a regular basis. If he were my man, I'd make it my mission to amuse him every day. Because when Jason loosens up, it's a beautiful thing.

When we sit down for dinner, Jason asks, "Who was the lumberjack?"

"Who?" I frown.

"The guy you had over the other day."

It takes me a moment before I realize who he's talking about. "Finn? He's the Vino and Veritas owner's boyfriend. A chicken farmer. He was checking out my designs for his website."

I'm not imagining that Jason relaxes after I say it, right?

The next evening, I'm poking around the kitchen when Jason walks in, dripping from the rain and holding two grocery bags.

"Hey, sugar daddy, what did you bring for me?" I coo.

He chuckles. "Not a sugar daddy, but I did bring some dinner. You interested?"

"Meh, I guess so. If it has you involved, then reluctantly. You're an okay cook." I smile broadly at him so he knows I'm teasing.

His eyes flash at first like he's hurt, then he catches my meaning and plays along. "I can force it down your throat."

I think of a few things he's got that I would happily accept down my throat. His tongue. His dick. "Oh, I swallow."

He laughs and starts to unpack the bags in the kitchen.

I need to stop flirting with him, because it's one-sided. Jason's just being nice. He sees hilarious gay Davey Murphy and thinks he's funny, so he plays along.

Meanwhile I'm over here getting my heart broken. No biggie.

Goddess, I need to stop pining over him.

But I'm a masochist, because I can't leave him alone. I *want* to be around him. Something about his solid presence calms me. I'm flighty, he's steady. I need anchors in my life, and I wish—oh, how I wish—he could be my anchor.

For now, I help him by scrubbing the potatoes and making a salad while he grabs a shower, and we eat dinner together, like I've never done with any other roommate.

But it's the best thing I've ever experienced.

I revel in it. I sit across from him, with his fresh-out-of-the-shower hair, and I try not to stare. When he gets up to grab another beer from the fridge, his loose track pants show all the goodies he's hiding. I sigh happily into my sangria.

After we've chowed for a bit, he looks across at me and bites his lip. "Can I ask you something?"

"Sure."

"How are you so unapologetically you?"

I shrug one shoulder. "As if I have any other choice?"

He shakes his head and holds up his hand. "Oh, no. You have plenty of choice. You could've squashed all this"—he gestures generally to me—"authenticity, but you don't. You don't worry about whether people accept you. *You* accept you."

Tilting my head to the side, I toy with giving him a fake answer. But I don't want to. So I put both hands on the table and look at him seriously. "Here's the thing. I can either listen to other people or I can listen to myself. And, spoiler, if I do the former,

I'm never going to be happy. So I came to the conclusion long ago that, since it's my life I'm living, I might as well please my damn self. Some days it's easy to be me. Others, I simply don't have the strength."

His eyes sadden, and again, I'm falling for the way this guy listens to me. He doesn't interrupt. He just lets me talk.

"Sometimes I'll put on this face"—I grin wildly—"but underneath it, I'm …" I trail off. "Sometimes, I wonder what's the use?"

Again, here's where he could chime in, but he doesn't. He's not making this about him. He reaches across the table and taps my hand, then pulls his hand back slowly.

He hasn't touched me since yesterday at the Ren faire, and I feel the ghost of his fingers for much longer than they were there.

"I used to feel like I was fighting all the time just to be me, because the alternative was hiding. But I know I'm fortunate. While I might stick out in Vermont—or a lot of other places—I have the freedom to be as fabulous as I want. If I'd been born a hundred years ago?" I shudder.

"Ever since I met you, I've thought you had something going on beyond the smile you show," he says. "Those with the brightest smiles can hide the most pain inside."

Goddess, *Jason*.

And because he listens, I find myself opening up about things I barely ever talk about. "I used to self-medicate. Club drugs. But after one too many mornings waking up at some guy's house and not knowing his name or how I got there, I quit that. It felt too dangerous. I've gotta admit, though, it also felt good to lose myself."

"Promise me you don't do that anymore?"

"Nah. Sangria is it for me. And occasionally a shot or a beer or whatever a handsome guy named Jason Falkner makes for me."

"I think you've got your act together now."

He seems sincere. It's nice. "Thanks."

"I mean, you pay your rent on time."

I laugh, but it's halfhearted, because he's reminding me of my place in his life. "Yeah," is all I can manage.

He looks around. "Wanna clean up and go watch something?"

I nod. We gather the dishes and tidy up, and I wonder how someone this genuine hasn't been snapped up yet.

Class, listen up. Jason's a good one! He cooks and cleans and does the dishes. And I bet he fucks like a beast.

Wait, I shouldn't think about that.

But I do.

The next afternoon, I'm wiping down the bar when I hear a familiar voice and get all tingly inside.

Raising my eyes, I see a big, Technicolor dream-haired hunk standing on the other side of my bar, wearing a suit and looking distinctly tempting. And a little out of place.

"What are you doing here?" I ask.

Jason smiles his crooked smile. "You told me it was okay if I came to see where you worked. It's only a few blocks away from my office."

"Ooh, can I come to your office sometime?" I ask.

He shrugs. "If you'd like. It's not really all that interesting." He scans the room. "This place is nice."

My manager comes over and joins us. "Yeah, it is."

"Tanner, this is my roommate, Jason."

They shake hands. Jason says, "We know each other. Sort of. From high school."

"Hey, man. How are you?" Tanner asks. "Long time."

"Good to see you."

"Want a drink?" I ask.

"Sure. You pick." While I pour him a glass of my favorite, Jason takes a more languid look around the place, which is buzzing, even though it's not much past noon.

I can't resist teasing him. "Sure the rainbows won't rub off on you here?"

He furrows his brow. "I thought you said this place was inclusive."

"It is."

"So, does 'inclusive' include me?"

"Definitely." I set the wine down in front of him. "We want this to be a safe space."

"But be careful," Tanner warns.

"Why?" Jason asks.

"You might end up learning something about yourself. Rainn thought he was straight, until he worked here."

"What happened to him?"

Tanner smirks. "He's off somewhere with his boyfriend, teaching hockey."

Jason chokes on his wine.

JASON

Closing my office door the next morning, I hit the green button on my phone and adjust my pants. They'd gotten tight after a few sexy thoughts I just had—ones involving a mouth on my dick and someone on their knees before me. The face of that person keeps shifting, though, and I'm getting mixed up. I pace, waiting for the call to connect.

When she answers, I say, "Marnie?"

"Jason! So good to hear from you. How *are* you?" A baby cries softly in the background, but Marnie seems cheerful enough, judging by the enthusiasm in her voice.

"Missing you."

Because it's true. At least, I'm missing her body, but it's insensitive to phrase it that way.

This morning I woke up with wood the size of the spire at the state house in Montpelier. I haven't counted how many weeks it's been since I've had sex, but it's too many.

And life's gotten weird since she left. I don't know if I'm only starting to think things because I'm now living with a gay guy, but I've had thoughts.

Weird ones.

Weird ones I'm sure will go away after a romp in the sheets with her.

Like remembering how my roommate felt pressed up next to me at the Ren faire, or before, when he got in my face after the thing with Ruben. He's strong and solid and lean. I couldn't seem to control the way my dick reacted.

And that shit—those sensations—have to go. I'm not attracted to him, it's just that being touched by another person triggered something. A need in me for human companionship. That's all. That's the reason for my awkward boners.

So I need to get laid.

"Aww," she says. "I miss you, too."

I don't hide what I want. "Are you coming back home anytime soon?"

She sighs. "Maybe at the end of the week. Not sure. My sister had some complications with her pregnancy—hypertension and then a C-section—so she needs extra help still. Plus, I can't get enough of my new niece."

"Is your sister doing better?"

"Much," she says decidedly. "She got to take a short nap today."

Even though she can't see me, I nod. "Good, good."

But this means I have to wait longer before I get laid, unless I want to drive to Syracuse. And while I'm horny, I'm not totally governed by my dick. I can keep it in my pants until she comes back.

As she chatters, I can't help thinking that this is one of the longest conversations we've ever had. And I can't explain why I'm not more upset that she isn't around.

When we hang up, I sag against the wall and let my head fall back.

Becky meets me for lunch at the diner. She slides into the booth across from me and orders a lemonade from the waiter right away.

I set down my menu to ask her a question and then notice Murph across the restaurant, eating lunch and laughing with another man. A date? A coworker? The other guy's stature is slight, like Murph's, but he's got black hair and olive skin.

It looks like they're having a lot of fun. Murph's super animated, practically bouncing in his seat, gesturing wildly while the guy with him cracks up. They shoo away the waiter and focus on each other.

"Jason? Are you even listening to me?"

"What?"

Oops. Becky looks me straight in the eyes. "I asked you if you wanted me to renew the tenants' lease in the downstairs unit."

"Oh, sure. Thanks."

She speaks very slowly, like she's explaining something to a child. "Do you want me to increase the rent?"

"No. I don't know. Do you think so? Sure. I don't care. Do whatever you think." I take a sip of my water.

The waiter returns to Murph's table with fresh sodas, and even he seems like he's flirting with Murph.

Jesus, does *everyone* flirt with Murph?

"Earth to Jason. Hello? Are you even listening?"

"Yeah, sorry. You were saying?"

"Do you want to do a month-to-month lease, or another year?"

"What do you think I should do?" I take a sip of my drink and glance up to see Becky staring at me. Then she looks over her shoulder to see what has my attention.

"What?" I ask.

She raises her eyebrows. "Nothing. Just. This is even more interesting."

"What's interesting?"

"Nothing."

I roll my eyes. "Keep it a secret, why don't you."

"Oh, I'm not the one keeping secrets."

"What the hell are you talking about?"

"Nothing. Nothing. Let's talk about something else."

I don't see Murph at dinnertime for a few days. But one night when he's off work, I notice the light on in his room and the door ajar, so I knock and walk in. He's lounging on his bed with his glasses on, reading a Robert Jordan novel.

I like looking around his room because he's constantly changing things—adding curtains or moving his furniture. Now he's hung some new high-concept fantasy art on the wall.

Murph's still got his nose in the book. "Hungry?"

"For what?" He sounds playful.

Because he's Murph.

I'm used to him. I'm not only used to him, if he weren't the way he is, I'd miss him.

"For food, dude," I say. "What did you think I meant?"

"Oh, I don't know. I can get hungry for all kinds of things."

"It's been a long week. Want to make me a drink, Mr. Bartender?"

He sets down his book and grins. "Sure."

"Here's the plan. I'll cook you dinner. You make me a drink. Sound good?"

"Sounds like the most perfect plan that was ever invented," he crows, then gets up and follows me into the kitchen.

Once there, he floats around, picking out two glasses, selecting ice like the cubes are fancy chocolates in a display case, and mixing drinks.

One advantage of living with a bartender.

"Hey," I say, aiming for casual and failing hard. "I saw you the other day in the diner." I focus on preheating the oven, then turn around to look at him.

He tilts his head, thinking. "Oh! I went to lunch with Tai."

"Is Tai someone I should meet?" I refrain from growling.

Murph smirks. "No. His boyfriend's a veterinarian, and they have a kid. I met him at V and V, and we get together for coffee sometimes. He has a charming Kiwi accent, though don't get him drunk, because he'll sing Crowded House songs." He blinks at me. "Jeez, if I didn't know better, I'd think you were checking up on me."

I rub the back of my neck. "Yes, we've discussed this, and yes, I'll stay out of it. But I still care, okay?"

"Aww," he coos. "You care."

"We've established I do," I say. "Very much."

My dad strides into my office like he owns the place—spoiler, he does—and stands over my desk, making me fold into myself like a closed umbrella.

I know there's supposed to be some sort of psychological thing about a desk and power—like the one behind it has the power, which in theory should be me. But when he looms like this, he's just being an ass.

"What's up?" I ask, keeping my thoughts to myself and focusing on my computer screen. Maybe I'm being an ass back, but it's hard working with your family.

"Looks like you have some new clients here."

"I do?" I cough, startled. "I mean, yes, I do." Without saying anything further, I sweep past him and go to greet the guys sitting in the entry.

I realize I recognize them, although I haven't met either officially before. One was in my living room with Murph, and the other must be his partner, the owner of Vino and Veritas.

I have the idle thought that I've been spending more time around gay men recently than I have in my entire life.

"Hi," I say. "I'm Jason. How can I help you?"

They introduce themselves. Harrison's in his forties and looks very professional. His partner, Finn, is perhaps a decade younger. While on the surface they seem like an odd couple—city slicker and farm boy—one look at the two of them and you know they're desperately in love.

They glance at each other, and Finn starts talking. "We're here to buy insurance for a home we're building together."

"Sure." I gesture to my now-empty office. "Follow me."

Once we're all seated, Harrison says, "At a minimum, we need to make sure the house we're building is covered. And I'm not sure what else we need."

I spread out my hands. "I'm happy to help." I pull out a few brochures and start talking about coverage. They chatter about dealing with Vermont red tape to build a new house on Finn's family farm.

As we talk about the different options, the thing that strikes me is how comfortable these guys are with each other. One will casually put a hand on the other's knee. They'll laugh at a shared experience.

And I have a lump in my throat because, for the first time in my life, I want this. A relationship. Someone to share my life with.

With all my friends moved away, my mom gone, my dad an ass, and my love life just an absent hookup, I'm jealous of the happiness these men share.

Who do I have in my life? A bossy little sister and an over-the-top roommate.

Although those two do make my life better.

Finn turns to Harrison. "We should talk about life insurance for each other, too."

Harrison's expression turns thoughtful. "Finn and I both lost our fathers when we were young, and my dad's very generous policy made things comfortable enough for me and my mom to live in New York on a librarian's salary. It's old school, but yeah, I'm open to that if I can get it."

I tilt my head. "What's old school about it?"

"Gay history, my friend," Finn says. "Before same-sex couples could get married, we had to get creative." He shudders. "There were too many horror stories about families keeping lovers apart through a mix of hospital rules and prejudice. Too many tragedies where a partner became destitute and homeless when the other died, because of inheritance rules. Naming your partner as the beneficiary of your life insurance policy was a way to get around some of the bullshit. Estate planning was another." He looks at Harrison. "Not that Audrey'd ever do that to me, or my family to you. But it used to happen."

I've heard these stories before. But today, for some reason, it's striking me as poignant that my company doesn't care who buys its policies. It'll simply do what is asked. If an individual wants to pay for another to get $50,000 or $500,000 or $5 million on his death, it'll do that.

But what a hug from the beyond for the guy left behind. What a way to take care of the love of your life.

I chew my lip, thinking about this. Wondering why it's hitting me so profoundly. Perhaps because I've been so miserable trying to sell people policies and thinking about actuarial tables and medical exams. I haven't been looking at the benefits to those insured. Insurance doesn't have to be a dry, boring thing that makes me focus on future death or destruction or loss. It's a way for people to get a sense of calm *now*. It's a way of living *now*. That way the buyer can relax and know the person they love is going to be okay even after they're gone.

I've never thought of insurance as romantic before, but dammit, it is.

MURPH

In late September, the days grow colder and Vermont starts to put on its autumn leaf extravaganza. Jason's busy at work. I take on extra shifts. But I try to schedule as many early ones as I can so I'm home to have dinner with my roommate.

Don't be hating. I like his face.

I also get the feeling Jason's working less than he used to. Before I moved in, his sister emphasized that I'd barely see him and I'd have the place all to myself because he was a workaholic. Hardly. He barely ever burns the midnight oil. It's more like, by unspoken agreement, we both try to get home in time to have dinner together. We text a lot to coordinate, too, and I like having Jason in my phone. And in my life.

One evening, while sitting across the table from me and picking at the remains of a rich chicken piccata, Jason asks, "So tell me more about Vegas." He's drinking a beer from the local brewery, and I'm sipping sangria, of course.

These conversations with him? Spending time with him? They're the best part of my day. And I've found myself being more honest with him than I am with anyone else.

"It's a weird place to grow up, because anything goes. Gambling, drinking, sex, guns, drugs. You can get anything you want at three in the morning. Taco Bell serves alcohol. People walk down the street in thongs and pasties. Almost everything is legal in Vegas, so when you leave, it's an adjustment."

"The glitz is mostly on the Strip, though, right?"

"Downtown, too."

"What's it like to live there?"

"I grew up in a cookie-cutter tract house on the west side of the Strip. The deed was in my mom's name, because my dad would've gambled it away. The only reason why we didn't get foreclosed was that her parents bought her the house. Land's cheap in Vegas."

He sips his beer. "How much time did you spend on the Strip? Or downtown?"

"Very little. I hate gambling. I'd rather spend a hundred bucks on what I want than probably lose it trying to turn it into more. In my family, drinking is no biggie. My mom's parents were French, so she gave me watered-down wine when I was five. And sex?" I grin. "I did go to strip clubs to find guys to hook up with. Sorry, I know I'm a slut."

"Don't use that word."

"Sorry?"

He chuckles. "That, too. But I meant slut. It's your body. Do what you want with it."

I'm dying to pry into his love life. How serious is he with Marnie? He says they're just friends with benefits, but Jason seems like the type to save for a ring.

"When did you lose your virginity?" I ask instead. "Since we're getting personal."

"Junior year of high school." He licks his lips. "With a college girl."

"You dawg."

"I know. It was nice."

"Nice? Sex shouldn't be 'nice.'"

"We ended up doing it five times in one night."

My eyes bug out.

"She was my sister's friend's older sister." He reddens. "I don't wanna think about how many of my sister's connections I've slept with. How old were you the first time you had sex?"

"Not that you're changing the subject, but I was eighteen the first time I let a guy fuck me."

Jason nods, and I can tell he's trying to be cool with the idea of men fucking even though he probably isn't. Something about that makes me like him even more.

Since I'm a masochist, I ask, "How did you first get together with Marnie?"

He pauses, thinking about it. "I went to a party, got drunk with her, stumbled back with her to her house, and ended up in bed. Then we did it again—the sex, not the getting drunk—the next morning. And for a few years now. Mostly at her house."

"You guys haven't dated at all?" My heart gives a flippity-flop.

"Nope. I have barely seen her outside the walls of her abode." He studies me. "Are you going to judge me for that?"

"Are you kidding? If it works for you both, who am I to say what you should do?"

"Okay," he says and smiles.

Although, as far as I can tell, he hasn't spent any time with her since I moved in. But that's because she's away.

When she gets back, is everything going to change?

I'm getting a wee bit tipsy. "It's easy to find a fuck." Except when I have a guard dog for a roommate. "It's harder to find someone you want to talk with." I sigh. "I guess my views on sex are typical—at least for your standard gay man. I don't equate sex and love. Sex is just biological."

"Agreed."

"But if I had someone to love? I'd want to give him everything. That might be a very heterosexual notion, but sue me. I'd probably kiss him a lot. A *lot*, a lot."

The idea of someone loving me and only me is such a foreign concept. I'm torn between the me who wants the love of the ages you see on screen and stage … and the one who gets his cock sucked in a back alley.

"Is that what you're looking for?" he asks, oblivious to the place my thoughts went.

I rewind. "A relationship?"

Jason nods.

"I don't know." Because the relationship I want, I can't have. I want one with character. One that's reasonably happy.

One that's right in front of my face.

"Me neither." Jason's face drops.

"What?"

"Maybe that's not true. I'm thinking of calling it off with Marnie. We aren't dating, so we wouldn't be breaking up. But part of me, I guess, wants something more."

I volunteer as tribute.

"Do you think you'll ever get married? Not to her. To someone."

"Dunno. Some guys think that way. I never did. Maybe I just haven't met the right person, but I feel, if I were the marrying type, I would've made more progress by now. Found someone in college. I haven't found anyone I click with." He grins at me. "I click more with you than I do with anyone else."

Isn't that the pity of it?

"Is this what you want from life, then?" I gesture around. "Own your own place. Go to work. Run. Make fancy dishes for your house in bright eighties designs?"

He smiles. "Yeah. I'm content with the way things are right now. As for marriage, my parents are a textbook example of why *not* to get married or be in a relationship. I'm sure my mom could file for divorce if she cared enough about it to bother. But my dad never will. He hates the idea of divorce. Must be some sort of old White man conservative thing."

"'Old White man conservative' explains a lot about behavior."

Jason grimaces. "Here's the thing. I knew I had a conservative upbringing, so I intentionally went to Brown, which is a very liberal school."

"I know."

"There, I got all this education and experience being around all sorts of people. Lots of diversity. I know I love a world that is multi- … well, everything. Despite that, my consciousness still has some of the racist or homophobic shit my dad—or his friends—would say when I was growing up. It's like it's in my pores."

"Maybe you need to go to a sauna and sweat it out."

"That's not a bad idea." He lets out a long breath. "I hate it, though. It's like I've bought into what my dad believes, and I don't even know it. And how do I fix it if I don't know I do it?"

I want to reach over and hold his hand, but I don't. "You're a really kind person. If you just let yourself be yourself, you might find that's enough of a compass. In other words, just follow your heart. And now, ladies and gentlemen, I've turned into a commercial."

"You're right, though," he says, saving me. "Heart. Gut. Soul. If I listen to me rather than anyone else, I'll make better decisions. I'm just so used to listening to everyone else."

"Want me to help?" I ask. "To remind you to pay attention to what you want? I can ask, 'Jason, is this your decision or someone else's?'"

"I think I can do it on my own."

"You sure?"

He looks at me. And pauses. "Actually, I need help. So, yes, whenever you want to remind me to make my own choices, I'd appreciate it."

Saturday afternoon, Jason stops at my doorway. "I have to run a few errands. Wanna come?"

Absolutely. But not in the way he means.

"No, thanks. You go ahead."

As much of a people person as I am, sometimes I need a little me time to sort out my head.

And looking at him in my doorway in a flannel and beanie and jeans and boots, his hands gripping the wall … it's getting to be too much.

Too many feelings and no action.

And I don't even need action per se. If I could get Jason to look at me and acknowledge that he likes me in that way, I could die a happy man. Not having that, though, chips away at my insides until I don't know if there's anything left.

I have to have some sense of self-preservation. Which means I need to distance myself.

After he leaves, I plop on the couch with a snack. I need medicinal sword fighting on television.

Not ten minutes in, there's a buzz from the street-level door.

I answer it and am surprised by who's there. But I let him in. It's been pouring buckets, and now there's a very wet man in my doorway. But it's not my roommate.

"Hey, Scott. How's it going?"

Scott's a hookup from a while ago. Actually, he's a repeated hookup. We've texted some recently, but I haven't made specific plans with him because reasons. Reasons like, I want Jason. But Scott's perfectly serviceable. He has a charming nose, and he's kind of a hopeless romantic.

"Am I interrupting anything?" he asks.

"No. What's up?"

"I, um, got this idea and decided to take a chance." He lifts up a basket lined with a red-and-white checkered cloth in one hand, two bottles of red wine in the other. "Unless you're busy, I mean. Sorry, this was stupid. You probably have a boyfriend. I didn't mean to assume—"

"It's fine," I say, touching my hands to my heart. "You're very sweet. Come on in."

I don't really feel much for Scott, but he is nice and has that extremely lovely nose.

"Thanks. I forgot to bring an umbrella."

"Let's get you changed." I step aside to let him in.

"That's one way to get a guy out of his clothes."

I laugh. "I'll put them in the dryer. Or maybe you can borrow something of mine?" I study him. There's no way he'll fit in any of my clothes. He's too big. "Well, I can get you a robe, anyway."

"I'm fine," he says.

And, in a flash, he tugs me to him and kisses me.

It's the wrong man, but it's a man, and that's what I want.

Someone to soothe my heart by way of my lips and the rest of my body.

JASON

I'm in a foul mood.

I went out shopping without Murph, and just about everything bad that could happen, happened. It started to pour, which is fine, except I ran over a nail and had to change the tire in the rain. I'm now soaked to the skin with water pooling in my boots.

The store didn't have the thing I needed.

A road was closed, and I got stuck in a detour on the way back.

Marnie texted me saying she isn't coming home for another week.

And my dad sent me six calendar invites for client meetings in the next week and a half.

All I want is dry clothes, my couch, the remote control, and a beer. And maybe some dinner. I find myself looking forward to a quiet evening with Murph.

Keys in hand, I race up the stairs, hoping I can change my clothes and order pizza and this will all go away.

I'm short of breath when I get up to the door and not in a better mood, because I banged my hip on the newel post and my toe on the loose step.

That'll need to get fixed, but I'm the one in charge here, so it's my responsibility. I'll add it to my list.

Unlocking the apartment, I step inside and shuffle off my boots, throwing my keys on Murph's dish on the side table.

Then I come into the living room, look at the couch, and see some sort of octopus made of men.

What the fuck?

My stomach lurches.

I march into the room, wishing I were still wearing my shoes so I could stomp appropriately.

Red-hot—no, white-hot—fire flicks up my spine and hits my neck and cheeks, so I can see nothing but buzzing, vibrating designs.

I can't watch him do this. I don't wanna know about this.

"What the fuck?" I growl. I immediately want to both take my words back and yell them again.

They break apart. Murph's hair is ruffled, and his lips are kiss-stung. He's short of breath, and I avoid looking down his body to see his erection.

"Oops. Sorry, Jason," Murph says, in a voice that doesn't sound that sorry.

"Sure you are," I mutter. I roll my eyes. "Just fucking don't do this in my living room. I don't need to see this"—I gesture at them—"when I walk inside. I shouldn't have to."

I race past his pale face and narrowed eyes. I've hurt him, and I've pissed him off, and I don't care.

"My roommate," I overhear him say as I tear down the hallway.

A small part of my brain scolds me. It's not rational to be pissed to see him doing this. He's gay. He can kiss men.

But he deserves better than this guy. Whoever he is.

After throwing on dry clothes, I storm back into the living room. "Who the hell are you?" I point a shaking finger at the asshole who's, thankfully, moved away from my roommate.

Is he wearing one of Murph's robes?

"*Jason.*" Murph's eyes widen in shock, but I don't care. I don't want this tool touching him.

The tool does his best to be calm and friendly. "I'm Scott."

I ignore him and turn to Murph. "How long have you two known each other?"

He squints at me, a *Here we go again* expression on his face. "What's it matter to you? You're not in charge here."

"Yeah, but you don't need to be fucking the first guy you see."

I can't stop the words from coming out of my mouth. And I really want to put a fist in his date's face. Just for existing. For touching Murph.

I've never had a problem with impulse control. Never. But Murph's dates bring out something primal in me.

"I think you should go home," I say to Scott the Unwanted, and Murph whips his head around to look at me.

"Uh, no. Scott can stay right here. You don't have the right to tell my date where to go."

"It's my house, too."

"For fuck's sake, Jason!" Murph shouts, getting up from the couch. "How many times are we going to go through this? It's none of your goddamned business!"

I've never heard Murph not say "goddess." He must be really pissed. And I know he's right, but that doesn't keep some irrational part deep inside me from insisting that I'm part of the decision-making process about who Murph kisses.

Murph stalks over to me, his chin jutting out, his eyes flashing with anger and hurt.

"Get out," he says quietly. "Or I will. Is that what you want? You want me to leave?" Then his face crumples. "It's because you can't really handle me. You're okay with the gay as long as you don't have to see it. That's what it is, isn't it?" He looks up to the ceiling. "Oh my goddess, why didn't I see it before? You're all alike. This isn't—" He stops. "This isn't working."

"It works fine when you don't have people here for me to walk in on."

"Jeez, you really are an asshole. I didn't think you were like that." He turns to his date. "Look, I'm sorry. Let me deal with my roommate. I'll call you later."

"Don't bother," I say. "I'll go."

Murph's cheeks flush with renewed anger. "Then get the hell out, and don't fucking scare my friends away anymore."

But they aren't his friends.

I grab my keys, phone, and wallet, shove my feet back in my wet boots, slam the door behind me, and run down the stairs two at a time. I get back into my car and make a call. Then I turn on the engine and squeal out of my parking spot, rain sloshing under the wheels.

"Becky?" My voice sounds broken, even to me.

"Honey? Jason? What?"

I'm quiet.

"Jason! You're worrying me. Do you need me to come get you?"

"No. I'm driving."

"You haven't had anything to drink, have you?"

"No, *Mom*." But I'm glad she cares enough to ask. So many people don't.

"Where are you?"

"Almost to your house. Can I come up?"

"Of course." She lets out a bitter laugh. "It's not like you'd expect me to be anywhere but home on a Saturday night."

"Thanks," I mutter. "See you in a few." We hang up, and I find a place to park.

When I raise my fist to knock on her door, it opens before I make contact, and she swerves to avoid me hitting her. I yank her out the door and give her a hug on the steps.

"Honey?"

I tremble. "I'm such an asshole."

She lets out a chuckle, and it sounds almost involuntary. "*That's* what has you all tied up in knots? It's never bothered you before."

"Fuck off," I say mildly.

"Come in. Sit down. Do you need food?"

I need to be bossed around by my baby sister. Sometimes decisions need to be out of my hands. Sometimes I need to not think. I know I do that too much, but I need her guidance. I nod.

"I'll make you a sandwich."

I plop myself on her new couch and put my head in my hands. She bustles in the kitchen. A plate pings on the counter. Plastic crinkles from the packaging of a loaf of bread. Condiment jars clink in the refrigerator door. A soda can pops open.

She's caring for me with food.

I'm both grateful and numb.

Becky sets the plate before me on the coffee table and turns off the TV, and I look up. She curls up in the armchair next to me with a glass of water.

"Okay," she says. "Take a bite and tell me what happened."

Automatically, I do as she says. The sandwich is good, even if my mouth's dry. I don't feel like eating, but I can tell my body needs the food. I'm not sure the last time I ate, because I think I forgot lunch. And maybe breakfast. This is another reason why I have to plan food in advance, because otherwise I don't eat.

Fuck, my life is unmanageable.

"I came home after running errands," I start, " and my roommate was making out with a guy on the couch, and I went ballistic."

She doesn't say anything, but her green eyes widen.

"This weird rage came over me, and I can't believe the things I said. I almost put a fist in the dude's face, and I told him to get out. I'm such a dick."

"Did you actually hit him?"

"No. But I wanted to."

"Okay. What did Murph say?"

"He yelled at me to get the hell out. Which I deserved." I look at her, broken. "Am I a monster? A complete bigot? I can't live with myself if I'm like that. I don't want to judge people. I feel like

I'm one step removed from Westboro Baptist Church." I drink a sip of soda, and somehow I feel better. As if coming clean about all this has made me break down, and I've got nowhere lower to go.

Becky doesn't say anything for a long while. She watches me as I squirm in my seat, take another bite of the sandwich, and swig another gulp of soda.

Finally, she says, "Do you really want to know what I think?"

I nod and brace myself. She's gonna say that I need meds. Or that I need to go on some retreat in a foreign country—a meditation retreat—where I can come to terms with life. Or she's gonna make me do some required reading on how to be a better person.

"I think you're jealous."

I scoff. "Jealous? Of what? I can get laid anytime I want. That's what Marnie's for."

Her eyes laser in on mine. "No, you're jealous of anyone who kisses your roommate. Because you want him for yourself."

I blink.

Uh.

She's swung her words like a bag of rocks that hit me in my stomach, and I suck in a sharp breath.

No.

But.

For a moment, my mind zaps blank. And then I start thinking about Davey Murphy. The sinuous way he moves. His tight skinny jeans that show off the curve of his ass and the length of his legs. The shoulder he so often bares. His elfin face.

And her words feel like the truth.

Yes.

Holy fuck.

I like Murph.

I blink at her some more, and her sharp eyes turn knowing as she watches the gears rumble to life inside my head.

"You know I'm right," she says. "If you're honest, that is."

My hand shakes and my thigh trembles, and all of a sudden, I can't stop moving. My body quakes like I've lost control of all my faculties. She immediately hops up and puts her arms around me, sitting beside me on the couch.

"Shh," she says. "It's okay. No judgment from me."

"Holy fuck," I whisper. "It's the truth. I like Murph."

Becky nods against my neck.

"I want to kiss him."

She laughs. "Spare me the details, big bro." But she pulls back and looks at me. "It's the only explanation that makes sense. Because while you can be gruff, you don't judge people based on stereotypes. You don't have a problem with people being gay or lesbian or trans or anything else. You just have a problem with other men touching Murph."

I nod slowly. "You're right." I blink away some tears. "So I'm not as straight as I thought?"

"Seriously? You haven't picked up on the clues before?"

She's shocked me again. "What clues?"

Becky rolls her eyes. "You keep yourself exceptionally well groomed with artfully messy hair, and your house is incredibly clean."

"Those things don't make someone gay," I sputter, but she holds up a hand.

"When we watch baseball games, you're watching the players' asses. Football, too. I've seen you completely ignore women to talk with guys about who knows what."

"But I love women."

"Maybe in the abstract. But when's the last time you loved a woman *like that*?" She holds up a hand again, cutting off my attempt to talk. "I'm not talking about family love. And we're not going to talk about how you listen to Broadway musicals in the car. You know all the words to *Moulin Rouge!* Or the fact that you secretly buy women's clothes for men."

"Just the one time, for Murph! And none of those things make me gay," I protest.

"Fair. But maybe they don't add up to *not* being into guys, either."

I voice the question I'm scared to ask. "How long have you suspected?"

"Since junior high."

"*What?*"

She nods.

"*Pfft.* No way. I haven't suppressed it that long."

"I don't think you've suppressed it. I think you just haven't thought about it. You're not very self-aware." My sister studies me and takes a deep breath. "While I don't really want to know the answer to this, I'm gonna ask."

"What?"

"You haven't had any experiences? No guy get you off in college?" She wrinkles her nose. "I don't want specifics. But think about it. Lots of supposedly straight guys have fooled around with another man and written it off as meaning nothing. Did you?"

I shake my head. "No. Never. The idea never even entered my head."

"That's so hard to believe."

"As you say, philosophy degree notwithstanding, I'm not one for navel-gazing."

"True. Have you not thought about it at all?"

I shake my head. "I really haven't. I guess I think about other things. As far as sex, well, recently it's only been Marnie."

"Again, I don't need to know specifics, *especially* about a friend of mine."

I tap my fingers on the table. "Does this mean I'm bisexual?"

Becky snorts. "Um, only you can answer that. But from the outside, I don't think you're straight."

I stand up.

"Where are you going?"

"I need to figure out what I'm doing. I need to find Murph. I need to apologize." I lean down and give her a tight hug. "Thank you."

"You're welcome."

I pause at the door, shutting my eyes, white-knuckling the door handle. My breath bursts in and out.

Jesus, I'm fucking scared.

But I need to tell him how I feel about him. Before it's too late.

MURPH

The door slams behind Jason, and Scott swivels his head toward me. The silence in the room almost vibrates.

"What the hell was that?" Scott asks, pointing his finger at the closed door.

I can't answer him, because I don't know. A wave of nausea comes over me as the world seems to slow down on its axis.

"Hey," Scott says, and his voice is gentle. "Are you okay?"

"Yeah," I say robotically, my eyelids hot. "I'm fine."

"No, you're not." He gives me a sheepish grin. "I mean, you are *fine*."

I laugh despite myself. And despite it not being the right time for that joke. Or maybe I laugh *because* it isn't the time for that joke.

But my laughter subsides, and my lower lip trembles.

"Let me get you something," Scott says. As he gets up, he tightens the robe around him. When he'd gotten here we'd made out for like a minute, and then I lent him a robe so his clothes could go in the dryer. Then, um, we found ourselves on the couch. But it wasn't long before Jason came home and threw a tantrum like a toddler who didn't get a toy.

Scott opens cabinets in the kitchen, then returns with a glass of ice water, which for some reason tastes like the best thing I've ever had.

I perch on an arm of the couch—the one where Jason and I have watched shows, discussed matters of the heart, and connected as friends—stare down at my hands, and wonder whether I've been getting through to him at all.

"Look," Scott says. "If I caused this, I'm sorry."

My head whips up. "Don't you dare. You're not responsible for his behavior. You're responsible for your own. But you didn't behave like … like him."

"Well, I did put the moves on you."

I reposition myself, taking a seat on the couch, my arms spread along the back and my chin up. "Only because I'm irresistible."

"Agreed." He pats my leg. "Need to talk about it? I mean, I came over for sex, but I can stay as a friend."

"Thank you." I sip the water and test out how to say what's bothering me. "I can't figure Jason out. He's so very nice to me, except in this one area. Whenever he sees me with another guy, he flips out. We've gone over it. He told me he'd respect my dates and not be such a dick. But he can't stop hulking out at them. It could be because, underneath, he's really homophobic and can't handle boys touching. I don't think so, though, because he touched me—platonically, of course—without turning to ash like I'm Harry Potter and he's Voldemort."

"Or?"

My shoulders droop. "Or he's closeted."

"There's a fine line between being in the closet and being a closet homophobe."

Scott's right. "It would honestly break my heart either way. Because if he's in the closet, he's not letting himself be who he really is because he's scared of what people will say. And if he *is* a closet homophobe, well, why'd he rent a room to me?"

"Maybe he needed the money."

"Maybe. He seems to be doing fine from a money standpoint. But he says stuff to me, like he appreciates how open I am. How he wants to be that way. Makes me think he wants me around."

Scott grins at me. "He's not the only one."

"Hey," I say. "Don't come on to me."

"I'm not. I'm just sayin' I really like you, Murph. And I guess I came over tonight to see if it could work out with us. But I'm getting the idea that it cannot."

"I'm sorry." Inadequate words, but I'm feeling so emotionally drained right now, it's the best I can do.

"You know what I think?"

I perk up. "No."

"Me neither," Scott says.

That earns him a chuckle, then I sigh.

Scott leans in. "So you really think he's into the D?"

The thought makes me pause. Because what if? What if, for real, Jason's sexuality includes men?

What if, even then, he doesn't like me the same way I like him?

"I don't know," I manage to say.

Scott inspects me, his head cocked to the side. "You're into him, aren't you?"

"Yeah," I confess. "And that's why this whole thing with him makes me even sadder. Because he told me he's not interested in me, but he yells at my dates so I can't have anyone else. He told me he'd stop interfering, but he hasn't."

"That blows. What are you going to do about it?"

"When he gets back, I'm going to yell at him. He hasn't listened to reason, so maybe he'll listen to volume. I swear, Scott, this is the last time he'll ruin one of my dates. He has to either sort out how he feels or leave me and"—I wave my hands around —"*whoever* alone. He can't have it both ways. I'm pissed."

"Pissed enough to leave? You could move out."

I heave out a deep breath and look around this cozy, beautiful apartment. "When it's only me and Jason, this place is amazing. But when I try to bring anyone else into my life, he's awful." I realize something. "Jason's probably hating himself right now. He's not a shitty person, not truly."

"Still, he was a dick."

"Yeah. I think it's because he's super protective of me."

"Do you want to come home with me?" Scott asks. "I promise I won't try anything. I just want to make sure you're safe."

"Jason would never hurt me—at least not physically. No. Thanks for the offer. I wanna watch something comforting until he comes back and I can give him a piece of my mind. I'll be fine."

But I'm not sure that's true.

"If you change your mind, come over."

"That's kind of you. Thanks."

I pull him into a hug. He doesn't feel like Jason. Smell like Jason. He's not Jason.

But he's nice, and until Jason walked in, he didn't feel that wrong. I hope he finds the right guy who will appreciate him.

Scott pauses before standing to get his things. "Will you tell me one thing? Are you in love with him?"

"With Jason?" I stammer.

He nods.

I sigh. "It's possible. Probable, even. I don't know. I've had a crush on him since I met him. And everything he does is so caring and loving. But he has it in his head that he dates girls only."

"Internalized homophobia?"

"Maybe. I don't think he recognizes it in himself. If he'd have me, though, I'd accept in the blink of an eye."

Scott rubs the heel of his hand against his chest. "I figured as much. I hope you can get your man, Murph."

"Yeah, it's not looking good right now."

We gather his clothes and basket, and I give him another small hug goodnight.

JASON

My grip's firm on the steering wheel, although inside I feel jolted to my core. Like I've been shaken and now I'm a blank gray Etch A Sketch waiting for someone to draw a new image on me.

Only, is that image gay? (Bi? Pan? Something else?)

The ringing in my ears stops, and I blink and look at where I am. I'm not sure how I got here. Must have been some sort of internal directive.

I'm parked in the lot behind Vino and Veritas. The back door is open. Light emanates from inside, like it's alive.

And I'm out here wondering if I belong in there. Not because it's inclusive and friendly. But because of those rainbow flags in the windows.

I need to go talk to Murph, but I have to figure out how I feel and what to say first.

Is my sexual orientation something I've been ignoring—consciously or not—for years?

I've always been open with my body. Sex is fun and natural. Does it matter who I do it with?

To my surprise, the answer that comes to me is both yes and no. They duke it out in my mind.

I'd figured the answer was no. As long as I'm having sex with a consenting adult who's into it—preferably really into it—it doesn't matter who I sleep with.

But maybe the answer is yes, it matters who I touch. Because maybe I want sex to mean more than it has. To not feel as empty as it felt—*feels*—when it's just sex with no heart.

So, what if the person I'm touching is a guy? Could I do that?

A rap on my window knocks me out of my thoughts.

A man crouches down and looks in my window, smiling.

I roll down the window—thankfully the rain's tapered off—only now realizing I hadn't turned my car off. I'm not sure how long I've been parked here.

"Hey, gorgeous. You okay? You were here when I arrived, then I went outside and noticed you hadn't moved. I wanted to see if you wanted to come in with me." The guy's tone is light and flirty and *oh my god, I'm being picked up by a guy.* While my first inclination is to be shocked, I take a deep breath and stare at him. Time to try out this new ... identity.

"Um," I say. Eloquently.

His smile falters. "Are you all right? You're not waiting for someone, are you?"

Is it just me, or is he brazen? And his confidence is giving me confidence. Because I could do this, right? Ask a guy out?

Or do I only want one specific guy?

I gulp and gaze at him, not sure if I'm grimacing or smiling. "I'm not sure," I say, honesty coming out. "I just ended up here."

"If you make up your mind and decide to go in, I'd be happy if you wanted to end up with me." He shrugs. And then he looks again, really taking in my face. "You are okay, right?"

I nod repeatedly. "Thank you. Yes. Sorry. I've just. Um. Had a weird night."

"I can take your mind off that," the guy says. "Right here. Or we can go back to my place. You're totally hot."

I inhale sharply.

What is even happening here?

His words make all my emotions rise, churning in a blender.

Mad and relieved and turned on and pissed and sad and curious and depressed.

For a moment, I have to restrain myself from opening the car door and shoving him up against the nearest hard surface.

And I don't know if I'd be doing that as some twisted hate crime—or if I'm turned on by the idea of this guy on his knees sucking me off.

I realize that in this short interaction I've noticed things about him. How his eyes are big and friendly with little wrinkles on the side, but not as lively as Murph's. How he smells good, but not as good as Murph. How his hands are big, with knobby knuckles and neat nails. But no nail polish like Murph's colorful hands.

I somehow am picking up on more clues than I thought.

As much as I don't want this random guy, I'm rejecting him not because he's a guy.

But because he's not Murph.

There's the clarity I wanted.

I just want Murph. My little roommate ball of fire.

"No, thanks," I croak.

"Okay," he says cautiously. "Don't be afraid to reach out if you need to." He gives me an apologetic smile. "I lost a friend in high school because he didn't reach out when he needed help. I'm extra cautious these days."

I choke out a startled laugh. "No, it's nothing like that. I just have some things to think about."

"Good."

I manage a weak smile. "Thanks."

He saunters off, and I think about Murph. And not just his spirit this time.

Specifically, I think about kissing him, and lo and behold, that makes my dick happy.

I rummage in the center console and pop a piece of gum in my mouth, because a guy can hope.

Bottom line, I want to find out what Murph tastes like. I want the intimacy of being in his face, close to those blue eyes. I want our lips to lock, and I want to touch him. I don't just want him for sex, although I'm starting to think I want that, too. Judging by my boners around him. Or, ahem, while thinking about him.

Plain and simple, I want *him*. I want to know what it feels like to share something intimate with him, because I like him.

I'm open to this new idea. Inhabiting a body that *could* allow a man to touch me.

And *that* shifts my worldview.

Becky accuses me of not thinking for myself. She finds my roommates. She shops for me. She thinks for me. Or Dad does. I do whatever he says.

But I'm thinking for myself about something *really* important, and making the decision is heady. This is who I'm meant to be.

Bisexual.

For the first time, I accept that word, and something clicks into place, finally.

I should've been paying more attention. I should've been more perceptive. And I don't know how to become more perceptive when I've been so clueless for so long.

Except to ask Murph for help.

I think about him. His small body and bright, impish smile. His love of all things nerd.

And I think about his lips and how horrified they'd been when I left. I spit out my barely chewed gum into the wrapper.

Murph kicked me out, and he doesn't know how much I want him. I'm worried I've ruined our relationship beyond repair, when what I want is *more*.

I need to fix this. I need to go fix this with him, now.

But before I can do that, I pick up my phone and hit a number. I'm not breaking off things with her by text.

She answers.

"Marnie? I have to tell you something."

23

MURPH

Scott's left, but I'm too jumpy to sit and watch anything like I said I would. So I spend my evening pacing around the living room. My eyes sting, but I refuse to cry.

One star. Not fun. Do not recommend.

After a while, when it's apparent Jason's not coming back anytime soon, I give up the marching band routine and flounce into my room to start packing.

I'm leaving.

I need to get some space between us. I don't know what his deal is, but I need to not see him for a while. Like at least for the rest of tonight. I'm much too attached, and I can't have my heart yanked around this way. It isn't healthy. While I don't know where I'm going, Reeve'll let me stay on his couch, I'm sure, at least until I sort out what I'm going to do next.

If I can even stay in this apartment after tonight.

My heart beats fast, and my face flames hot. I pull out my duffel bag and start throwing clothes into it.

Then I sigh and take them back out, lining them up neatly on my bed. If I'm going out in a blaze of glory, I'm gonna make sure I have complete outfits set up. With accessories.

But the more things I gather to pack and the more I stew, the madder I get, until I'm spitting like a wet cat. Also, packing means I have plenty of brain time to compose my magnum opus telling Jason off.

I have half a mind to call him right now, but I think it will be more effective in person. You can't really slam down a cell phone. I'm hoping I can at least slam a door.

Underneath it all, though, I'm in agony. I'd honestly thought, even if I couldn't have him romantically, at least we were friends and he cared in his own way.

But apparently I was wrong.

Way wrong.

After I've packed two bags, I hear the door open. I sprint down the hall, livid, targeting my jackass roommate. I skid to a stop, glaring at him. "Come home to disturb another one of my dates?" I spit out, ready to launch into parts one, two, and three, along with subparts A through Q, of my dissertation entitled, "Why Jason Needs to Leave Me and My Potential Hookups the Fuck Alone."

Jason's somber, guarded face tries to tell me something. I have no idea what. He takes a step toward me, seriously in my personal space. I take an equal step away from him, my back now against the wall, feeling like he's the dogcatcher and I'm headed to the pound.

He asks in a deadly quiet tone, "Does he mean something to you?"

I throw my hands out in exasperation, trying not to touch him, but he's kind of all over me. "Does Scott mean something? He's a person, so sure. People all mean something."

Jason draws a breath in and releases it before he speaks. I can smell minty gum on his breath. And again, his words almost feel like a threat. "You know what I mean."

I lean forward, my face getting dangerously close to his. "He's just a guy. He doesn't mean any more or less than any other human on the planet. But where I put my tongue is my own business. Who I spend my time with is my own business, too. *I* get to make that decision. *Not you.*" My voice rises by the end of my little speech, and I wouldn't be surprised if steam's coming out of the top of my head.

Yes, I'm advocating for Scott even though it wasn't my idea for him to come over, because it's the *concept* of Scott I'm fighting for. Not the actual Scott, who, even with his darling nose, doesn't make me feel a particle of what I feel for this bastard who's crowding me against a wall.

Jason's face morphs from fierceness into something gentler. And he reaches out and strokes the side of my face.

I'm so confused.

But then he starts talking, and the sincerity in his eyes bowls me over. "I realized something, Davey." It's the first time he's called me that. "And I'm sorry it took me so long. I'm sorry I had to put you through the wringer to come to this conclusion. I know I've been an asshole."

"Yeah, no kidding—"

"It's because I'm jealous."

The silence in the room engulfs us, and my thoughts skitter to a stop. Then my heart starts beating so fast, I think something's physiologically wrong with me. And maybe something's wrong with my hearing, too. Because nothing computes right now.

Somehow he's three inches away from me, and I have no idea what this means. A flicker of desire rises in my chest, but I don't want to fan it because I've spent so much time trying to put it out.

All I know is his big, strong body gives off heat like a barbecue, and I'm on fire.

My voice drops. "Jealous? What do you mean?"

His finger traces my cheek, and I close my eyes. "I think—" He stops and takes a deep breath. "No. I *know*. I know *I* want to be the one kissing you. Not him."

I shake my head like a dog in a cartoon, and he moves his

hand away. *Stupid move, Murph*. But he puts a foot between mine so our knees knock. Anyone looking at us would think we're making out, we're so close. Still, none of his words make sense. He's my straight roommate. The one with years of booty calls with the same girl. The one who chews out all of my hookups. The one who's kept me from getting any since I moved in.

I have to ask, eyes now wide, "What? I mean, I heard you, but *what*? Are you serious?"

Instead of answering me, he glances up at the ceiling, then his fiery eyes laser on mine. His low, husky voice arouses me, and we really need to stop playing this game, because someone's gonna get hurt. He asks, very simply, "Would it be okay if I tried something?"

I can barely get the words out, hope—and other parts of my body—rising. "Tried what?" My voice cracks.

"Kissing you."

Oh holy fucking fruit trees. All I can do is stand there, mouth open like a guppy, and nod. Sensations zing all over my skin, like electric charges between us, from him to me and then back again, the same as when he touched me at the Renaissance faire, only more so.

Jason moves so his hips and chest touch mine, and his soap scent wafts over me. He looks nervous but resolute. He trails a finger down my face again, feeling my stubble, and a look flickers behind his eyes like he can't believe he's doing this. But he leans in, and his lips touch mine.

And it's everything.

Jason kisses like Prince Charming. Sweet and insistent and giving. His lips press to mine, soft and sexy, and a quiet noise rumbles in the back of his throat. A very turned-on noise.

I whimper and kiss back with vigor, because I don't know what else to do. I try to express my feelings for him through this kiss, because I don't know if this is a one-time shot. When our tongues finally touch, lightning courses through my veins.

Goddess save me, because I might die right now, when I've finally gotten what I want.

He draws back, gasping and blinking. Then he shakes his head, his lips red, his eyes still unsatisfied, his hair mussed from where I apparently played with it.

I hadn't known my hands had made it into his hair, but they're there now.

Oh, and yes. It's very soft.

Very gently, he drops his forehead to mine, and his breath fans me, and I almost dissolve into a puddle of goo on the floor. "That answered one thing."

"What?" I mumble.

"Evidently I have no complaint about a guy kissing you, if that guy is me."

"Holy shit," I wheeze. And I reach my arms around him and kiss him again before we even catch our breath. Lips colliding and tongues doing the cha-cha and our bodies wrapped together tight.

It's *wonderful.*

How did my life go from sinking to the bottom of a fish tank, covered in algae and fish poop, to soaring? Am I in an alternate universe?

But there's no mistaking the large, corded muscles holding me tight to him. Or—can you hear the chorus of angels singing?—that impressive erection I can feel rubbing against mine.

Jason Falkner likes me.

My apparently not-so-straight roommate's kissing me.

Is this my life?

This fantasy can't ever end. I force myself to stay still, because I don't wanna wake up. But our tongues slide together, and my hands move from his hair down to rub his beardiness, and he shoves me even more forcefully against the wall.

Fuck yeah!

He tastes like mint and tangy man, and I may expire on the spot. Rather than call for smelling salts, though, I shamelessly rub against him, wanting the friction, and his posture goes rigid.

Oops.

I pull my hips away. "Too much?" I ask, feeling dizzy.

"Not enough." But he swallows hard.

"What's wrong?" I can't quite meet his eyes, but he puts a finger under my chin and tilts it up so I'm looking at him this close.

And goddess, he looks good. His green eyes have flecks of gold and some darker bits, and he has one kissable freckle on the outside edge of his cheekbone, like a male Marilyn Monroe.

His voice dips to a low, gravelly register. "I *really* like kissing you. But I don't know how ready I am for anything else."

"Baby," I say, and I watch his eyes soften. "We never have to do anything you don't want to do."

I can't believe I'm saying those words. Not because they aren't true—they *so* are—but because I never thought I'd be in the position to even have a chance at Jason in my arms. Or—*goddess*—my bed.

"Okay." And he leans in and kisses me again, this time more chastely. Then he grins, and his grin turns into a full-on chuckle, which makes him collapse into a belly laugh. He steps away from me and doubles over.

"I've never known someone to have this reaction to kissing me before," I say tartly, my hand on my hip, watching him like I'd watch a goat eating a can—amused and wondering if I should do something to stop it.

When he composes himself, he chokes out, "No, Murph, you don't understand. I'm just so happy to have figured it out. All this time I've been afraid I was some homophobic prick. But I just didn't want anyone *else* touching you."

His words thaw a frosty place inside me. I jump up and wrap my arms around his neck, and his arms come around me instinctively, gripping my ass and holding me up. We stagger back to the couch, and he sits down roughly, then lies down lengthwise on the cushions. I straddle him and toy with the bottom of his shirt.

"You're the sexiest man I've ever met," I admit. "I've had a crush on you since the day I moved in."

"I think it might be the same for me. I mean, I'm pretty damned sure I've had a crush on you, too. This entire time." And his admission is so endearing, I think I might die all the deads all over again.

JASON

I kissed a boy, and I liked it.

I'd thought that kissing Murph and admitting my feelings to both of us would make things absolutely clear, like I got to the top of a mountain and could see all the land below. And in some respects they are: I'm not straight, I like kissing him, I like *him*. Very much.

But it's not that easy. The view from here tells me there's so much more landscape to traverse. I'm still a mess, and I start repeating, "I'm so, so sorry. I am just so sorry."

"It's okay, sweetie," Murph says, his lips on my skin, which feels utterly right.

I grip his waist. "You don't have to forgive me that fast."

"You kind of made up for it epically." His eyes catch mine. "I'm serious. I was about to move out—at least for a few days or, um, hours—but you coming in here like some gay avenging angel, telling me that you like me? Well, it's not making me want to pack up my pantyhose anytime soon."

"What *does* it make you want to do?" My throat thickens, and my voice drops an octave.

His tenor matches mine. "Get to know you better. A lot better."

I relax into the couch. "Thank fuck."

That said, I don't know if I'm ready to do anything more than kiss Murph. This is all so new.

My body, however, seems to have other ideas. It's knocking on a window, holding up placards that say, "GO GET NAKED!"

"I wanna go down on you," Murph murmurs, apparently reading the signs, and the image of his mouth around my stiff dick makes me light-headed. He scoots back and holds up his hands. "I know you don't want to go fast. I'll respect that. But I'm also done pretending I don't want you."

I cock my head. "I've seen you get your flirt on. Have you *ever* pretended you didn't, um, you know, want me?"

"No," he acknowledges. "But I also want you to know where my thoughts are and, well, they're in your pants. Not that you asked my opinion, but you need to be sucked off, and now, and by me."

I groan so loudly our neighbors can probably hear it across the street. Everything inside me goes to war—my head and my heart and my conscience and my cock and the rest of my body and my soul. All fighting.

And I'm not sure what they're fighting about, because they all want Murph.

He catches the look on my face and pulls back even more, so his ass is on my knees instead of his cock grinding against mine. "Ooh-kay. That's too fast for you."

"I don't know if it is," I admit.

"That means it is." He kisses me chastely. "Let's tone it down."

"I don't know if I want to," I also admit.

The smile on Murph's face lights up the outer reaches of space, and it makes my heart surge. Other parts, too.

He repositions himself on the large leather couch, straddling me closer to my groin, and I notice where we are and grimace, remembering who he was kissing here earlier. He pulls back, understanding dawning on his face.

"I swear I'm not a harlot," he says, yanking his shoulders away from me.

My hands fly up in a surrender position. "First, I never said you were. And second, there's nothing wrong with being sexually free. Haven't we discussed this? We agree on that point."

"But maybe I don't wanna be sexually free. Maybe I want to be tied to you." He bites the tip of his finger and smiles around it, gazing at me through his lashes. And that one coquettish move makes me even harder.

I groan again. "Don't say shit like that. It gives me ideas." He offers a light little grind on my dick as a preview. Couple that with his sly grin, and I'm officially done. "You're such a tease," I whine, my palms flat on the couch on either side of me.

"But I'm not," he protests. His eyes drop, and he picks at nonexistent lint on my shirt. "I want you so bad it hurts. It's hurt for weeks."

"C'mere." I beckon him closer, and he stretches out on top of me, his mouth meeting mine. My hands cup his round ass, and it makes me wild.

He feels good.

He feels more than good.

"I like you," he whispers against my lips. "A lot."

If it were possible to sink farther into the couch, I'd be doing it right now. "I like you, too. And, um, my jeans are getting very uncomfortable."

The anguish in Murph's eyes is palpable. "I dunno what to do. I can't stay away from you, and I don't want to pressure you. At all."

"I appreciate that." I shut my eyes. "I don't want—" I let out a breath and start again. "I don't want to lead you on. I don't want to play with your emotions. But I really, really want to try going further. I want this. I want *us*. I like you too much not to try."

I open my eyes to Murph blinking away tears and tracing my face with his fingers. "You're serious, aren't you?" He sniffles. "Today's the best day of my life. It'd been so shitty, but now I have you. I do have you, don't I?"

"Yes, Davey." I try out his real name again. "Can I call you that?"

"You can call me almost anything." He cuddles into me. "I feel so happy in your arms."

"It's where you've belonged from the start. Only I was too oblivious to know."

"That's okay. You just needed to figure it out." Murph starts doing that speed-talking that I find charming. "We put so much pressure on ourselves when we believe we should already know everything. But if that were true, when would we be able to *learn* anything? We really aren't fair to ourselves. We're supposed to know how to do everything perfectly already, and we get reprimanded when we don't. But how are we supposed to know unless we learn?"

"You have a point."

He grins. "I guess you simply needed to learn that you like dick." He puts both hands over his mouth. "Wait, goddess, we don't know if you actually do like dick."

I wrap my arms around his waist and hold him to me. "I'm almost sure I do. And I can't wait to confirm that," I whisper as I palm his butt. "I know for certain that your ass is mighty fine."

"You noticed my ass?"

"Since you wore your purple towel—and only that purple towel—the first week you moved in."

"Hmm." He wiggles it. "Same. I mean about yours. It was hard to follow you up the stairs move-in day. And by hard, I mean …"

I throw my head back and laugh. God, I'm feeling this tremendous freedom. I've heard all these phrases—like I'm free from shackles or breathing fresh air for the first time after being underground. But it's so true. I feel like I'm finally just, I don't know, *right*. Not right in the sense that I'm right and you're wrong. But right as in this deep sense of authenticity.

I don't want to frighten him, but I think part of that feeling is associated with the thought of being with him for a long time into the future. Like, in perpetuity. Because I couldn't have had this fierce of a reaction to Murph if I didn't feel something really deep for him.

Also, I haven't felt this horny in a while. Yes, women turn me on. But what I feel for him is different—stronger—and I don't think it's only the thrill of the unknown or the fact that it's been a while for me. At least, I hope it's not.

I don't want this to be a phase. This isn't a test. This isn't me trying something out.

This is me being real and true to myself for the first time in my life.

This is me becoming who I was always meant to be.

I study his face. "Are you hungry?"

"No. I'm sleepy. Or, at least, I'm ready for bed." He grins at me. "Come with me."

"There's no way I could stay away." We get up, and he tugs me out of the living room.

We brush our teeth side by side for the first time, and I keep from touching him because otherwise I wouldn't finish the job.

It's a different sort of intimacy. I have this cute guy smiling at me in the mirror. Not me, LOL. When I glance down to spit out the toothpaste, I see the fish dish I made, now being used as a soap dish. And it somehow has pieces of both of us in it.

Then I stare at him in the mirror as he brushes.

I like a dude.

I'm still not positive I like all dudes in general, but this small, vivacious one I live with?

I like him a fuck ton.

My brain truly is expanding to let me accommodate this new definition of myself.

We walk into his room, and he shucks off his shirt and stalks over to me. My arms automatically wrap around him, and then I can't get my own boots and shirt off fast enough.

Warm skin next to warm skin feels really, really wonderful. Where I'm used to smooth curves, Murph's lean muscles are sexy in a completely different way. My hands cup his ass, and I realize my cock is rubbing against his and I might come from this if we keep it up.

"Yep," he murmurs.

I guess I said that out loud while he was sucking on my neck. I shuffle with him to the bed, pick him up, and kind of throw him on it.

"Oh, fuck yes," he hisses.

I fall onto him, noticing how he feels beneath me, somehow foreign and familiar at the same time. While I'm obviously familiar with what a male body feels like, I'm not used to touching someone else's.

He lets out a moan, and his hands start exploring my torso. Then he backs off. "This okay?"

"Yes. It's new." He stills, but I lean into him, encouraging him to keep going. "But I really like it. I'm into you, in case you hadn't gotten the memo." I fall to the side and take him with me.

"I don't care what we do, as long as you touch me. Actually, you don't even have to touch me. Just breathing the same air—" His eyes widen in horror, and he shoves his fist in his mouth. His words come out garbled, but I pick out, "Fuck. I didn't mean to say that out loud." He moves his fist. "Pretend I didn't say it."

"No way. I like that you say what you think." My voice lowers.

"You do?" His vulnerable question makes my heart squeeze. *This guy.*

"I do," I assure him. I kiss him before he says anything else. Whatever he wants to say gets lost on my tongue, and that idea fascinates me. Like what he said is now part of me. Like we're becoming one.

He wiggles out from under me and shimmies off his pants. He's wearing tiny, sparkly pink underwear. "I'm thinking I want to do this," he says and climbs on top of me.

Yeah, I'm not straight—or at least not as straight as I thought.

I can feel how hard he is. And I'm hard under him. Hell, I was hard when I came home.

Moving my pelvis away from him, I keep our lips touching.

"You're sexy." I run my hands through his thick hair. Messing it up gives him bedhead, which adds to his allure. *Slow*, I tell myself. *Keep things slow.*

He whimpers. "You're in my bed. This isn't a dream?"

"I am. You're not dreaming. This is real." I pause, remembering something. "When I told you I was crap at my previous relationships, I thought it was because I was falling for the wrong girls. But maybe I was just looking for you."

Murph's eyes fill with tears. "Oh my goddess." His hands fly up to his mouth. "Can I touch you more? Please."

"Yes. I want that so badly. But—" I pull back and groan. "Fuck."

His expression darkens. "Look, we don't have to—"

"I don't know what I'm doing," I blurt.

"Sweetheart." He strokes my arm. "No one does—"

"And I'm kinda shocked at how natural it feels."

"You're thinking too much, Jay Jay. Just let your boy toy take care of you."

I snort. "My boy toy?"

"At your service. Tell me if you want me to stop, and I will. Immediately. No questions asked." He leans back and gazes at me, seeking permission. Consent.

He has it.

This. I want *this*.

"Okay," I whisper.

He pounces and starts kissing down my torso, and I'm weirded out at how *not at all* weirded out I am by any of this.

When he gets to my hips, he peers up at me. I shrug and nod, hopelessly gone.

Murph tugs down my pants and lets out a quiet moan. "Fuck, you're hung. I want you in me." He rubs his hands together as he scoots down my thighs for access. "Oh, I'm *drooling*."

His naughty grin's so sexy, it takes my breath away, and, not for the first time tonight, I seriously believe I may pass out.

Perhaps because all my blood's taken up residence in my dick or perhaps because so many emotions are swirling around inside me that I'm spinning. But before I know what he's doing, he's pushed my remaining clothes off, and he's holding my dick.

Another man's hand is on my dick.

And I *really* fucking like it.

Before I can react, my dick's encased in the hot, wet luxury that's Murph's mouth. He inhales and hums around it happily. If I were standing, there's no doubt I'd fall down.

Whatever he's doing, it feels different than it ever has before, and, well, holy *everything*. I grit out, "You're gonna make me come embarrassingly fast—"

He pops off and holds up a finger. "Correction. Not embarrassing. It's called a compliment."

My laugh sounds slightly unhinged. But I manage, "'Kay."

Murph uses his tongue to rub underneath my shaft, taking big, long sucks, staying still, letting his warm mouth engulf me. It's amazing, mostly because it's *him*.

I'm so gone I may very well burst out and tell him something mortifying, so I shove my forearm in my mouth and chomp on my wrist.

The word to describe what Murph is doing is worship. The man's worshipping my dick, making me feel like a goddamn prince. He's treating me with reverence, as if he's put my dick on a velvet pillow so he can lavish it with attention.

I've never experienced such a good blow job. I'm not even going to sort through old memories to compare, because this, right now, is mind-blowing.

"Oh my god." Now I'm the one whimpering, as he does something around the tip.

He stops for a moment to lock eyes with me, then pulls off and beams. "You okay there, big guy?"

All I can do is nod wordlessly. He opens his wide, wet grin and takes me in once more, and I gasp, then bite my lip, unable to express what I'm feeling right now.

He goes back to blowing me, and while I've got no idea what I was thinking for every day of my life before this one, I know what I'm thinking now.

I'm thinking I'm completely gone for my roommate.

He stops again, though. He's driving me bananas. I make a noise of protest.

"Shh," he says soothingly. "I want you to come in my mouth. Think you can do that?"

I nod rapidly again, and he chuckles. "I'll take that as you're good with this."

Then he dips his head down, and this time he starts bobbing up and down in earnest, his other hand caressing my balls, then stroking me along with his tongue, the perfect pressure, the perfect tension, the perfect—gahhh, I'm going to explode.

"*Ungh,*" I say, and my back arches involuntarily. My hands clench the sheets, and my eyes water. I realize I'm shoving myself down Murph's throat, but he doesn't seem to mind. In fact, he doubles down, and it brings me to the edge of orgasm and over it, and my mind goes blank, my body pulsing over and over again in waves of pleasure as I release into his mouth, his throat working to swallow everything.

Murph laps at me as I come down, then sucks me clean. He kneels between my legs, grinning up at me and licking his lips like a satisfied cat.

"C'mere," I say and tug him up along my body. He snuggles in happily and lies still. Again, I enjoy his weight on me. I cradle him, and he kisses me. As he lies on my chest, he smiles smugly against my skin.

"Yeah, okay," I mutter. "We should have done that ages ago."

"You like?"

"Like? Yeah. I guess." Then I wrap him tighter in my arms. "Holy fuck, Murph, that was a religious experience. I think you transported me to a different dimension. Like real-life *Rick and Morty*."

"Excellent," he mumbles against my neck. "My evil plan worked."

"Seriously, you *are* evil. It would've been more ethical if you'd injected me with heroin. Because that was the most addictive thing I've ever experienced."

He sits up again, straddling my waist, and his expression sobers. "I'm glad. For real. I wanted to show you." He takes a breath, and his next sentence comes out at Murph speed. "I wanted to show you how I feel about you."

"Mission accomplished." I stare at him. "I don't think I can top that. You've given me performance anxiety now. There's no way on god's green earth that I can make you feel the same way."

"Here's a secret. You already do." His eyes warm. "Just seeing you come apart. Knowing I did that. Having you let me into your life, in this way? It's enough."

But his hard dick pressing against my thigh means his body's not satisfied.

"I want to try," I whisper, and the joy on his face lights up the stars.

Once I catch my breath, I roll us over and let my hands start exploring his body.

I'm not ready to suck his cock, but I can hold it. I think.

I lean down and kiss his lips, then kiss his collarbones and between his pecs. Murph whimpers, letting me touch him while his hands fuss with my hair. I explore, tonguing each nipple in turn, enjoying his gasps. His hands move to grip the sheet below him in a kind of voluntary restraint, and his intense eyes watch my progress. I trace a line down his body, licking his belly button, then going lower. He has virtually no body hair anywhere. I slide down and reposition myself between his legs, loving the muffled curse he makes. His hand eases from the sheet to skim my shoulder muscles, then his nails scratch my scalp with the gentlest of touches. But it feels like he's about to snap.

Very slowly, I drop light kisses, making my way down to his pelvis. I nuzzle into him over his underwear, enjoying his scent.

Murph always smells great, like soap and aftershave, but he also has this hint of man underneath—a little musky or salty—and I really like it.

Then, gathering my courage, I shove down his underwear and his cock springs free.

It's nice looking.

I hold my breath and grasp it, and he shudders under me. And I relax.

It's a body. I love bodies.

And it's not just anyone's body.

This is *Murph.* My funny, sexy roommate who's bowled me over since I met him. Who I feel this undeniable attraction to. Who I want to make feel amazing. Whose whole body is vibrating in tense anticipation.

His cock is velvety skin over thick hardness, and, well, it's generally very familiar. *Obviously*. I decide this is no big deal.

I carefully tug on him the way I like it done to me, and he responds immediately, his voice a hoarse whisper. "Jason."

"Yeah, baby," I say, trying out an endearment. I glance up, and his eyes are brimming with tears. "Hey." I kiss his inner thigh, then move up to kiss his face and hold his whole body in my arms. "Need me to stop?"

He shakes his head. "Jason. You're not a unicorn. I mean, you *are* a unicorn, but you're a real unicorn, not that unicorns are real except for you."

"You're so fucking cute," I say and kiss him, then go back to stroking him.

His eyes widen comically and then scrunch tight like he doesn't want it to stop. His hands seek my shoulders. "Do your worst," he says. "I'm not gonna break. Do what you like to do to yourself."

"Hang on a sec," I say and scoot toward his bedside table. "Got lube?"

He startles. "What?" The beginning of a grin tugs at his lips.

I give him a playful shove. "Not for that. I want to make this feel better."

He reaches over to the drawer and pulls out a bottle, and I notice some personal items there that I want to see him demonstrate. Later.

I squirt lube into my palm and stroke him faster. "This okay?"

"*Uh-huh*," he groans, still and stiff, his limbs clutching at the bed and his dick hard in my hand. In that moment, I can feel he's going to come. The trigger is pulled and the waves start crashing, and I'm mesmerized because while I've felt it myself, I've never experienced anyone else doing this. Well, any other man.

When he's mellowed and pushes me away, I look at the come on his chest and poke at it with my finger. He watches as I trace designs in it. Then I put my finger in my mouth. I manage not to get a mouthful of lube.

He sits bolt upright. "Oh my goddess, did you just do that?"

I smile and kiss him. "Let me help you clean up." I crawl out of bed and go to the bathroom to get a wet washcloth.

After wiping him down, I stare at him. He looks so defenseless lying nude, but also so beautiful, his hair messy, his body flushed and satisfied, his spent dick lying against his leg. I have to tell him. "You are utterly beautiful."

Then I realize I'm naked, too, and he's taking in my body as much as I'm taking in his.

"Come to bed," he whispers. I crawl in behind him.

I drift off to thoughts that aren't of my nascent gay tendencies, nor of sex. Instead, I'm enjoying holding someone I'm really, really attracted to. In this moment, there's no fallout. There's no coming out.

There's just us. Cuddling on a bed.

I'm good with that.

MURPH

On Monday, Jason goes to work and I, well, go to work, too, and it's really hard for me to shut up. Auden tells me all about his weekend: the movie he saw, the farmers market he went to, and the amazing meal he cooked for his boyfriend.

I, on the other hand, am silent. Tanner notices immediately, since I'm normally a chattering magpie. But I can't tell a single soul in a 300-mile radius that the straightest guy in Vermont kissed me. And did more.

Don't get me started on learning that Jason's a Sunday-morning cuddler and that he makes the sweetest waffles I've ever had—not sugary sweet, but kind-and-generous sweet, going to the effort even though it was just us. That he spent the day watching movies with me and fooling around on the couch.

I don't want to keep this a secret. But it's not my business to tell anyone.

Still, I think Tanner's on to me. Because he keeps eyeing me, opening his mouth, and then thinking better of it.

I'm grateful for his self-control, because I have little to none, but I still might implode.

Because Jason didn't just kiss me and have his hands all over my body.

Nooo.

He admitted he liked me and that he'd been a douche because he was jealous.

Jason Falkner. Jealous. Over guys touching me.

There really is a goddess, and my prayers have been answered. My crush likes me!

I'm nearly levitating, because I can still feel his lips on mine. I can hear the way he sounded when he came. Note, that sound's made me constantly hard as I replay it in my mind over and over again. I should've recorded it … although that would be pervy, so no.

But gah. The boy is *fine*.

Thankfully, we're busy at work, so I'm pouring my little heart out. Pouring wine, that is. And my hands are sure today, so no breakage on my part.

The repetitive actions of take glass, fill with wine, hand to customer leave me free to daydream about how Jason's shoulders are much bigger than mine. What his beard felt like against my chin. And parts below.

The feral look in his eyes when he said he wanted to kiss me.

I'm such a fairy princess right now, I could spin. And wave a wand. And dust everything with glitter.

Tanner stops me again. He goes to say something, but I'm saved by Jake, a customer. I could hug said Jake the customer, even though he's always a righteous ass, because he saves me from having to explain myself.

Finally, in a lull, Tanner tugs me over to the side. "Did it finally happen?"

"What makes you think something happened?" I ask, raising an eyebrow.

"Don't give me that, David Murphy. Spill."

"You full-named me. That's an ouchie. I thought we were friends."

He chuckles, then schools his eyes into a glare.

So I relent. "Okay, okay. I had a good weekend," I confess.

"I knew it."

"But I can't talk about it. I'm sorry, and it's killing me, but I can't."

He narrows his eyes like he's piecing together the puzzle and coming to the right conclusion. But I don't want him to do that. I hold up my hand. "Don't go guessing. Don't go sticking your nose in anyone else's business."

"I don't do that." I give him a look. "Very often," he amends.

"I know. But in this case, I'm pleading with you. Don't ask too many questions. Just know I'm happy."

He smiles. "I can tell." Putting a hand on my shoulder, he squeezes it. "I'm glad. You're like Cinderella today."

"I'm scared of what happens after the ball. Because the ball—can it be a ball with only two people?—well, it was amazing. And it went on well past midnight. But what happens now?" I start speaking faster. "If you're figuring anything out from my words, please please for the love of the goddess do not. Don't figure it out, don't repeat it, don't let anyone know."

Auden walks by. "Let anyone know what?" he says in his Scottish accent. Tanner eyes his utility kilt. Auden pushes the dress code as much as I do.

"Argh!" I sputter. "I have a secret, and I can't tell anyone, and you are not going to make me tell you, because it's not my secret."

"We're sorry," says Tanner. "We won't press or try to figure it out."

"Speak for yourself," says Auden, but after laughing at the panicked look on my face, he eases off. "I'm only taking the piss."

Tanner gazes at me. "I'm glad you're happy, and when you can talk about it, come tell us who it is—even though we've already guessed—and how happy you are. Because all we want is to see you happy."

"Precisely," Auden says.

I nod.

A customer comes in, and my thoughts of what's actually

happened with my new boy keep me from worrying too much about what's going to happen in the future.

As the day goes on, I realize another reason why I can't blab: I'm scared this will all go away. If I speak of it, it'll be an alternate reality I can't return to, like when Rick Sanchez can't get back to a certain world because the equipment broke. That isn't the best thought, so I stick with *it's not my secret to tell.*

But I have a secret, too. That I'm really fucking falling hard, and if this is only an experiment for Jason, I might get broken into pieces that can't be put back together again.

I've never felt like this for any other guy. It's not just Jason's looks, mouthwatering though they are. There are plenty of hot guys in this state to choose from.

But there aren't that many who are as responsible as Jason is. As open and willing to try new things. As generous with time and food. As kind. As patient a listener.

He's a good one, and I want to keep him.

So I stay quiet at work. I don't text him.

I don't want to rock the boat. I don't want to upset the preliminary balance we came to over the weekend, because it means too much to me. I think it meant a lot to him, too, right?

And not just the watershed moment of touching a boy with his tongue. All of it.

I need to stop thinking before I stress myself out. I go back to my game plan. Pour wine, keep my mouth shut, and hope that Jason wants to kiss me again tonight rather than kick me to the curb.

When I get home after my shift, I'm nervous as I put the key in the lock. The magic of the weekend has passed, and we've both gone back to our real worlds. Will the man in the gray flannel suit forget his sexual adventures and go back to being straitlaced? I very much hope not.

I didn't see his car, but he doesn't always park it in the same place. Still, the apartment is quiet when I open the door. He's not home. I don't know if I'm relieved or bummed because it delays answers to my questions—will he want to pretend it didn't happen? Will it be uncomfortable? Will I get to taste him again?

Not knowing what else to do, I pretend it's a normal day and start making a casserole from the *Betty Crocker Cookbook*, wearing a frilly apron I picked up once Jason and I started cooking together. While Jason's the better cook, with his help I've figured out a few things.

After browning meat, cooking noodles, and putting it all together in a dish with veggies and a few cans of condensed soup, I hear the key in the lock, and I panic.

Get it together, Murph.

"Sweetums!" I call. "Did you have a nice day at the office?"

Because I'm me. I can't help being me. And I'm gonna milk this situation for all it's worth.

Jason comes in the door, sexy and rumpled with his tie loosened, his suit jacket over his shoulder, and his sleeves rolled up. I try not to admire how good he looks, and I fail.

He smiles broadly as he puts his jacket down on a chair and enters the kitchen. "Hey, Murph." His eyes crinkle up, and I lose myself in them. He walks over to me and hesitates. He shifts his weight, and his hands twitch. Like he wants to kiss me but isn't sure if he should. Isn't sure how this is going to work. If we're going to have our hands and mouths all over each other all the time, or if it was one and done. Two and done.

I'm not having any of that. So I grab him behind the neck and yank him to me for a blistering kiss.

He grunts, then leans in, parting his lips and slipping me his tongue.

And I'm in heaven. I have big hands holding my ass, gripping it tight. A beard rubbing my cheeks. Plush lips touching mine. I'm getting aroused under this frilly apron.

"God," he groans. "You make me come undone."

I shove him up against the refrigerator, and he gives another grunt of surprise, but he attacks back just as much.

"The thing about being with a boy," I pant when we break apart, "I told you, is it's okay if you get a little rough."

A wicked light shines in his eyes. "Is that so?" He bites my lower lip, and I whimper. Then he bites harder—and my dick goes stiff as a board.

"Fuck," I whisper. "Is this reality? It isn't, is it. I've been sent to a different plane. This isn't canon. I'm not here."

His lips go down my neck, and he murmurs against my skin. "Why are you denying it?"

"Because if it's true, then it can be taken away."

I didn't mean to say that, and I think he knows it, because he leans back and cups my face in his hands. His eyes go serious. "The last thing I want to do is hurt you."

"I know. But it's rule number one, Jason: don't fall for the straight guy."

He tilts his head, happiness spreading on his face—which is also flushed from our kisses. "Are you falling for me?"

My cheeks burn. I want to turn and run. I *should* turn and run, because this is too personal. So I do my usual: deflect and turn it into a joke. "I have great balance, so I rarely fall."

But he doesn't take my bait. "Maybe that rule doesn't apply, since we've established I'm not straight." And he tilts his head and kisses me softly.

He's going to break my heart. Or he isn't going to break my heart, and this'll be the most amazing relationship of my life.

One or the other. No pressure.

"I'm proud of you," I say, wrapping my arms around his waist and trying not to drool on his dress shirt. "Letting a guy touch you. You're so open-minded. Exploratory. Intrepid. Brave."

He talks into my hair. "I accepted two blow jobs. Big deal. You make me sound like I'm Ernest Shackleton."

"Who the fuck is that? And did you sniff my hair?"

"Shackleton? An old-timey explorer. And yes. I like the way you smell."

"You kind of are an explorer. We're not gonna talk about your man-smell fetish."

"I kind of am not. And it's not a fetish. It's just you."

I chuckle. "Okay, so it's true. You're not an explorer. Because you're not really boldly going where no man has gone before."

Jason processes my words and then howls with laughter. And somehow I think everything's going to be okay.

At least I hope so. And hope is a very dangerous thing.

JASON

Every day this week, my office computer's in the same place it usually is. The phone sits where it normally sits. My inbox looks the same. Emails pile up as always.

But I've changed.

I've got all these feelings that I've never had before. Not for a woman. Not for my family. But for Murph.

I'm fixated on Murph.

Murph's inspired me ever since I met him, no doubt. To have more fun. To do more creative things. To be more myself.

But now he's also inspiring me to take a hard look at the things in my life that aren't going so well and to change them.

After all, he changed things for himself: no club drugs, no Vegas, no dead-end relationship.

What do I need to change? I look around my drab office and can't even start counting, because I'd never stop.

Becky called and crowed about how she was right. Yes, she was.

Marnie's been silent, but I suppose that's understandable. During our last conversation, I didn't give her details or reasons. Just said that when she returned we needed to talk, but I'd found someone and couldn't see her anymore. She seemed cool with it on the phone, but I'm suspicious she isn't.

And that someone?

This week, he's cooked me dinner every night for a change, then we do the dishes together and play video games or watch movies. We joke and laugh and talk about our days. It feels like I could talk with him forever—I want to know everything about him, down to the last detail.

And we've made out on the couch. In the kitchen. In his room. In mine.

I want more. I want much more, and it's so natural, even though it's new. Increasingly, I'm struggling with pulling myself back. I want to do things with Murph. I want to go out of the house holding his hand. I want to see him naked all the time. I want my mouth on him. I want to let him do things to me.

I'll admit to being weirded out about ass play—even if I've experimented on my own. And about sucking another guy. It's not that I'm not gonna do it. I just want to make sure I'm ready for it when I do.

I'm close, though, because he turns me on like no one else. And I'm curious about what it's like to fuck a guy. Or be fucked by one.

But I need to let things unfold. I don't want to push it. The worst thing that could happen would be for me to go beyond my comfort zone, get scared, and shove him away. No matter what he may say about rough play, when it comes to his heart, I need to handle Murph gently. He's too special.

I'm definitely not going to treat him like his asshole ex. I can't kiss him in private and then disown him in public. Never.

God, I'm falling for him, aren't I?

I am.

It's not only sex. I want to get Murph all the presents. Take him to all the experiences. Make him food. Travel everywhere. Cradle him all night.

But my mind right now is on all the very dirty things I want to do to him. Things I never really thought about in this kind of detail before, but now that I am, I'm on board.

The kind of things I shouldn't think about at work, because I'll get hard.

So I'm fighting a tent in my pants from just thinking about Murph and his talented lips. Those eyes on me. The way he kisses me back, almost fighting me.

It's fucking hot.

He's just … perfect.

I discreetly run my palm down my pants to try to shove my erection away, but it doesn't sag.

Fuck. Murph's a distraction.

Oh well. He's a spicy one.

I don't make many sales calls this afternoon because all I can think about is getting home to him. Instead, I spend the time looking up articles on insurance for LGBTQ people, inspired by talking to Harrison and Finn, since that's marginally work-related. Then I start reading Wikipedia articles on the Mattachine Society, *One* magazine, riots and protests and marches—

And then my dad walks in.

Great timing, Dad.

Also, I need to figure out how to come out to you.

"Jason. How are you doing on the McKinley account?"

McKinley account. McKinley account. Ah. "They're switching from term to whole."

He raises an eyebrow. "That's a good decision for them."

And it's a good commission for me.

"They have a daughter your age, you know."

Gah. No.

I manage to say, "Yes, I've met her. I think we went to lunch with her a few years ago?"

"She's back in town."

"Dad," I start, a warning tone in my voice. And then sigh. "I'm not looking to date anyone." Anyone *else*.

"We talked about this before. People want their insurance salesmen to be solid family men."

I should be braver than this. I *am* braver than this. I don't mind standing up to my father. I have before.

Right?

I can't think of a single time. I'm sure I have, though.

Right?

Fuck. I'm not this weak. I can hear Becky telling me I'm not weak, he's overpowering, and when you fight with him, he fights back.

Somehow I find myself saying, "Oh, that's bullshit and you know it."

He looks at me as if I've slapped him.

No wonder Mom left. He's too much to deal with. Some people are like that. They only think of themselves, never of others. And it hurts those around them far too much.

But I also don't want to pick a fight with him.

Still, I find some source of strength inside me and say, "Do you mean that gays, lesbians—hell, single people can't be insurance salespeople?"

"Of course they can," he says placatingly.

"But ..." I prompt.

"But with you, it would be a good image ... No, dammit, Jason, it's more than that. I just want you to be happy."

"The way to keep me happy is to stay out of my business." I'm impressed with my own momentary assertiveness.

"I'm your father."

"And I'm an adult."

He sighs. "Act like it." He leaves, and I feel deflated.

I don't think I did that quite right. But I'm not sure how I could have done it any better.

WWMD? What would Murph do?

Redecorate, for sure. And sass right back to my dad. I'm sure I'll come up with all the right words sometime in the middle of the night tonight.

My phone buzzes.

Marnie: Can we talk? I'm back

Jason: Course. When?

Dammit. I'm not looking forward to that conversation, either.

I'm going to have to let people know I'm bisexual at some point. Between this conservative job, my dad, and my own shit, it's not going to be the easiest thing I've ever done. But do I have a choice?

I guess I do.

But it isn't only my life I'm dealing with now. I have a boyfriend. And I'm not hiding my attraction to Murph. So I guess this means I'm going to come out to everyone.

I let out a breath and nod to myself.

At least that feels right, even if it scares the crap out of me.

I arrive home extremely late because I got stuck on an emergency claim, and Murph's asleep. He left a plate out for me with a note: "Feed yourself, Seymour."

I chuckle.

And then my heart squeezes.

I eat dinner, then go into the bathroom, brush my teeth, and get ready for bed. I pause in the hallway. Should I go into my room? Or Murph's?

I don't want to be alone. Murph's door is open, and I peek inside.

He's curled up on his side, facing the doorway, and he looks so young and vulnerable, my chest gets tight.

I know I'm creeping, but I linger longer, inspecting his room. He shudders and lets out a light snore.

I'm not even capable of conscious thought, seeing his slim

form all inviting like this. I shuck off my shirt and pants in the hallway and pad over, slipping into bed behind him.

I put my lips on his back and kiss him as I cuddle him, wrapping my arms around him. He's warm and snuggly and hard in the right places. But he's too tired to do anything I dreamed of at work.

"Mmmm," he says sleepily. "Is this a booty call?"

"No. It's better than that." I kiss his neck, sucking on his skin. He nestles his ass against my crotch, and I groan. "I hope it's for always."

But he's still not awake. He yawns and folds in closer to me. "Good."

His quiet snores resume. I chuckle.

I hold him until I fall into a deep sleep, content.

MURPH

I wake up to this darling man holding me. I don't know what time it is, but the gray dawn tells me it's early. I think I felt him come in late last night, but I was dead to the world after being on my feet all day.

In fairy tales they don't tell you that when the prince wakes you from a slumber, he has a glorious cock the size of a cucumber poking you in the back. That then makes your normal-size cock want to greet the day with a glad eye. My morning wood is definitely giving my tailored pajamas a custom profile.

Yawning, I scoot more into Jason and apparently wake him up. Or maybe he's been awake for a while, judging by how lucid his next questions are.

"Murph," Jason says. He nuzzles the nape of my neck. "Can I ask you something?"

"Of course."

"Something sexual?" he amends.

I sit up in bed so fast you'd think it wasn't morning. "Now you have my attention."

He lounges on the bed like it's his, and I love that he's so comfortable. He's only wearing boxers, and I can only resist so long. But I'll let him talk. His voice is raspy, and I can tell he's been struggling with how to bring up whatever it is he wants to talk about. "I'm, um. Well, I'm adventurous when it comes to sex."

Is that all? I lie back down on my stomach and smile into the pillow. "This is outstanding news."

"But I've never done it with a guy."

My man is so cute. "I know, honey." The pillow muffles my voice.

"I mean, I assume I know the logistics. But, like, how do you decide who, um—" I lift my head and watch him rub his face. "I don't even know the terminology."

I like the way this conversation is going. "Who bottoms?"

"Yeah," he says, relief in his expression.

I scoot over and kiss him. "You ask. My experience is, if you go to a gay bar, most guys in there want to bottom."

Jason wraps his arms around me, and if there's one place I'm happy to be, it's in his arms in bed. The heat from the blankets keeps us cozy, but not too hot. I'm with a male Goldilocks. He speaks against my hair. "That surprises me."

"It won't once you get your prostate pegged."

He smiles into me. "I do like my prostate massager."

I raise my eyebrows. "You have one?"

"Yeah. Like I said, I've always been sexually open. But is that what you want? I mean, do you like bottoming?"

"Oh, hell yes. Can you feel my dick right now? It says yes, please. But I'll top, too, if you want. I prefer to bottom, but I'm vers. Versatile. Meaning both."

"Ah." He chews on his lip. Then he leans over and chews on mine.

After he kisses me leisurely, I break away and ask, "Are you nervous about penetrative sex? Because we have to be able to talk about it if we're going to do it. And there's no pressure. Seriously."

He blinks up at the ceiling, and I sprawl on his chest. His hand tousles my hair. "I am, and I can't articulate why. Maybe because it feels new."

"It's really not. It's just touching bodies. Making them feel good. The parts are slightly different, but, you know, it's all in the execution."

He lets out a sigh. "I guess that's it. I'm confident with women."

My heart melts even more. "You could do anything to me and I'd probably come, simply because it was you."

This earns me a smile. And then a look passes over his face. "Part of me just wants to maul you. And the other, saner part wants you to have a lover with some finesse."

Lover. Jason Falkner is my lover.

"Have you ever been with a woman?" he asks, not hearing my inner cheerleader.

"I kissed Kaitlyn Torres in junior high. No tongue."

"Doesn't count. Anyone else?"

"No. I knew early on I liked boys."

"That makes one of us."

"Hey," I protest. "No judgies. Just because it took until you found me to realize it, doesn't mean there's anything wrong with you."

"Maybe it means I'm meant for you."

I nod. "And vice versa."

"You look happy."

I must have a huge grin on my face.

"I am." I let out a breath. "Look. You don't need to worry about performing in bed or anything like that. In the moment, if something hurts, I'll tell you. And if it feels awesome, I'll tell you. Unless I can't talk, in which case you'll also know you're doing it right." I shrug. "Like we discussed, sex is a bodily function. It doesn't need a judgment. We just do it."

He rolls us and settles between my legs, which makes my heart speed up, because I can feel his cock. "Not with you. It's not just a bodily function. It's more."

And as he says the words, I know they're true. With Jason, sex is more than sex. The way food can be more if it's done with love —like the way he cooks. With Jason, being in bed with him is always *more.*

"Don't worry." I kiss his nose. "I'm up for anything."

He nods. "Me, too." He gives me a sheepish grin. "I still worry, though."

"It's because you care."

"I do."

I meant that he cares about his reputation or how he does things. But the way he says it, it feels like he means he cares about me. All these warm feelings expand in my chest. I'm not sure what to do with them.

So I do what I do best: I shove him on his back and straddle him.

His eyes go wide and then a little hazy. I love seeing them that way.

I lean down and start kissing all over his face. "Wanna practice?" I rub my pelvis against his, our hard cocks against each other.

"God, yes," he groans. His big hands grip my ass, and I grind into him.

It must be that it's been so long since I've had sex on the regular—since he scared away my dates—or maybe it's that it's him and it matters more. Or maybe it's all the talk. But I have zero stamina right now. I'm nearly coming like a teenager.

His hands find their way under my clothes, and he caresses my skin. "You have the sexiest body." Now it's my turn to groan.

"Off, off," I say, shoving down his underwear.

I kiss down his neck and bite his shoulder, still trying to keep our dicks in contact.

I'm bendy.

When I lick his nipple, he practically convulses. I grin wickedly. "Oh, that's a fun trick. Does it work on the other side?"

"Oh, yes," he whispers, and it's the prettiest whisper I've ever heard. So simple, but he says it so reverently. His hands alternate between gripping me firmly and holding back, hovering over me like he's wondering whether he can keep me. He's making up his mind.

"I'm yours," Jason says. "Do what you will."

So I lick my way down his torso to his erection.

I cast my eyes up at him. He heaves a heavy, turned-on breath.

"I think," I say, "I'll play with you exactly as I want."

"That," he says, urgently. "That. Please."

My mouth descends to his cock. It's so damn yummy. And I swallow him whole just to see his reaction.

He writhes on the bed with a muttered, "Fuck," and it's another pretty sight. And sound.

"Wait," he says, struggling up after a moment. "I don't want to come yet."

I wipe my mouth with the back of my hand and grin at him. "No?"

"Can I do something?"

"Course," I say. I shuck off my pajama shirt and pants so we're both naked. Warm, soft skin touching warm, soft skin. Muscle against muscle. Belly to belly. Cock to cock.

"God, this feels right." He snakes his arms around my back and flips me so he's on top. Now he's doing the journey I did to him. He's kissing me under my throat, along my collarbone. His hands trace my shoulders, my arms, and then skim down my torso.

Jason looks me in the eye, and I can see the moment he decides. He's going to suck a dick. *My* dick.

His large hand grasps my cock, and it's the relief I needed. He's got the right touch. Not too light, not too hard.

A small smile flits across his face, and I'm falling even more for my brave man.

But then his tongue darts out and he gives me a lick. Just a little one, but it's a paradigm shift for him. My thoughts go to a place of rainbows and unicorns and sparkles, because his mouth on me is all that's beautiful in the world.

Then he tries again. And this time, he swallows more of me.

Oh, and that tongue? It's divine.

"Weird?" I manage to ask.

"No." His voice has turned husky. "It's weird how not weird it is."

Then he sucks on me for real, and I lose the plot. My brain's zeroed out to where there's only pleasure and sensation—only, well, my deepest fantasy being played out for real in this bed. Or at least my main fantasy besides me sucking him off. Because what gay boy wouldn't imagine Jason doing this?

Even though he's new to this, he's clearly paid attention in class, because he's doing all the right things and goes at it with an intensity that matches the way he does everything. Jason does everything for real and the right way.

All I feel is hot, wet suction on my cock and strands of Jason-colored hair occasionally brushing my skin. His skin is tan, and I can see the muscles in his shoulders and biceps shiver as he holds himself up to suck me.

And then my body goes into that kind of lock—the halting before I'm going to come—and as much as I don't want to stop, I think coming in his mouth might be too much for a newbie.

"Let me finish us together," I say. "Because otherwise I'm coming in your mouth, and I'm not sure—"

"I want that," he says.

I hate that I'm asking this, but … "Next time?"

He nods. "If that's what you want." His expression goes thoughtful. "I like doing that. It's meditative. And I like to see how you react, especially since I know how good it feels." Then he slides up to me and kisses me soundly.

I align our dicks and take over, and he breaks the kiss and watches in wonder as I jack us at the same time, both of our dicks wet with spit.

Jason makes these great noises in the back of his throat as I bring us both closer and closer to the edge.

We kiss frantically until I can't take it anymore and pull back. He buries himself in my neck, and we both come. I don't know who started first. I think it was me, because I nearly blacked out, but his hot spurts landed on me at almost the same time. And it's wonderful.

When our breathing evens out, he kisses me softly and tenderly.

"Let me, uh, grab something," he says. "To clean up."

I'm sated, sprawled out under him, and it's all I can do to nod. "Okay." My voice isn't higher than a whisper.

In a moment he returns with a warm washcloth from the bathroom and wipes me off.

"Sorry," he says. "I kind of made a mess on you."

"Oh, don't you say you're sorry, toots. No apologies for that treat of an orgasm you gave me. Absolutely not."

He chuckles. "Okay."

When I'm clean, he arranges us on the bed. I'm the little spoon. Naked. With Jason. Talking with each other.

I was born to be Jason's little spoon.

I don't know how this is my life now. But I hope it never ends.

A few days later, I have the day off work, so I bundle up in a cream-colored beanie and light-blue puffer jacket and go for a walk downtown. Right off the bat, I see two men holding hands, and when I walk into the diner, I see another gay couple.

I'm still buzzing from being able to touch and kiss Jason, but am I ever going to be able to show anyone else how I feel about him? I haven't asked him, because I'm scared to. I don't want a repeat of what happened with my ex. My ex who pretended in public he didn't know who I was, even though he fucked me all night long.

If I'm just going to get my heart broken again, maybe I need to step away.

Then I come to my senses.

I'm going to act like an adult and have a proper conversation about my concerns, even though it makes me almost have a panic attack right here on the sidewalk.

I dial Jason.

"Hey, babe." His voice is quiet, and I realize I never call him.

"Jason," I whisper.

"Davey? What's wrong?" He barely ever calls me that, and I love it when he does.

"I just missed you. Am I a sap?"

I can hear the smile in his voice. "Yes, you're a sap. But I don't mind that. I'll be done with work soon. What are you doing?"

"Going shopping. But—" I cut myself off.

"But what?"

"I just saw a couple, and I wished it was us. Like, two guys. Holding hands. Out in public. And I was scared—"

"Murph. Listen to me. We're going to do that."

My heart soars. "Are you serious?"

"I am. I'm proud to be with you. We're boyfriends, right?"

I nod before I realize he can't see me or the overwhelming happiness on my face. "Yes. We're boyfriends." This thrilling electrical pulse runs up my arm and into my heart, where it settles, content.

"Good. It feels so natural and easy to be with you that I forget we need to actually talk about these things. Maybe because we were friends first? But now we're way more."

I fucking swoon.

He continues, "I admit it's an adjustment for me. It's something new for both of us, but I'm not going to hide you. Especially when I know your history."

"But that means you're going to have to come out—"

"Yes, I will. But my sister knows, and she's the main one who matters. I'll tell my dad soon enough." He pauses, and I hear him take a breath. "I'll be honest: that one will be hard to do. No matter what, though, I'll be so honored and proud to tell everyone you've chosen me."

Break the cycle, Morty.

A tear slides down my cheek, and it's too cold for that. I'm sure my nose is red, and I don't know if it's from the cold or from rubbing it. But I couldn't be happier.

"When it's time to tell your father, it doesn't have to be a big confrontation. You can just quietly do you."

"I'll do *you*," he jokes.

And I'm again stunned by my good fortune at finding this man. "Please," is all I manage.

"I'll try to leave work early, so we can talk about this."

I nod. "That would be super."

"Everything's going to work out," he assures me. "Don't worry."

"You can't promise me something like that."

"I can promise I'll do my best to ensure it."

I inhale. "That's a good promise. I can live with that."

A few hours later, when Jason comes home in his yummy suit, he sets down a bag of groceries on the counter. Carefully, he takes off his overcoat and jacket. Then he stalks over to me, holds me in his arms, dips me, and kisses me like he's a soldier returned from overseas.

I like that very much.

"Hey," he says, still holding me sideways.

"Hi."

He sets me to rights. "Did you have a good day?"

I nod. He kissed me speechless.

Jason smiles. "Excellent. Now, this is my plan. I've been thinking about it since you called. Let me know if you're on board."

"Okay."

"I'm going to make us dinner. We're going to drink sangria."

"Ooh! Fine idea. I'll make a pitcher."

"Already did yesterday."

I stare.

He grins.

"Then we're going to talk about every single thing your ex did, so I don't do it. Next, we're going to go to Church Street for dessert and hold hands the whole time. And then we're going to come home so I can fuck you into your bed."

My legs give way.

But he catches me.

I close my eyes. "Don't get my hopes up, sweet pea. I might expire on the spot. Just let me enjoy this."

"I hope you enjoy all of it," he says. Then he kisses me again and goes to change his clothes, leaving me blinking in the kitchen.

When we're sitting at the dinner table, I find myself being shy, which is rare.

"Tell me what kinds of things Dirk did," he urges. "I know it'll hurt, and I'm sorry to do this to you. But I want to make sure I'm nothing like him. Remember, we'll get pie afterward, and then I'll—"

My nostrils flare. "Don't talk about fucking me anymore, because I won't survive dinner." I take a deep breath. "Where to start? When Dirk and I met at any kind of party or event, he'd shake my hand like he didn't know me."

Jason makes a disgusted face. "The fuck?"

"We'd go to movies, and he wouldn't sit by me. He'd make his sister sit between us. Because goddess forbid he touch a queer. It might rub off on him."

"But he was your boyfriend?"

I nod.

"That's fucking awful." He pauses and sips his drink. "Is it all this kind of shit? What he did to you, I mean?"

"Yeah."

"Then I'm not going to make you go through with telling me all the rest of it. That was a bad idea. But please, Davey. Don't be shy about telling me anything. Especially if I fuck up. I want to make sure I do nothing he did. Even unintentionally. So please, help me to become conscious." He scrunches his eyes closed and opens them. "I'm attracted to you. I ignored it. Or suppressed it. Or whatever the word is. I was completely oblivious. And I don't want to be oblivious anymore. I want to be fully present. I want to be with you. But old habits die hard, and I'm not very good at self-analysis. So if I'm doing something that hurts you, tell me, and I'll stop." He looks down at his plate. "Sound good?"

I gulp. I'm overwhelmed. "Yeah."

"I still have this knee-jerk reaction that no, there's no way in hell I could be gay. Or bisexual. Or whatever. And then I have to analyze it and remind myself who I am. Because the idea feels right. Denying it is just old programming."

"Old programming sucks. Much better to watch a new show."

"Absolutely. It's like in *The Wizard of Oz,* when Dorothy opens up the door in the sepia-toned house to this huge, bright world of color. Did you know, by the way, that the whole scene was filmed in color? They painted the house sepia and had a stand-in wearing a sepia dress who opened the door to the Technicolor world and a Technicolor Judy."

Says my Technicolor dream-haired boyfriend.

I remind him, "Um, haven't we discussed Judy Garland? You don't have to be gay to love her."

"But that scene explains how I'm feeling. I never knew this amazing, vibrant world existed. My life before was sepia, but now that I know there's this other, bright place, I can't ever go back. I just can't. And it's all because of you."

"That's beautiful." I reach across the table and hold his hands. "I think you've always liked color, though. That's why you do your glass."

He squeezes my hands back. "I think you're right. Time for pie?"

I nod. Though I'm looking forward to what comes after pie even more.

When we enter the pie shop, Jason greets the waitress. "Hey, Darla. Good to see you."

She looks down at our joined hands. "Jason. It's been a while. How are things?"

He smiles. "They're terrific." And then he says his next words so naturally, it's as if he's been doing it all his life. "Darla, I'd like you to meet my boyfriend, Murph. Murph, I went to school with Darla. Her parents own this place, and she's going to own it someday, too. They're clients."

I stick out my hand and shake hers. Her words come out a little breathy. "Jason! I had no idea you were. I mean. You're gay?" She smiles. "It's nice to meet you, Murph. What kind of pie would you like?"

And I don't think I've ever been more proud of another human being in my life than I am of my boyfriend right now.

"We're doing this?"

"Of course."

It's one thing to come out to acquaintances. It's another to come out to your family. And it's yet another to come out to your friends as being in a relationship. But I guess we're doing a lot tonight.

Jason holds my hand as we walk into Vino and Veritas after dessert. Not only did he walk into the pie shop holding my hand and introduce me as his boyfriend, when we left, once we were outside, he pressed me up against a wall and kissed me breathless. In public.

Now we step inside the busy wine bar, and I know people notice us. Partly because it's my day off. And partly because I'm cuddled into my Jason.

The first person to see us is Harrison, who's counting cash at the register. He looks up, does a double-take, and then gives us a gentle smile before going back to what he was doing.

Tanner, though. He shoots me a knowing look that morphs into something fierce. I know he's seen this before—the straight guy falling for another guy. But he also has a protective streak a mile wide.

If only he knew Jason does, too. And Jason would protect me from everyone, including not only himself but me.

It's a heady feeling, to be so secure.

Reeve leaves a conversation with Oz and bounds over to us. "What is this?" He gestures at our joined hands.

Jason grins sheepishly. "What can I say? I fell for the guy. I'd like you to meet my boyfriend, Davey Murphy."

"Aww, that's so sweet!" He looks from Jason to me. "God, you guys look good together."

I kiss Jason's cheek. "We really, really do."

28

JASON

When we get back to our home, I chase Murph up the stairs and kiss him against the door while we laugh. I don't know what it is with me and pushing him against hard surfaces, but I can't seem to get enough. He scrabbles against me like he's trying to climb me, and I love it so much.

I don't even try to open the door. I just kiss him and laugh against his lips and skin, enjoying the contrast of his soft lips and scratchy stubble. How smooth his neck is and how hard he is against me. In all the ways he could be hard.

"I'm gonna make a very big mess," he mutters right into my ear as I suck on the area right where his neck meets his shoulder, "if we don't get inside right now."

I step back so he can stand on two feet and give him a wicked grin, reaching for my keys. "Then let's get inside." Once we step into the apartment and I lock the door, we pause, studying each other. He drops his coat on the floor, and I do the same. And then his sweater follows.

My heart starts up like I'm sprinting.

We're really going to do this.

Raising a hand to touch him, I pull it back. "Do you need to, um, prep?" I ask. "You know what, never mind. I can figure it out—"

He steps into my space, his lips a whisper-breath away from mine. "Wanna know a secret?"

I nod carefully, so as not to knock into him with my noggin.

"I'm ready now. I've been wearing a plug since I went to the men's room back at V and V. You could bend me over and fuck me right here, right now." His cobalt eyes glitter. "In fact, I want you to."

My pulse soars, and I'm nothing but desire. My wants and needs are lasered on just one thing—*him.*

I crash into Murph, my hands cupping his curved ass as his arms curl around my neck. We're a struggling coil of sloppy kisses shedding clothes onto the floor in the dark apartment while we stumble to his bedroom, which has a dim light on. Somewhere in the hallway, I pull at the hem of his T-shirt, and it comes off over his head to expose his toned, slim torso. My shirt hits the floor. And his shoes and socks.

My boots require more work, so I do this weird dance where I untie them while walking and holding onto him and trying to kiss him. That doesn't go so well, but I eventually manage and shove off my socks, too.

With brisk efficiency, my belt is undone—presumably by him, but it felt like elves did it—then he wrestles open the buttons of my button fly, and my erection fills out the knit of my boxer briefs.

I unbutton his pants and unzip, only to discover he's wearing minuscule red briefs.

"Figures," I mutter, amused, hooking a finger into the elastic and tugging them off. I hurriedly shuck mine off, too.

Naked, we pause in his bedroom like we did at the entryway, chests going up and down, fingers twitching to move, only this time we're so close I can feel the heat from his body even though we aren't touching. Our aroused dicks stand at attention.

Then Murph takes a half step back and adopts a territorial look as he eyes me from head to toe. It's a different expression than his previous flirtiness. Now it's like he's soaking in the truth that we can be together, and he likes that idea quite a lot.

I'm doing the same thing as I look at his perfectly proportioned body. He's got cut shoulders, a narrow waist, and long legs. And that cock of his is really handsome—not too big or too small. Just lean like him.

"You're really fucking beautiful," I say, and his eyes go from focused lust to fuzzy happiness. I've said it to him before, but can you really ever say that enough to another human being?

"Thanks, but I'm the one looking at the art that should be in a museum. If you look up 'ideal man' in the dictionary, there's this picture of your face."

I laugh, but it's strangled because I'm so turned on. I want to be in him. Connected. Together.

If you'd asked me a month ago if I'd ever have a boyfriend, I would've asked what kind of drugs you were on. But now I'm drinking in this bundle of energy standing in front of me—

This man I'm attracted to—

This man I want to make mine—

And I'm soaring because being with him is *my* decision, not anyone else's. Being with him is me listening to myself and my own heart.

Screw everyone else.

I choose him.

Now, though, it's time to listen to him, because this next part is all about Murph. I trace a finger along the outside of his arm and watch the goose bumps rise. Feel the intake of his breath. Watch his stomach as he breathes in and out.

He nuzzles my wrist, then grabs it. "Jason," he says urgently.

"Yeah," I say, my voice cracking.

"Manhandle me as much as you want."

I blink. I know this, he said it before. But it's still ingrained in me to be careful during sex.

"I'm serious," he says, and he scratches his nails down my torso—not enough to leave a mark, but enough that I know he means his words. And I like the jolt of it. I feel so fucking alive right now, and I remember our talk from so long ago about how the purpose of life is to *be alive*. "I get off on a bit of a fight. Be pushy. Be aggressive. I know you're not really going to hurt me."

I study his face, looking for his sincerity. And finding it.

It's so different. Usually, when I'm with a woman, I hold back and spend time trying to build up her arousal.

But with Murph? Apparently I don't need to do that, because he's just like me. Ready to go.

Damn, that's hot.

So I push him against the nearest wall—I can't get enough of that—and a laugh bursts out of him. "That's more like it."

I drop to my knees, and his inhalation is so loud and sexy it urges me on. Sticking my tongue out, I do an exploratory lick up his shaft, and he squeaks.

As I take long, drawing sucks on him, I grab the base of his cock with one hand. While I want to check out the toy he's wearing, I feel his knees weaken, so I grab him behind the thighs with my other arm, holding him up. I hear the back of his head thump on the wall, and he murmurs a curse.

I feel powerful and protective. Like his pleasure is my responsibility, and I'm going to do whatever I can to make him feel amazing.

"Don't wanna come this way," he whines, a tone of desperation in his voice, and I look up at him through my hair. "Oh, goddess, you're gorgeous." He tugs on my shoulder and I stand up, then we finally wrestle through his room to the bed.

I flip us, pushing him into the mattress, pinning him down, and he groans.

"Yes," he says. "Please. Want. Now." His legs lock me against him, and I chuckle.

Yeah, okay. I adore this. I want to experience everything with him. I am so in—

I don't want to finish that thought. But I've never felt about another human being what I feel about him.

Like, it's never enough. I always want to spend more time with him. I'm entranced by him.

And while I expect I'll get this right, I also trust he'll guide me if I do something wrong.

I cock my head at him. "You're serious about being prepped?"

He nods vigorously. "I didn't want you to have to—"

Silencing him with a kiss, I whisper, "I'll do whatever you need me to do."

"I'm good to go," he assures me. He reaches over to his nightstand and gets that bottle of lube and a condom and hands them to me. I set them down right beside my knees.

And before I do anything else, I kiss him yet again. I can't seem to stop kissing him, our lips locked, trying to swallow each other's tongues.

While we're sharing this intimacy, something inside me moves and lodges in my heart. I've had plenty of sex that didn't mean much. This—when it means something? When I want to show my partner how much I care?

It becomes big.

Scary.

And incredible.

Our hands explore, and it's not desperate like just a moment ago. His hands roam, cupping my ass and sliding all over my shoulders. Mine are on his balls, his cock, his taint. I'm feeling dirty and sensual and fucking erotic, and eventually he settles his head on a pillow and lifts up his knees, exposing the purple plug. "Can we do it this way? Facing each other?"

I gaze at him, biting his lip. My hands shake as I tug on the plug, popping it out. "We can do anything you want."

I let out my breath and take another deep one, then rip open the condom and unroll it on my erection while he watches me, his fingers alternating between caressing my thighs and using his nails to abrade the skin on my legs.

I lube myself up generously, then take more of the cool fluid on my fingers and explore him.

But he's absolutely correct—he's ready. He's hot and loose and looks debauched beneath me, his hair askew and his cheeks pink.

I kiss him one more time.

"Okay, baby," I whisper. "Here we go." I line up and press my sheathed cock into him inch by inch, my attention divided between the gripping, unbelievably hot sensation in my own body and Murph's overcome, pleasure-filled expression.

When I make it in all the way, we're both breathing hard. I'm feeling this mind-melting pressure and joy. And I'm staring at the guy who means so much to me.

He's blinking away tears.

I cup his face. "Davey? Are you okay? We don't have to—"

"No! Don't you even think about stopping. It doesn't hurt." He gives me a small smile. "Dreams coming true just get to a guy, you know?"

As he says this, my eyes water, too. *Fuck.* So, to distract from all the feels, I make an experimental move, pulling out a little and then thrusting into his body.

Oh, god.

I stutter out, "This okay?"

"Stop asking." He grips my forearms, which are braced on either side of him. "I want to be here. With you. Right now. Fuck me hard, lover."

"Okay," I say, letting out another breath and nodding repeatedly. "I can do that."

And I do. Or at least I try to. I start out careful and intentional, but I'm not holding anything back. Long strokes into him and out, experimenting with angles and watching his face to see when I—

"There," he whispers, shutting his eyes tight. "Holy goddess, *there.*"

I repeat the move. Again. And again.

I wrap my fingers around his cock and match my thrusts with my hand movements. "Yes," he hisses. "Oh fuck. This. All this."

And now that I know he's getting what he needs, I start focusing on what I need—more speed, more thrusting, more—

He's going to come, and I absolutely love it. His body tenses, then his eyes flutter open, his cock starts to pump in my hand, and I fuck him through it. He spurts on his chest, and then I'm letting go, too, helpless to control the movements of my body, my own release white-hot and powerful.

And the best I've ever had.

Period.

When I come back down, I carefully pull out, but before I can go do something with the condom, he draws me onto him and starts kissing me.

I fall into him, not caring that we're literally a hot, sticky mess, and then roll so he's straddling me.

I'm sure my blissful expression is the same as his.

"So this is what getting what I want feels like?" he asks. "I am very much on board."

"Me, too." I look down at our torsos.

I don't want to push him, but he doesn't seem to want me to move, either. After a moment, I ask, "Wanna go get cleaned up?"

He nods. "No, but I'm not going to turn down a shower with you."

"First times for me all around tonight." I smile and get off the bed, then hold out a hand to take him with me.

"First time for me to have my reality better than my dreams."

While I wait for the shower to warm up, I ditch the condom. I don't bother turning on a light. The night-light is enough. Murph goes to the kitchen and returns with glasses of water, which we both need.

We get in, and our shower is a soapy tangle of kisses and limbs. Lips on my dick. Then mine on his. The house is dark and quiet, and it feels magical. I even end up dancing a little with him in my arms as he hums under the spray.

When we get out, he dries off with a purple towel. I finger part of it at his waist. "You and color. That's what you give me. Color."

"Eh, even if you're the man in the gray flannel suit, I like you regardless." He whips off the towel and tousles my hair with it, then steps back to admire his handiwork. "Color looks good on you, though." He beams at me. "Race you to bed."

And he takes off naked across the hall to his room.

So, of course, I chase him. Tackle him. And hold him all night long.

29

MURPH

I skip into work the following day, still soaring on a sexual—and emotional—high.

I mean, Jason. Me. Together. *OMG all the yeses that ever existed!*

I can't stop grinning. I can't stop humming. I'm quivering with happiness.

The man is really good at reading what I need and giving it to me. This was the opposite of a quick hookup. It was exploratory and from heaven. I've never had better sex.

But it's more than sex. It's ... *everything*.

"You're glowing," Reeve says as he helps Tara unpack boxes over in the bookstore side of V and V. She smiles and takes a stack of the latest bestseller over to a table to display, leaving us alone. He squints at me. "Did you get laid?"

"Inappropriate question for the workplace!" I cry.

Tara glances over at us with a smirk. "Sometimes those end up being the best part of a workplace."

Knowing the story of how Tara met her girlfriend, I smirk, too.

Reeve puts his hand over his mouth, his face reddening. "Oh my god, I'm sorry, I didn't mean to pry."

"I'm kidding," I say. "You're my best friend, not some jackass." I stare far off into space, remembering the feel of Jason inside me

—how *full,* how *right,* how … well … *loved* I felt. "And maybe I did. And maybe it was the most amazing thing that has ever happened to me in my entire life."

What did I say about me being the musical star on stage, singing for all to hear? That's how I usually am. And I know I don't need to hide who I'm with at my work, because he walked in here with me, proud. The guys here all know about us. That fact makes me gooey inside.

But for the first time in my life, I'm wanting to keep some special things to myself. The look on Jason's face as he entered me. How his hands felt on my body. The way he moved inside me.

I shiver. Those things are too precious to be shared with anyone else. Even my best friend.

I'm the first man Jason was intimate with. I'm the first one who touched *him.* Now I'm getting greedy, because I want to be the *only* one to touch him. *Ever.*

Is that too much to ask?

Reeve smiles and pats me on the elbow. "I'm glad. You deserve happiness. And he seemed to be really into you."

"I so want to trust that it's going to work out. Because it feels *stupendous.*"

"Then do it. Is there a reason not to?"

"It's new for him. For two people who were only into hookups, we've become very attached to each other very fast." I tap my lip. "He's slipped into all of this so easily that it scares me."

Reeve nods. "I get it. You're still wondering if he's for real."

"Yes." I bite my lip. "But … Reeve?"

"Yeah?"

"I'm in love." I want to tell Jason first, but this—us—is so new. If I tell him right now, I'll make him close up like a flower at night.

Not that Jason's some sort of flower. That's me.

But still.

"I can tell. You have this calmness about you instead of your manic energy. Now your energy's smoothed out."

"Never figured you were that much of a mystic."

"You're the one with the abundant energy, Showgirl. Not me."

I laugh. "True."

"But you're bumping up against our deepest fear. It isn't that something bad will happen. It's that something *good* will happen. That we'll be wanted by someone else. That we'll be enough for them. Because it means that we're enough for ourselves. And it also means responsibility. We have to take responsibility for our own lives—and for loving someone else."

His words hit me in the solar plexus. Because he's identified what's been nagging me. That I'm not good enough for Jason. He's so much better than me in so many ways.

So I change the subject. "When did you get to be so deep?"

"Last night. With Oz."

I snicker. "Atta boy."

I head over to the wine bar part of Vino and Veritas. For the rest of my shift, I pour wine and sweep floors and tidy. But my thoughts remain with one big, burly Vermonter with a heart of gold.

The following day at work, I'm wondering how far he intends to take this relationship with me.

I guess I don't trust that it's real, given my history. True, Jason told people that he's bi—in a very safe place, V and V, where everyone knows not to out someone without their consent. And obvs, he had sex with me, but he says he's a very sexual person. Sex is easy to give.

The bigger question is, do I have his heart? I think I do. I *hope* I do.

Because he has mine.

I manage not to break anything, and Tanner gives me a fake award. "This is the Molly award," he says ceremoniously, and I laugh. Molly's likely to put waffles in a Blu-ray. "Why now? Why didn't I get this when I broke everything?"

"Didn't think of it then," he grunts.

And everyone laughs, including me.

When get I home, it's late, and Jason went to bed early. But I crawl into his bed, and he tugs me to him as he sleeps.

It's the best sensation in the world to be snug in those comforting arms. Arms that make me feel like I'm not some misfit from a disreputable city where nothing's real. An embrace that makes me feel like it's okay to be me, and it's okay for me to be with him.

"Jason?" I murmur against his neck, wondering how many times I've called him by his real name. Not many. But late at night, sometimes we just need to speak the truth.

"Hmm?" He yawns creakily and then draws me closer to be the little spoon.

I speak against his bicep, then kiss it. "Can I tell people about us? Not just people at work?"

"Of course," he mumbles.

"That means I'm outing you, you realize. Just because you come out once doesn't mean you're done. You kind of have to keep doing it over and over again, and that's not something you do to someone else without their permission."

He shifts so he can look me in the face in the dark. Now I've fully woken him up. "I told you, I'm not doing a damned thing your ex did. I'm fucking claiming you every chance I get. We are together. Whatever I need to do to prove that to you—because you're the only one I need to prove it to—I will. Want me to make a video of us kissing and put it up on social media? Fine. I'll change my status to 'in a relationship.' I'll post over-the-top pictures of us doing anything. I want to be with you."

Oh, those words. A tingle goes up and down my spine at his sleepy vehemence.

"Why do I feel like it isn't that simple?" I still have to ask.

"Because your ex fucked you up."

"You seem to be changing your identity pretty easily, though. I mean, you're no longer straight. How does that feel?"

He digs his cock into my ass. "About like this." I laugh and tug one of his fingers into my mouth and suck on it. He groans. "I *was* sleeping ..."

"Not sorry for waking you up."

"Not sorry to be woken up."

And somehow my underwear fall down to my ankles, Jason's fully awake, and I'm enjoying life, with his mouth on my cock. And then his cock's inside me.

When I lie breathless and spent in his bed, I decide I can trust what I have with him. Because he's figured out what was holding him back, and he's being true to himself.

He's the one who needed to change, after all. Not me.

But that's not true. I've changed drastically since I met him, and especially since he came into the apartment, got all up in my bidness, and kissed me senseless. I'm beginning to believe in something for the first time. Some*things*. Like ...

I don't have to be alone.

I can have a partner.

I can have love for real.

Because Jason's mine. I think he's been mine since the moment I met him.

The next morning, before I go to work, my phone rings, and it's my mother. "Davey?"

"Hey, Mom."

"It's good to hear your voice." I don't hear any noise in the background, which means she's calling me from home rather than a casino.

"How's it going?" I ask.

"Nothing much here has changed. But I worry about you. Isn't there going to be snow soon in New England?" She has it in her head that I'm going to turn into an icicle in Vermont.

"Just think of me as a penguin. I'll be fine." I bet I'd look cute in a red scarf and black suit. Or do penguins wear turquoise?

"I miss you. I worry."

If only she'd done more of that when I was a kid, I might not have some of my issues. But is there a person who hasn't been fucked up by their parents? Talking things out with Jason has helped me realize I'm years past blame and well into the land of acceptance.

And apparently also into the idea of being a penguin in Vermont.

I'm distracted when she asks, "Are you happy out there?"

I don't even hesitate. "I'm happier than I've ever been in my entire life."

"I'm delighted to hear it. Why? Have you met a young man?"

One thing you can say about my mom—she accepts my sexuality without question. I know many queer kids don't have that, but she's always been supportive. At least in words, if not in, you know, deeds like being awake when I got home from school.

"I've found this great guy." Again, my normal enthusiastic self would tell her everything. Well, not everything—she *is* my mom and doesn't need to know *some* stuff. But the feelings I have for Jason are private. Tender. "He's just." I sigh. "He's just really special to me."

He said we're boyfriends. That means we're exclusive, right? I should make sure.

I can hear the smile in my mom's voice when she says, "So my son has fallen in love for real at last."

"I have," I whisper. I didn't really want to tell my mom before I told Jason, but it's okay. Guess it's my trend.

When it's the right moment to tell him, I'll know it.

After talking with my mom, I grab my coat and head out the door, whistling. Mom promised to come visit sometime, although she's not so sure about the snow. That's okay. I'll be happy to show her Vermont in the spring. Late spring. After mud season's over.

The past few days have been amazing. Ever since Jason showed up with fire in his eyes, sweet words on his lips, and a hard-on, my life has gone to a place it's never been before.

As I walk down Church Street to Vino and Veritas, I pass by a restaurant.

And inside I see a very familiar figure.

Jason's giving a girl a hug. She's tall, with a lush head of curls and long, slim legs in jeans.

It can only be Marnie Madison.

It's a big hug, and then I see her face moving toward his. Like for a kiss.

Horrified, I freeze, and I'm brought back to a scene with Dirk. I saw him at a party—while we were dating—making out with some girl. Because he couldn't acknowledge that he was with me.

I was too stupid, and I believed his excuses. That *she* kissed *him*. That it didn't mean anything. That it was only him making a show for the world.

But it was awful, and all those horrid feelings start drowning me.

I'm torn between moving on as fast as I can and stopping and seeing it play out.

My sensible side wins out, despite my fears. It didn't look like Jason kissed her back. And he's just telling her nicely that he's with me. No problem.

I'm amazed I can be this rational, because I want to whirl in there like a Tasmanian devil and break them apart.

I'm stronger than this. I'm better than this. I can do this.

But my dramatic little green monster tells me Jason's acting exactly like Dirk.

This—having a different sexual orientation—is new to him. How do I know it's for real?

He says all the right things, and I desperately want to believe him.

I believed what Dirk said, too, though.

And is Jason, like Dirk, going to decide that it's simpler to go back to his hookup than to deal with that Murph, the one who attracts all the attention?

I look down at my silver glitter cowboy boots that Tanner will roll his eyes at.

Why'd I have to go and fall for the "straight" guy? Rookie move.

But I can't help it. I *have* fallen for him.

I force myself to scoot to work.

JASON

I sit across from Marnie in a sticky booth at the diner, because if I'm going to have this conversation with her, I'm going to do it face to face. With access to alcohol for confidence.

Even at lunch.

Good thing I'm my own boss, although my dad would look at it differently.

And while we could have talked in private at her house, I'm chicken. Guess I'm hoping there's less chance of a scene if we're in public.

That might be wishful thinking.

Marnie looks like she hasn't slept in days. And while I know she's been taking care of a newborn and a new mom, I believe the fatigue in her eyes and the dullness of her skin have something to do with me.

Fuck.

She kissed me when she saw me, even though I told her on the phone we weren't getting together anymore, and even though we barely spent time in public before anyway. I had to disentangle myself from her carefully, because I didn't want to embarrass her.

Now she sits across from me, bracing herself—as she probably should, given that she can likely sense what I'm about to do. I don't know any way to do this without hurting her. I wish I didn't have to, but my actions have consequences, and I have to deal with the fallout.

I clear my throat. I'm ripping off the Band-Aid. I'm going to say this as truthfully as I can. "I wanted to tell you in person, because you deserve that. I've found someone. When I called it off with you the other day, I meant it for good. Not only for that night."

Her face falls, and I feel like the biggest heel on the planet. I swivel my head, scanning the restaurant, but no one's watching us. Thank god.

I never, ever wanted to treat her badly. But we weren't going anywhere, and both of us knew it, even if we didn't say it.

Still, I'm rethinking my venue, because at her house she could have let the brimming, unshed tears flow. But she recovers, sucking in her cheeks and taking a deep breath, then squaring her shoulders. "Okay."

"Marnie, I'm sorry. "

"It's not you, it's me?" A mean smirk twists her lips.

I resist rolling my eyes, but barely. "We were never like that, and you know it. But yeah, I found someone I click with, and it's special. I can't see you anymore because I'm exclusive with this, uh, new person." At least I assume that's true.

"But we can still be friends?" She can't keep the acidic tone out of her voice, and it bruises my heart.

This is going worse than I thought, and maybe I completely underestimated *everything*. Maybe Becky's right, and Marnie had feelings for me that I didn't reciprocate. *Has* feelings? That thought nauseates me. I aim for a warm smile. "We'll always be friends." I take a deep breath, gathering my courage. "I have to tell you, the person I'm with? It's not who you'd expect."

"Not some hot girl?"

I chuckle. "You're the hottest girl I know."

That gets a reluctant grin out of her.

"So, no," I continue. Then, heart pounding, pulse racing in my ears, I lower my voice. "Actually, it's not a girl at all."

Her mouth forms an O, and her eyes pop open, no tears present anymore. "*What*? Are you serious?"

I nod. "Yeah. Who'd've thought I'd be into a guy?"

She shakes her head, her face now confused. "What the fuck? Since when are you bi?"

I keep my voice quiet, although hers has risen. "Since probably my whole life—I just didn't realize it until now. He's special, though."

Marnie sneers. "Please. You? It's not like you actually have feelings."

Ouch. "Hey. I have feelings," I protest.

But I'm processing the way she's trying to keep her lip from trembling, and I'm remembering times when we were together and she acted like she wasn't interested—playing on her phone, not paying attention to my words, letting me leave as soon as we were done.

Crap.

She's been into me this whole time. I'm such a fool.

I tug at my hair. "And you have feelings, too, don't you? For me."

She sniffles and nods, and for some reason that pisses me off. This isn't the way it was supposed to be.

Hot indignation wants to explode from my insides. "Every time we said it was casual, you agreed! Most of the time *you* were the one insisting."

Her temper flares, too. "That's because it was the only way I could be with you! I'd rather have you as a fuck buddy than not at all."

"God, Marnie. I'm sorry. I didn't mean for that to happen. It just wasn't like that for me."

"That's fucking obvious now," she mutters. "I can't believe it. I leave for a few weeks, and you get together with someone else. I thought I meant more."

I throw up my hands. "You've been a friend. I found someone who means a lot to me. What am I supposed to do?"

"You were supposed to stay," she whispers. And she gets up and storms out.

I'm not in my office ten minutes when Becky appears in my doorway.

I sigh. "Do your worst."

"I hate to say it, but I told you so."

"So don't say it."

She crosses her arms over her chest. "I told you Marnie was into you."

I'm at my wit's end. "She's an adult. I thought she could handle it. I was wrong. I feel bad. What more can I say?"

Becky shakes her head. "I know. Marnie was the one getting herself into more than she could handle."

"Did she call you?"

"She was sobbing, Jason."

"That was why we *weren't* dating. So things like that would *not* happen."

Becky gives me a half smile and pats my shoulder. "I know, big bro. You're just a dunderhead. I'm glad you figured out how not to be a dunderhead with Murph, though. Are you ever going to tell Dad?"

"Are you going to tell Dad what?" A voice sounds behind her, and our father looms in the doorway.

"Nothing," I say at the same time Becky says, "He broke up with his girlfriend."

I'm sure I'm as convincing as a five-year-old with chocolate on his face denying he ate a cookie.

"I didn't think you were seeing someone," he says, staring at me.

"I wasn't. But I am now."

He furrows his brow, clearly lost. Then he hands me a file. "Here's a new client for you to handle."

"Thanks," I say, grateful he seems to have dropped it for now.

I'm going to have to come out to my dad. Sooner rather than later.

I told Murph I'm proud to be with him, but what kind of pride do I have if I can't tell my own father?

Not that what I do with my body or my heart is any of his business.

Becky notes, "You didn't get The Look."

"Not yet. I'm sure I will once he finds out about Murph."

"No kidding." She heads to my door, then turns and looks at me. "I'm rooting for you, okay? I'm just sorry Marnie had to be collateral damage, because she's my friend, too."

"I'm sorry, too."

It's been the worst day I've had in a very long time, and all I want to do is crawl back home into Murph's arms. And forget that anyone else exists except me and him.

MURPH

Hours into my shift at work, I'm still frayed and edgy from seeing Jason with Marnie. From trying to make sense of it. Trying to tell myself I'm not making a colossal mistake.

"Talk me down," I say to Liam, a musician and regular, as I careen into his space at V and V.

"Talk you down from what?" He cocks his head and strums his guitar.

"From full-on panic mode."

He smiles at me. Okay, so I have a habit of turning to anyone and telling them everything about myself. Maybe I need to keep a little more of Jason inside me.

Heh, he can be inside me all he wants.

But seriously, I don't know what's going on and I have to talk with someone and Liam's close because it's open mic night.

"What does it mean when I see the guy I'm dating and a girl is kissing him?"

"That doesn't sound good."

"But he says he's into me. I mean, really into me. So talk me off the ledge. Please?"

"What did you see?" he asks.

I tell him.

"And you say he swore he isn't going to do anything your ex did?"

I nod.

"Then give him the benefit of the doubt. Maybe he was clearing things up with her so he could be with you. Go home and ask him. It could be a miscommunication. Don't let that happen to you. Text him. Ask him. Find out. Don't let it fester."

"Okay," I say.

New, improved Murph can do this. I pull out my phone.

Murph:

Murph:

Murph:

God. I stare at the screen and then peer up at Liam's sympathetic expression. "I don't know what to say to him," I moan.

"Did you actually see him kiss her?"

"I saw her giving him a kiss, but he didn't look comfortable or like he was returning it."

"Trust that."

I stare at him. "I'm so scared, and I'm making this more complicated than it should be."

"Sometimes your brain functions turn off when you're scared. Don't worry. That's why you have so many friends around to help you." He picks out a tune and stops. "I am curious why the first thing you thought of wasn't to go ask him."

"Probably some more mistakes from my past that I have to excavate."

"Just because you made a mistake before doesn't mean you will again. And also, can you really call a relationship a mistake? I'm sure you got something out of it, even if it was only life experience."

"Is everyone at this place a fucking relationship guru?"

"No. Just a little farther down the path than you, that's all."

"But if I don't learn from my mistake, then I'm being obstinate."

"If you learn from your mistake, then you're smart. Not that I'm agreeing that you made a mistake. Remember, opening yourself up again when you've been hurt or scared is the bravest thing you could do."

"Or the stupidest," I mutter.

"It's not stupid to want to have companionship. Support. Respect. Does he give you all those things?"

"He gives me *everything*," I whine.

He wrinkles his nose. "Then what are you complaining about?"

"Because I'm getting what I want."

"Uh-huh."

I bite my fingertips. "Oooh, but what if it's bad?"

"What if *what* is bad?"

"What if he really is seeing her on the side."

He looks at me like, *Seriously, Murph*? "Do you honestly believe that?"

"No."

"Then there's your answer."

I hate it when people are all reasonable and sensible. Makes me feel like an utter fool.

"But maybe I'm a cynic."

"You aren't. You're new to this relationship and trying to figure it out. Don't be so hard on yourself."

Letting out a breath, I say, "Thanks," and let Liam prep for his set.

I manage to get through the rest of my shift without doing anything too stupid. A major accomplishment.

When I get off work, I head over to the bookshop part of Vino and Veritas. While I love the camaraderie of the wine bar, there's something about being surrounded by all these stories and ideas. I simply love it over here. I notice that a few books are on the side waiting to be reshelved, so I do it.

"You don't have to do that," says Harrison, popping up out of nowhere. "I'm not paying you to work here, too." But he says it with a grin.

"I'm not organizing books as an employee. I'm doing it as a concerned citizen," I say. "Books must be set in the proper place. It's a crime otherwise." But I'm kidding, and he knows it.

"I see you spending a lot of time here," he says.

"And a lot of my paycheck," I say under my breath.

"Do you want to work over here? At least some of the time?"

I blink at him. "Are you offering?"

"Sure. To fill in."

For the first time today, I feel a bit better. Like everything's not all gone to hell because my boyfriend kissed a girl. Like maybe the things I want—more time with books, a real relationship with Jason—can actually come true.

I've spent all day so down in the dumps that a minor offer feels amazing.

"Let me think about it." I know I should jump at the chance, because I'd be happy over here helping people find the books of their dreams. But the tips on the wine bar side are better. They help feed my book habit, which is only slightly less expensive than my clothes habit. But I need the clothes to wear to work. It's a vicious circle.

"Okay, well, offer stays open. I can put you on the schedule and see if you like it. I know you already know where everything is over here."

"Thanks, Harrison. That's nice of you."

"Nice has nothing to do with it. I think you'd sell a lot of books."

"Your mom does that."

"She does. But she isn't the only one who can talk a customer's ear off."

I give him a mock gasp. "Are you saying I do that?"

"I'm not saying you *don't* do that."

With a laugh, I give in. "Okay, fine."

"Just give me a heads-up. I'm fine with you splitting your time, if that's what you want."

I nod. "You really are the best."

"If I hire good people, everything seems to work out."

Briar comes up to me. "Couldn't help but overhear. You gonna come to the dark side?"

"I hardly think books are the dark side," I say.

"Exactly. You'll do well."

"Why do I feel like I'm interviewing for a job I didn't apply for?" I see a row of cookbooks not in order and straighten them.

"Because I offered to hire you for a job you didn't ask for. But in your heart you know you want it." Harrison puts a hand on my shoulder. "You can have anything you want, Murph. You just have to believe it."

But does that include love?

At home, in short, I drive myself up the wall. Jason's not home yet, and I'm trying to figure out if two guys with commitment issues—because hello, we both only did casual, me with an ex who hid me, and him with a girl he never saw in public—will ever work out together.

Or—what I'm starting to wonder—if I pressured him into being with me. Did I manipulate him by pursuing him nonstop since I've been here? Even after he rejected me on my knees?

That's how I got Dirk to be with me. Flirted with him until he finally gave in.

After all, I did have Operation Get Murph Laid and/or Jason Out of the Closet. Now that Jason's come to the not-straight side, does that mean the operation was a success?

If so, why do I feel like a failure?

The feelings I have for him are big. Bigger than roommates or a fling. Bigger than people who share space and fool around in bed.

I think he's opened up to me—and it's now my job to open up to him. Tell him how I feel. But I don't know if I can.

Okay, I do know. I can, but it scares the crap out of me, because this is real.

Despite what Jason says about thinking he's into me, the fact remains that he was with Marnie today in a way that looked rather close. Can I live with that in a responsible, adult-like manner? Because I want to rip him away from her so he can be mine, which is a childish response. But jealousy is childish.

Fuck jealousy. I hate it.

I try to slam the kitchen cabinet shut, but it has those fancy hinges that keep it from banging. Unsatisfying.

So I open the fridge and slam a can of soda down on the counter, but that sucks because when I open it, it fizzes over, making a sticky puddle. I hop over to the sink to grab a dish towel.

The world is not letting me have my temper tantrum, goddess dammit!

I mop up the mess, wondering why, oh why, do I have feelings at all?

Angry tears flood my eyes, and I blink them away. I fold to the floor, sliding down so my ass hits my heels. I put my head on my crossed arms.

Fuck.

The front door opens, and I don't move. Instead, I curl into myself more, wishing I could disappear. But the tears come, despite my attempts to scrub them away.

Keys click on the entry table. Shoes tap on the floor. "Murph?" Jason's gruff voice calls. "Where are—" His feet round into the kitchen, and he stutters to a stop. "Hey." His kind voice has a tentative note. "What's wrong?"

"Life." I throw my head back, tears running down my face. I hiccup. And then I scramble to my feet, clenching my fists.

"What?" He's genuinely startled, and for a moment I feel sorry for him as I see the confusion on his face. I know coming in here to my meltdown is not what he expected.

"This." I point between him and me.

He blinks, and his face gets ashen. Then dark clouds gather behind his green eyes. "Mind telling me what exactly the hell is going on?" By the end of the sentence, his voice has gone from a whisper to deadly calm, but not raised. Jason wouldn't yell at me.

"You like girls." The accusation comes out like a dart, pricking him but not bowling him over, because I can't hurl it hard enough.

He tilts his head to the side, again with the bewildered look. "Yes. You know that." His expression reads, "Why are you saying this, Murph?" Out loud, he says, "I'm missing the problem here. What's wrong with me being bisexual?"

I can tell it's one of the first times he's said that out loud, because he looks like he's tasting the words.

And I let out all my fears at once. "You want to go back to women. Because I'm not enough, and I'm never going to be enough, and I don't have the right equipment, and you're ashamed of me. And I manipulated you into this." All of that comes out so fast I can't stop myself. It feels like I've just vomited, expelling my deepest, most cynical beliefs onto him.

Jason's face morphs from confused to heated to pissed to calm and sympathetic, and I can't handle the kindness in his eyes. He doesn't make a move for me, and all he says is, "There's a lot to tease out in what you just said, but can we start with what brought this on?"

"I saw you with Marnie."

"Ah. I'm betting you saw when she arrived. She kissed me before I could do anything to stop her."

My heart sinks. I don't know if it's worse or better that he's not denying it. Dirk would have made excuses.

But Jason steps forward and holds my hands, and as much as I don't want to hold his, I do. They're bigger and warmer than mine. "I didn't kiss her back. I was only there with her *to tell her about you.*"

Another heaving sob comes out of me—this one of relief—and I do my best to shove it back down my throat, but I'm getting a little snotty.

"Baby, I did," he continues. "I told her about you. About us. She deserved to know why I wasn't going to see her anymore, and I told her I only wanted to date you. Or whatever it is we're doing. Date's not the right word, because for me, it's more than that. Anyway, I wanted to get everything that was between us—her and me—out of the way. I wanted there to be nothing keeping me from you." He gives me a sheepish grin.

"Holy shit," I whisper, slumping against the kitchen counter, a balloon expanding in my chest that feels an awful lot like joy. "You do like me."

He tilts up my chin with his index finger, so I can see into the depths of his eyes. "I really do. A lot. Davey Murphy, I like you a whole hell of a lot." Then he leans down and kisses me, and it's a great kiss. Soft lips to my firm ones, and my tongue darts out and meets his and they twist together in long strokes.

So the kiss gets hot, because I'm emotional and, well, I'm a little OTT sometimes.

Plus, I have big, solid, warm Jason Falkner in my arms, who's just told me the things I had barely dreamed he'd say. With him embracing me, kissing me, how could I not feel all the feelings?

"You're too good to be true," I say, my voice still low. Because he is.

"No. I'm not." He corrects me in a gentle tone, and his lips trail down my neck. He's making me forget my issues, which is a good thing.

JASON

Note to self: I need to talk with Murph about all that he just said.

Note to self: No time like the present.

I pull back from him and sit on the floor. He sits beside me, his shoulder against mine.

"What's this about you not being enough and not having the right equipment and all that shit?"

"Oh, yeah." Murph's face falls. "That all spilled out of my piehole, didn't it?"

"Yep."

"I'm scared I'll never be enough for you."

"You don't get it, do you?" I hold both his hands. "You're enough. You're *everything*."

He closes his eyes tight. "No one's ever said anything remotely that nice to me before."

"The world is full of boneheads. What can I say? I'm not one of them. I see you, Davey Murphy. I see your light."

"I am kind of fun," he admits. "Although I can be an acquired taste."

"I seem to have acquired you."

He butts his head against my chest, hiding a smile.

I keep talking. "You're the best person I've ever met. And

anyone who can't see that is seriously missing a few screws in their head."

"Most people don't have screws in their head. Basic anatomy. I know they don't teach that to you insurance agents."

"Fuck off," I say good-naturedly. "Come here and kiss me some more."

Instead of kissing me, Murph curls up in my lap, tucking into my chest. "But what's gonna happen when your dad finds out you're with a guy? And a guy who isn't at all subtly gay?"

That arrow hits the mark. There's a part of me that's scared of what my dad will think and how he'll react. "You're worth it," is all I say. "Let me deal with him. There's no one else in this relationship except me and you. Got it?"

"Okay."

I press my mouth to his hair and say, "I swear that I will always be truthful with you. Yes, ingrained patterns are hard to overcome. But I've never felt for any person what I feel about you, Murph. You make me feel like I've got this bubble of happiness inside my chest. I feel better about myself just being around you. And I also think you're the sexiest being on the planet." He opens his mouth, but I shove my knuckle in it and keep going. He gives it a love bite, and I groan. "If you're scared it's a phase, I really don't think it is. I believe it's a sea change. What I used to think about myself is so far gone, I don't know where it went."

He bites my knuckle again. "Can I talk now?"

"Yeah."

"You've made me feel better."

"I could make you feel even better than that," I say with a smirk.

Murph nods. "I like the way you think."

A few days later, I walk into the restaurant where I've agreed to meet my dad and a client for lunch.

"I'm meeting Forrest Falkner," I say to the host.

"This way, sir."

When we reach the table, my dad isn't there. Instead, I recognize Darla from the pie shop.

Oh, god. *Dad*. He's setting me up.

"Hey," I say.

"Jason! Good to see you again. Your dad said he wanted both you and him to be here." She looks behind me. "Oh, there he is."

I glance over my shoulder and my stomach lurches. Because it's not my dad, or not just him.

It's Travis. One of the drunk dudes from the Ren faire.

He's glaring at me. And my dad is close on his heels.

Great.

Might as well open up a hole to the center of the earth where I can go live after this lunch is done. Because three out of four people at this table think (or know) I'm into dudes, but the fourth has no idea.

I silently plead for them to keep their mouths shut. To focus on insurance. There are how many billion people on this planet? They can tell every single one about me having a boyfriend except the very person in front of us right now. I mean, I *am* with Murph. I just want to tell my dad on my own terms.

The two of them sit down, and my dad shakes Darla's hand, then Travis's. "Good to see you. I'm glad you all got started."

I'm not sure how he came to that conclusion, since all we have on the table is water and a bread basket.

Apparently we're here to talk about Darla taking over the pie shop from her parents. And I guess she's engaged to Travis. I internally shake my head at her life choices—about Travis, not the shop—but that's not for me to judge.

We chat about current events until after we order, and then things take a turn for the worse.

My dad asks Darla about business, and with a big grin, she gestures at me. "I'm glad to have customers like Jason and his boyfriend."

While I don't move, I feel like I've shrunk into a smaller version of myself.

"What do you mean, Jason's boyfriend? My son? No. He's not gay. You're thinking of someone else." He turns to me and gives me The Look.

Which makes my self-esteem shrivel up like a raisin.

Darla can tell immediately she did something wrong. But I don't blame her. She didn't know I haven't come out to my own father.

"Dad," I say, my voice hoarse. "There's something you don't know."

I'm not phrasing it as something he needs to know. Because he doesn't *need* to know. He could go his whole life without knowing his son has sex.

I never thought I'd have to discuss sex with so many people. Like, mind your damn business.

But I'm not going to hide like Murph's old boyfriend.

It's tempting, I have to admit. I've hid in so many ways my whole life. Not picking a career I like. Not choosing much of anything for myself. Not showing anyone the secret parts of me.

Murph's inspired me to not hide anymore.

Dad furrows his brow, then clears his throat. "We can talk about that later. Turning to the needs of your company going forward ..."

When our meals arrive, I don't really eat, and a buzzing in my ears keeps me from following the conversation. My mouth's dry, and I feel faint. A flush creeps onto my cheeks and stays there, prickles of heat making my skin burn.

I can do this. I can be the person Murph thinks I am. Or at least he person he deserves. Because he deserves someone who will be proud to be by his side.

And I am.

I'm going to do this. I'm going to stand up to my dad. Not just for me, but also for Murph.

But fighting with my dad frightens me. Seeing The Look on his face—utter confusion mixed with revulsion—fills me with dread.

I'm now a serious disappointment. And that's hard to live with, because I've always wanted him to be proud of me. I guess I haven't outgrown the need for his approval.

Somehow, I make it through the meal.

Back at work, Dad corners me in my office.

"What were you saying at lunch? Is that some kind of joke? You can't alienate our customers like that."

"It isn't a joke, Dad. I have a boyfriend. It didn't seem to bother Darla. And it's none of your business."

He gazes at me as if I've said something in Klingon. "Your business is literally my business. You work with me. Whatever you do reflects on me. And people don't want to do business with a pervert."

I blink at him.

When I find my voice, I say, "Don't be a bigot. Being gay—and, for the record, I don't think I'm gay, I think I'm bisexual or maybe pansexual—doesn't make me or anyone else a pervert."

"That's not what people think. That's not what people in this town think."

And he again gives me The Look. The one my sister and I have feared all our lives. Like he has evaluated us and found us wanting.

I blink at him some more. Red heat flashes on my cheeks, and I don't know if it's anger or embarrassment or both. But my hands are steady.

I don't want to argue, but I'm not backing down.

"I have a boyfriend, and I don't care what people in town think."

"You need to keep something like this quiet. Do you know

how many clients you'd scare away if this got out? For god's sake, Jason, use your head."

"No, Dad. I'm using my heart. This isn't a phase, and it's not me testing something out. This is real."

He's looking at me as if he doesn't understand a thing I'm saying.

Maybe he never will.

"Bullshit. You don't know what's real. You can't decide a damned thing for yourself. That's why your sister picks out your shoes for you."

"I can—"

"You listen to me. You are not going to be seeing this guy—"

"His name's Murph, and I'm pretty sure you can't tell me that—"

"Or you won't be working here."

My pulse shifts into another gear.

Is he serious? Booting me out of the business because I'm romantically involved with a guy?

And it *is* romance. I think everything I've done with Murph has been romance.

Still, threatening my job is threatening another one of my identities. I'm only now getting used to this new identity as a guy who likes other guys in addition to women, but I'm also an insurance agent and a homeowner and a nerd and all these other things.

Now he wants to take away my livelihood.

I want to tell him that he doesn't have a say over me or what I do, that I quit.

But that's a huge step. I don't want to say those things in anger. Because once I say them, there's no going back.

If I'm all in with Murph, though, doesn't that mean there's no going back? *Could* I back away from Murph?

Not on my life.

"What the hell are you talking about, Dad? This is my life, not yours. And the way I live it is up to me. Not you. I don't live under your roof."

"You work for me."

"I'm an independent agent."

"Here with my permission."

"If you're going to discharge me for my sexual orientation, I think the courts will have a lot to say about that."

"Did you just threaten me with a lawsuit? Your own father?"

"Did you just threaten to kick me out of your life? Because I happen to be dating a person of the same gender?"

He adopts a "let's be reasonable" air, but I know he's pissed. "You have lived twenty-six years dating women. I have no idea why you're doing this to yourself. To your family. It's just not right. It doesn't make sense."

Here's the problem: A part of me is listening to him, wondering why my sexual orientation hadn't come up before.

Right now, though, I wish he'd just let me have the time and space to process it for myself. It's still so very new.

And maybe that's all I need to say to him.

"I'll talk to you later," I mumble, feeling sick.

He looks at me as if I'm abhorrent, lower than bacteria on his shoe. "I have no idea who you are anymore. When Jason Falkner returns—when my son is back—let me know. Until then, we have nothing to say to each other."

He leaves the room, and I put my head down on my desk.

33

MURPH

I head to my car in the dark, bundled up against the late fall chill. A few steps away from the wine bar, a woman emerges from the shadows.

It's Marnie Madison.

I stumble to a stop.

"Um, hi," I say.

Even under the dim streetlights, I can tell her eyes are bloodshot and she's angry.

"Are you Murph?" Like it's an accusation.

I try for a smile. *Keep your cool, Murph. You've got the guy, and if your positions were reversed, you'd be scrambling, too.* "Yes, and you're Marnie."

"So you're Jason's new roommate."

"Boyfriend," I correct.

She winces. "Whatever."

I hold up a finger to argue that she needs to take that attitude and go put it in a different zip code—so much for keeping my cool—but she keeps talking.

"I came to warn you."

Despite the alarm bells going off in my head like I'm being chased by a cop, I can't help but ask, "Warn me about what?"

"Jason Falkner."

"Thanks, but I don't need your help." I turn to leave, but she steps out in front of me.

"Actually, you do. This is for your own good." Her words come out in a rush, like she's been taking lessons in how to talk from me. "I've known him since his sister and I played in the sandbox. So that's a whole lot longer than you. And he's never, not once in all that time, had a steady anyone. It's only been me. Whenever he's gone out with someone, he's always come back to me. And he's going to come back to me when he's done with you. Because I'm the only one who can give him what he needs."

The better, more mature part of me wants to remember she's upset because she lost him, and she's lashing out. If I lost him, I'd be panicking, too. She doesn't mean it.

But I can tell from her voice that she does. And the words go right to my weakness. That I don't have the right parts.

Make an insight check, Murph. Like in Dungeons & Dragons. Roll the dice to see if you're getting lied to.

My internal dice roll lands on a two. Shit. I'm on my own.

"Just because he's with you now doesn't mean anything. Jason doesn't do relationships. He has playthings." She looks as miserable as she's making me.

I'm going to stick up for him. He'd do it for me. "Maybe Jason didn't have commitments before. But now he does. He's not like that anymore."

"You don't know him as well as I do," she snarls.

"No," I say. "But I trust him. I've been trusting him, and I'll continue to do so."

She makes a face. "I'm sorry, but you have to know it isn't real. He just goes along with what everyone wants. He's super polite and can't say no to anyone. He thinks if he said no to you, you'd be hurt. So he gave in. But it won't last."

I hate what she's saying, but I feel like she has a point.

She keeps going. "He works at a job he doesn't like to please his dad. He has his sister take care of all of his real estate. He doesn't do relationships." She winces again. "You're just a speed bump who talked him into it somehow. But he always comes back to me."

God, every word she says cuts into me. Because Jason can be that way.

A little voice inside me says that he's been doing better.

And that speed bumps don't talk.

But her words still bore into me, because they have the ring of truth. He ignored his sexuality for so long, and my life is too short to be with someone who's mixed up about who he is.

I want to help him figure out his sexuality and feelings, but I'm scared I'd be telling him what to do. Jason needs to make the decisions about his life on his own, not influenced by anyone else.

Including me.

She grimaces. "You know I'm telling the truth."

I stare at her. I want to tell her to fuck off, but instead I take the high ground and say, "This isn't helpful."

But she's watered the seed of doubt I've always had.

And I hate that. I hate that I can't go back to the time when I was happy in his arms and blissfully unaware that anything was wrong. Blissfully unaware that I needed to know anything other than what it felt like to hold him.

Her words are poisonous.

The trouble with poison is it gets into your bloodstream, and all I can see are the ways she's right.

I *don't* trust that Jason prefers me to girls. What's worse is that I can't believe he'll choose me if left to his own devices. I'm the one people are ashamed to be with, deep down. I'm the one who is too much to handle, the one they have to hide. And while he hasn't hidden me so far, he will. I'll embarrass him, like I do everyone else. It's just the way I'm made.

I want us to be real. But I live so much in the land of swords and princesses that I forget that sometimes there's just a landlord and a roommate, experiments and the thrill of the unknown, and that's not enough.

She looks so sad. "It's for your own good, you know?" And then she turns and walks away, leaving me in the cold and dark.

When I get home, I don't know what to do. I should text Jason, talk to him, although I'm not sure what to say. But fuck not communicating. Marnie's wrong about one thing. Jason *can* make decisions for himself.

I start with something simple.

Murph: Marnie came and visited me

Jason: WTF?!

My phone rings immediately, and I exhale and answer it, sitting on my bed. "Hello?"

"Murph?"

I feel the blood drain from my face. It's not Jason. It's Dirk, my ex.

I should've looked at the caller ID before I answered.

"Yes," I say warily. "Why are you call—"

"I have to tell you somefin," he interrupts, his voice ugly and harsh. Oh, goddess, he's drunk.

My voice gets prissy. "I made it clear a long time ago we don't have anything to say to each oth—"

"I'm gettin' married, see? And I'm marrying a *woman*. Because I'm not gay. Never was."

A call comes in from Jason. Even though I should hang up on Dirk, he keeps talking, and I'm frozen in place.

"I never shoulda fucked 'round wit chu," he continues, and I swear I can smell the alcohol over the phone. "You pushed me into it, see? Messin' 'round with ya. You always think ever-thing's the way you wan it ta be. But it's snot. I mean not. It's not."

My heart seizes up, and I don't feel like I can breathe.

"Why are you telling me this?" I manage.

"I'm not gettin' married to my wife without clearing the air. I'mma fix my past mistakes. You were a mistake. You pursued me. For a tiny guy, you're fuckin' aggressive, man."

And that? It's my worst fear come true.

Not about Dirk. I don't care about him anymore. But dread spears through me as I wonder if I forced Jason into something.

I get a sour taste in my mouth, and my chest tingles.

"Is that all?" I finally ask.

"Yeah," he says, and hangs up.

I stare at my shaking hand. An overwhelming need to flee comes over me. I need to go somewhere I can't hurt Jason. Where I won't be a bad influence on him.

The second I put my phone down, Jason calls again.

"What did Marnie say to you?" he demands.

I struggle to calm down, and then I tell him. He starts to protest, but I interrupt. "There's more." I grip the phone tightly. "She has a point."

"No, she does not at all have a point."

The line is silent for one second. Then two. Several heartbeats pass.

"Jason. I have to tell you something." I swallow, worried I'm gonna hurl. Everything gets blurry for a second while I try to spit out the words. "You see, I had this plan … I, uh, I wanted to push you into getting together with me."

"What are you talking about?"

"I coerced you into a life that isn't really you. You're giving up all these things you used to have—a steady girl, a stable family. For me. And I'm worried … I'm worried I'm not worth it."

I'm pushing him away. I know it, and I can't stop myself. Because I need room to breathe, and I've never been able to think clearly with him near me. And because he needs to make the choice without my influence. Without my pushy ass holding up giant neon road signs.

"So you think I like you because of some diabolical plan you had?"

"Yes," I say, my voice barely above a whisper.

"That's bullshit."

I want to shove my face into my pillow, but instead I tell him the truth. "Jason, I'm manipulative."

"You are not. I'm the one who decides what I'm doing with you. You didn't decide anything for me."

"But is us being together the right thing for you?" I sit on my free hand to stop it from trembling.

"Yes." He doesn't hesitate. "You agree, don't you?"

My pause is answer enough.

"Davey," he whispers. "We can figure this out."

"Can we?" I ask, my voice broken. I feel like I'm caught in a tornado of emotions and soon a house is going to land on me.

"Have some faith."

"That we'll get back to Kansas, Toto? I don't have ruby slippers."

"What are you talking about?"

"Dorothy had something to believe in."

"You do, too."

But I don't. "Jason, you haven't told your dad yet."

"Actually," he says, surprising me, "he found out today. It didn't go very well."

My heart aches for him. "What happened?"

"Darla from the pie shop outed us. She didn't mean it in a bad way, but ... Oh, and she's dating one of those tools from the Renaissance faire."

"What? I'm so sorry." Anger at myself scorches my body. "And great. Now I've ruined your relationship with your father."

He lets out a sigh. "I'll be honest. The whole experience sucked. But I don't care. Actually, that's not true. I do care what he thinks, and that's a problem. But it'll work out or it won't. No matter what, I want to be with you."

That's what he thinks. But he's wrong.

"Do you, though? I mean, we're two guys with commitment issues. Don't you think we might have trouble with it?"

"Are you having issues?" he asks, his voice quiet.

All I know is that I'm so in love with him I can't stand it.

"No," I say. "Yes. Maybe?"

"Fuck."

I hate my next words. "I need to go be by myself for a little bit and think about this."

What I really mean is that *he* needs to think about us without me being around. I'm giving him a chance to come to his senses.

"Davey," he says, his voice shattered. "I don't want you to go anywhere. Just wait a second. I'll be home soon."

"I'll be gone," I say, deciding. "At least for a while. Until I figure this out."

Until you decide you don't want anything to do with me.

"Murph—"

I hang up and burst into tears.

And I know I have to be out of here before he comes back, because he'll just pull me into an embrace and I'll forget everything.

No. I need to go somewhere where I can think about this. Where I can figure out what's right for both of us. It's the best thing I could do.

I pull out my phone and text my best friend.

Reeve hands me a Kleenex.

"Here, baby boy. You need this. You're as snotty as a toddler."

I'm curled up in the corner of his couch as tight as I can get, my knees to my chin and my hands wrapped around my ankles.

My best friend gathers me in his arms and holds me, and I cry on his shoulder.

"I'm not going to tell you to calm down, because that has never in the history of the world helped any person calm down.

And I'm not going to tell you to relax, because ditto. I'm just gonna tell you I'm here for you. If you need to cry, cry. If you need to be silent, I'll be silent with you. If you need to talk, I'll listen. And if you want a distraction, I can provide it. Food or a movie or something to drink or whatever."

"The only thing wrong is I'm in love with Jason Falkner. I just am."

"This is a good thing," Reeve says.

"No, it isn't. Because why does love hurt this much?" My tone turns bitter. "Easy hookups were so much … easier. No emotions. Just physical. This emotional stuff hurts worse than anything."

"I know," he says sympathetically. And while I'm grateful for his embrace, I notice it offers a different kind of comfort than Jason's does. It's the comfort of a friend. Jason's arms make me feel like I'm more. More loved. More me. And now that they've been taken away … okay, now that I ran away?

I miss them.

Reeve lends me a T-shirt and sweats to wear, because I'm too depressed to go out to my car and retrieve the bags I packed. He also gives me a pillow and a quilt. I barely move from his couch.

"I'm being an ass," I say. "It's been all about me. Tell me how it's going with your beau."

He gives me a smile. "Let's just say that if something happened to me with Oz like what's happened to you, I'd feel exactly the way you are."

I muster up a watery smile back. "I'm happy you found someone. The *right* someone."

"Do you really think all is lost with Jason?"

"I don't think he can be fully satisfied with me."

"Did he say that?"

"No," I admit. "It was his ex-girlfriend. Well, I thought she was only a fuck buddy. But she said some shit that made me question everything. About how easily swayed he is. And I got to thinking how manipulative I am."

"That's complete crap, and you know it."

"I feel like I'm this aberration. Like he's gone his whole life without ever questioning his sexuality, and then boom, I'm here, and suddenly he's bisexual? I call bullshit. As much as I hate to say it, because it's not in my best interests, I'm scared I'm using him. Because he takes such good care of me."

"And what do you give him?"

"Nothing more than a good fuck."

Reeve rolls his eyes. "I think you inspire him. Give him strength. And you give everyone the ability to have fun."

"Like any of that is unique or important," I mutter.

"How rational is your thinking right now?"

"Not very. But Jason's going to have to give up so much to be with me. His life, his identity. And who am I? Just a scrawny bartender." I roll my eyes. "Some prize."

"What we are going to do," Reeve says grandly, "is stop putting ourselves down. Let me feed you before I go back to work. And then tomorrow, you're going to take a sick day and do whatever it takes to make yourself feel better."

I nod.

"Hey," he says. "I have an idea. Why don't you make him something? Something that can occupy you so you're not just boiling in your skin."

"Jason's the one who makes things. He makes delicious meals, and he makes beautiful glass bowls and glasses and …" I sniffle. "I can't make anything besides websites."

"So make him one of those."

I look up. "Will it be a goodbye gift?"

"Not if you make the right decision." He touches my forearm. "Let me feed you. You just need to clear your head. I think you'll decide you can trust him. You'll feel better soon enough."

I hope he's right.

34

JASON

It's late, and I should go home. I have at least three people I need to talk to—Murph, Marnie, and my dad. And I'm not sure of the order.

My instinct is to call Becky and ask her. But that's something old Jason would do.

New Jason?

He's not putting up with any of this shit.

I'm making my own fucking decisions. I'm not letting Marnie hurt Murph. I'm not letting my dad hurt me. And I want to tear home and stop Murph from going, but if he needs time … well, I don't like it, but I'll give him some.

But, goddammit, I'm fucking fighting for him. Because what we have is *real*. It's my choice. *Our* choice. He didn't force me into a damned thing, and there was no coercion or manipulation. He's flirty, yes, but that's just one of his attractive traits. I like him exactly as he is. Murph made sure he had my full consent in everything we've done. Bottom line, I think I'm one of the few who sees beyond his glitter—even though I adore his glitter—to the very true human being in there.

The one I've fallen in love with.

And hell yes, I've fallen in love with Murph. I'm going to show him, too. Not just tell him. I take a deep breath.

How to do that? And how to clean up this mess?

I'll start with the person in closest proximity.

Dad, I need to talk with you about a few things.

I respect you. I respect your business. But you need to understand that you're not living my life. I am.

I've made some decisions. You may not like them, but they're my *decisions.*

I take a deep breath. I can do this. He doesn't get to decide who I'm in love with or what I do with my body or how I live my life. I've let everyone else's opinion matter for far too long. While I'll still be polite, Murph's taught me to have a backbone.

I knock on his door and enter. "Dad?"

He swivels in his chair behind his huge, dark wood desk and stares blankly at me. He doesn't say anything for a moment, and that might be more intimidating than harsh words.

Finally, he sighs. "Jason, I don't know what's gotten into you."

Murph, I think. Murph's gotten into me.

Well, not literally. But I can fix that.

I hope.

"I've fallen in love," I say simply. "You don't have to understand me or even respect me. But yes, I have a boyfriend."

He shakes his head. "I don't see how you can come to that conclusion in such a short period of time."

There he goes poking at the weak spot. Because, yes, it's new.

But when I'm sure, I'm sure.

Right?

Fuck.

"I can come to that conclusion because I know my own mind."

"Please." His sarcasm knocks the breath out of me, and my chest hurts. "When have you ever known your own mind?"

"Maybe I'm a late bloomer, but I'm becoming more and more the man I want to be."

"And that man wants to have sex with other men?" He rolls his eyes. "Modern society's gotten out of hand."

"This has nothing to do with society. This has to do with who I'm choosing to spend my time with."

"With some fairy? He's trapped you."

"No, Dad. It's nothing like that."

I think about how flirtatious Murph is, but how genuine he seems with me. My dad has to be wrong.

Right?

"Jason, listen to me, and understand me clearly. If you insist on this … *perversion*, you will not be working here. Don't answer me right now. Think about it. But I won't work with someone who embarrasses me the way you have."

"You have no business interfering in my life."

Finally, I get out something strong.

"Then you have no business working with me. Close the door on your way out."

Fuck.

That went about as badly as it could.

On autopilot, I turn to leave. But then I stumble on the carpet and look around our drab offices. Am I willing to leave this to be with Murph?

I think about his color. About how much he brings to my life. And the answer is obvious.

If my dad's kicking me out, then yes, I'm out of here.

What will I do? Insurance is all I've ever known.

But there's no way I'm giving up Murph, because not having him by my side is breaking my heart.

My natural tendency is to discount my feelings—I shouldn't make decisions based on emotions—but for fuck's sake, I *should* make this type of decision based on my true feelings.

My true feelings are telling me that I'm in love with Murph.

That I've been attracted to him since we met. That he fascinates me and supports me and lets me take care of him.

That I don't want to live without him. That I want to be with him for the rest of my life.

That's a big decision to make, and it's not my decision alone.

For my part, though, I've never felt surer.

Taking in my office, I search for anything that I couldn't give up. Any sign of myself in here.

There's none.

I pick up my keys and wallet, put on my jacket, and head out to my car. I told Murph I'd give him time, but he's just going to spin out of control. And besides, he's got it all wrong. If we talk and clear the air, and he still needs time after that, fine.

For now, I'm going to try to catch him before he leaves.

"Murph?" I call, my heart pounding from more than racing up the stairs.

Though his car's gone, I still couldn't help but hope he was here.

But he's not.

"No. No, no, no," I murmur, getting louder each time, but it doesn't stop the echo in the house. A quick glance in his closet tells me he took a suitcase or two.

Shit.

I pull out my phone.

Jason: We need to talk.

But it doesn't show that the text went through. He must have turned off his phone, because I don't think he'd block me.

Right?

Where is he? I need him.

I need him more than I need air or money. I need to make this right. I can't have him thinking—whatever it is he's got going in his head.

That he forced me into a relationship with him or that this is some test case or experiment.

I don't know anyone who would know where he is. I don't have Reeve's number. Or Tai's. Or any of his other friends'.

Okay, deep breaths.

I slide down to the floor and sit, staring at my phone.

What do I know to be true?

My name is Jason Falkner. I'm an insurance agent. I own a house. I like to run and slump glass and cook. I'm attracted to women.

And I like men. I probably always have. Maybe it's a little late to be realizing that, but I suppressed it so long that acknowledging that it goes beyond Murph feels like I'm coming up for air after being underwater. Like I can finally breathe again.

But while I may like men in the abstract, I really don't care about that. Because there's only one man who matters.

Davey Murphy.

The cute, sweet, funny, impish guy who's taken my world and turned it inside out and upside down. The one who's made me come apart at the seams.

And that's all there is to it.

Maybe one of the guys at V and V will know where he is.

There's something I need to do first, though.

I knock on Marnie's door. I don't even know what time it is, but it's dark.

When she answers, her eyes first light up, then sour at my expression and the anger I'm sure I'm showing.

"What the hell, Marnie? Why did you say those things to my boyfriend?" I demand.

She tugs at her hair and narrows her eyes. "Because they're the truth. You don't think for yourself. You only do casual. You just go along with what everyone says so you won't hurt their feelings. And you'll always come back to me."

I suck in a breath. "What the actual fuck? You had no right—absolutely no right—to interfere with my relationship with Murph." My nails bite into my palms as I clench my fists.

"That's not a relationship," she sneers. "You don't have those. You never have."

"I do now. That was a mean thing to do, to go up to him like that. You hurt him, and he never did anything to you. I don't know what got into you."

Her eyes flash fire, then her face crumples, and she turns away.

"What?" I say, my tone harsh.

"I only ever wanted you back," she says quietly. "I know we said it was casual. And I tried pretending it was. But it was never casual. Not for me. I've been in love with you for years, Jason."

Shit.

My heartbeat's pounding, and I want to shake her. At the same time, my brain interrupts my emotions to tell me she's hurting. I clench my jaw so badly it aches. But I can do this calmly.

I take a deep breath.

"I'm not going to excuse what you did. It was wrong, and I think you know it. I'm pissed. We have a long history, and you're an amazing, beautiful woman. But you deserve someone who wants all of you. That's not me. If you think about it, I'm sure you'll agree. I care about you like a friend. But I'm not in love with you. I only wanted to do what we agreed to do."

She wipes her eyes with the back of her hand, and I have to stop myself from hugging her. "It's my own damn fault," she says. "I tried to act all cool, when really I wanted you the whole time. I wanted you to stay. I wanted … so much."

Goddammit. My heart couldn't sink any lower if it tried.

"Marnie," I whisper. "I never meant to hurt you. I'm sorry."

"You're in love with him, aren't you?"

"Yes."

Because it's true. I'm completely in love with Murph. I never thought I'd be in love with *anyone*, but here we are.

"I'm still pissed at you," I continue. "You scared him off. You *hurt* him."

"If he's scared off so easily, maybe he isn't for you."

I open my mouth to argue, but she holds up her hand. "I know, it's wishful thinking. And I wish I could take it all back. I just wanted you." She lets out a breath. "Now it's time for me to be the big girl I said I was."

"It is." I repeatedly run my hands through my hair. "Just so you know, you're wrong. I've started thinking for myself."

"I'm glad," she says quietly. "And for whatever it's worth, I'm sorry. You're a terrific guy, Jason, and I'm sorry I tried to muck with your relationship. Truly. We had a great run, even as friends, and I wish you well."

"Thanks," I say, my voice strained, and I don't know what else I have to say to her. "I, uh, gotta go."

"Bye," she whispers.

I turn and leave.

I need to find Murph and tell him—what?

That he needs to ignore Marnie. That I've changed. And I will continue to change.

That I can't live without him.

That I love him.

That's what he needs to hear. He needs to know I love him.

I didn't think I could fall in love. I was a guy who didn't get emotionally involved.

But it's not true. I'm overwhelmed with emotion.

And if he doesn't return that emotion, I don't know what I'll do.

My car skids to a stop in the parking lot of Vino and Veritas. It's been enough time, right? I don't want Murph hurting a second longer than he has to. I barely remember to turn off the engine, let alone close the door. I have no idea if I locked it. It doesn't matter. All that matters is that I find Murph.

I sprint into the bar.

Tanner looks up at me. "Can I help you?"

"Murph. Davey Murphy. I need him. Do you know where he is?"

He looks at me warily. "He's done with his shift for the day."

That doesn't answer my question. "I know. But I need to find him."

He blinks. "Then call him."

"I have," I pant out. "He's not answering. He's got some idea. I think it's ... it's all wrong." I'm not making any sense.

"Whoa, whoa." He holds up his hand.

Reeve comes by and pauses. I almost grab onto his lapel. "Is Murph with you? Is he staying with you? Is he safe? Is he okay?"

Reeve blinks. "What do you care?"

"I'm fucking in love with him. That's why I care."

I hate that I'm telling Reeve and Tanner before Murph, but it's the quickest way to get my point across. They eye each other.

I scrub my face with my hands. "Look. My ... she's not even an ex, she told him things that aren't true. I need to find him."

Reeve puts a hand on his hip. "If Murph wanted to talk with you, he would."

"That's the thing. He's got this notion in his head about us that's all wrong. I have to explain."

I can tell that Reeve's finally listening to me. He sighs. "He's at my place."

I let out a breath. "God. He's safe. Good."

I can see he's surprised at my reaction. "You really like him, don't you?"

"*Love* him," I repeat.

Reeve smiles at me. "Okay. I'll tell him to call you."

"Not sure that's good enough, honestly." I wring my hands. "I need to talk with him, *now*."

Reeve shares another look with Tanner. "Okay." He scribbles an address on a napkin. "Here's where I live. I'm trusting you to not screw him over."

"That's the last thing I want to do."

He nods.

I run out, and I can hear the murmurs behind me as I leave.

I don't give a fuck. I need Murph.

MURPH

Jason stands before me at Reeve's front door, wild-eyed and beautiful.

I'm not sure I could look any worse. My eyes are red and puffy. My nose is running.

It's all I can do to not throw myself at him. Wrap my legs around him and bury my nose in his neck. Take shelter in his arms.

But it's not right.

It's not right for him, and it's not right for me.

"Murph," Jason starts. "Davey. I went and talked with Marnie, and she admitted she tried to sabotage my relationship with you by telling you a bunch of crap. She apologized to me. And she needs to apologize to you."

That makes me feel a little better, but also a little worse, because that's not the only thing that's wrong.

The real problem is I shouldn't have tried to reach for love, since it's not in the cards for someone like me. I'm cute and amusing. Someone who skims through life like stones skipping across a lake.

The fact that I inconveniently caught real, deep feelings for

Jason doesn't matter, because I'm never going to be enough for him.

"What happened with your dad?"

Jason bites his lip. "He told me if I was going to be with a man, I couldn't work there."

My mood swings to rage, and my hands start shaking. "What? That's illegal!"

"Like I'm going to sue my own father. So … I think I'm getting a new job—"

My stomach sinks to the floor. "You can't change your whole life because of me."

"Don't you see?" he asks, stepping closer. "Everything already *has* changed. Before I met you, I was the man in the gray flannel suit. And now? You're everything to me."

"Jason," I whisper, and the bottom drops out of my world. "I can't be everything to you."

The anguish on his face tears me apart.

"You don't want me?" he whispers, closing his eyes.

"It's not that."

Now I *do* want to tell him I love him and that he's the most amazing person I've ever met. I want to tell him no one else exists who I'd rather be with.

But it's not fair to him to say that. Because I can't push this guy who's been pushed around all his life into loving me. I've already pressured him enough.

"Tell me what's wrong, so I can fix it," he says. The way he's hovering without touching me makes my heart ache.

A tear slides down my face. "I think you need to go."

He crosses his arms over his chest. "No."

"Listen to me. I've known I was gay since I figured out I had a penis. But you? This is new for you, and our relationship has just started. It's going really fast. Us getting together has already had major consequences. You've lost your job—your family legacy—because of me. Take a moment to process. I couldn't live with myself if I didn't give you time to make a smart decision."

Jason reaches out as if to hold me, but I step away. "Murph. I don't need any time. I know what I want. It's you."

But this is all too much. He *does* need time to himself, without me as a distraction, to figure out if being with me is what he really wants.

Giving him space to evaluate whether he should choose me or the life he knows scares the crap out of me, because I'm not the logical choice. If I let him cool off, he's not going to pick me. But I'm going to let him do it if it's the right thing for him.

So, since I'm the manipulative one, I use the only argument that'll make him go think about this. I lift my chin up and say slowly, "It's not fair to me if this is an experiment for you."

That makes him still. "It's not—"

"I believe you when you say you're proud to be with me. And I believe that Marnie apologized. But it doesn't change the fact that I've been shunned by someone I thought I loved because he couldn't come to terms with his own sexual orientation. And while you don't think you'll do it, how can I trust that? You're so new at this, and it seems like you've just assimilated so easily."

"Because it's right," he says, his feet planted wide in front of me.

"Is it?" I ask.

I just can't be with him if he's going to lose everything he's ever had because of me. I can't hurt him like that.

He throws his hands up. "Murph, I'm waiting for you. I'll give you this night because you want it. But I'm not giving up on you. We can make it through this."

All I can do is nod slowly and let him out.

I call up Reeve, sniffling, my back to the door. I haven't moved from there since Jason left.

"What's up, Showgirl?" he asks.

"Jason came by and asked to have me back."

The bookstore and bar noises sound in the background. "I know, he came by V and V. That's wonderful news!"

"No. It's not. It's horrible. Because he's not ready for me."

Reeve's tone sharpens. "How do you know that?"

"Because he's not."

"Are you ready for him?" he accuses.

I shut up.

Because I am, right? I'm ready for a real relationship. He's the one who isn't.

"Goddess, I don't know. Now that I pushed him away, Jason seems so fearless, and maybe I'm the one afraid of everything."

I'm mostly afraid that I've fucked it all up beyond recognition, and I have only myself to blame for that.

"Your ex did a number on you, making you think you aren't worthy of love. That you're someone to hide. You're not. He kept you a secret because *he* was ashamed of who he is, not because you're someone shameful. Big difference. You did not deserve to have someone that toxic in your life. But do some thinking for yourself. Does Jason treat you that way?"

"No," I admit. "He never has."

"So let's accept that as a truth. Until the evidence shows otherwise, Jason, your very kind, generous, and gorgeous boyfriend, is not embarrassed to be with you."

"I'll think about that," I mutter. "But I'm still scared I forced him into being with me."

Reeve is my best friend because he doesn't minimize my fears. And he demonstrates that with his next words. "While I don't know Jason as well as you do, it's pretty hard for someone to fake liking you—or anyone, for that matter. Dirk liked you for real, he just had his own biases and prejudices to deal with—and, again, those issues weren't your fault." He takes a deep breath. "You have to understand that you have so many friends not because you're some fun twink who gives everyone a good time, but because you're caring and joyous and enthusiastic and inspiring.

Even though you attract attention and are all sparkly and pretty, I think you use that flamboyance as a front sometimes."

I let out a noise of protest. "But I *am* sparkly and pretty—"

"You are. We want you to express your true self. You brighten up a room. But sometimes I think you're extra because you're afraid if someone knew the real you, they wouldn't like you."

Goddess. He's not wrong. I press my lips together, sliding down to the floor.

"You're still listening?"

"Yes," I whisper.

"We all love you because we see the real you. Jason wants to be with you because he sees who you are and accepts all of it. At some point you have to realize what's holding you back is you accepting yourself."

I don't say anything.

"Promise me you'll take the time until I get home to think of a few benefits he gets by being with you. And if you say 'a good fuck' again, we're gonna have words. For starters, I think you cheer him up and are helping him navigate the wide and wonderful, but sometimes intimidating, LGBTQ world. You also give him someone to care for, and it sounds like that's something he needed."

"Reeve?"

"Yeah?"

"You're the best."

I can almost hear his smile.

We hang up. Reeve did make me feel better. I just wish I didn't feel like I'm a shiny new toy that Jason will throw away once he gets tired of it.

But maybe that shiny toy is worthy of love, no matter who plays with it.

JASON

How could everything wreck so quickly?

When I get home to a dark and lonely house, all I can think is, *I gotta win him back.*

Murph needs to know that I'm for real. That this isn't a joke. He's not a test case.

I've fallen so deeply for him, and I don't care who knows it. Not my dad. Not the world.

I have to do something to *show* Murph that this isn't a phase. That I'm not messing around with him. That he's not some sexual experiment.

And he didn't trick, coerce, or manipulate me into being with him.

I don't know how to show him other than over time, but I'm not patient enough for that. Actions are important, because Murph's been told too many things. His gambler dad and showgirl mom probably told him he was loved but never showed him they cared. His ex was simultaneously attracted to Murph's Murph-ness and mortified by it.

Murph deserves complete and total love. I'm going to figure out how to prove it to him.

I get ready for bed, gazing at his darkened room and wishing fervently that he were home.

It's late, and I'm scrolling through my phone and drifting off to sleep when I come across a GIF of a superhero, and a random memory comes to me. One I'd shelved long ago.

When I was in second grade, I wanted to be Wonder Woman. My dad said no. But I still asked my mom for the gold bracelets, and she bought them for me.

She also said she bought me the invisible jet, and I believed her. Hey, I was gullible.

But did me wanting to be Wonder Woman mean I had different ideas about my sexuality, even back then? Because now that I think about it, I didn't want to kiss Wonder Woman. I wanted to *be* Wonder Woman.

I scoot to a sitting position.

What else?

I should call Becky—but no. It's my turn to think on my own. I get up and start pacing my room.

Think.

Yes! I collected *I Love Lucy* paraphernalia when I was in sixth grade.

I used to have a purple glitter pen I loved.

Have I ever thought about men before Murph? Even if I wrote it off?

I shake my head, then start nodding. Because it happened.

There was that time I got a stiffy in the high school locker room shower and figured my body was just being shameful.

But I'd been looking at the hockey team dressing.

I scramble to open up my laptop and start typing a list. Because Murph needs to know this. His clueless boyfriend's starting to find clues to put the puzzle together.

The next morning, I don't have a job to go to. And I'll give Murph a little more time, even though seeing his empty bed makes my chest tight. I'm too antsy to sit still, though, so after a few cups of coffee, I put on a suit out of habit, get in my car, and find myself at my old office.

Because I need to tell my father something.

When I walk into his cavernous office in the back, he looks up from his impressive desk, his expression unreadable. Then it morphs into weariness. He sighs. "Unless you've come to your senses, you're not welcome here. I thought I told you my views on your situation, Jason—"

"No," I start. "Or, well, you did. But I didn't tell you *my* views." My dad's eyes start to narrow, but I continue, for once talking over him. I stand over him, too, my shoulders back, my chin out. I'm tempted to wag a finger at him, but I don't. Instead, I put one palm flat on his desk and lean toward him, getting in his face. I'm startled by the fatigue in his eyes, which almost makes me falter. But I don't.

"Dad, I let you walk over me for so long, because I wanted to please you. I wanted to get along with you. I wanted you to be proud of me. But what I didn't understand is that I need to be proud of myself, too. My very gay boyfriend"—he shudders, but I don't stop—"taught me by his example that I have to stand up for what I believe in. That's the way he lives his life. He doesn't hide who he is, while until recently I did it every day. But he's full of rainbows and joy—"

He hisses, "I can't believe you're together with a fairy—"

"People like you look down on him because he's feminine, but that's what makes him a fucking warrior. He's brave enough to be himself no matter what. I've talked some with our same-sex clients and done some research into their—*our*—history. Queers who couldn't hide who they were? Who couldn't blend in like me? Those warriors were on the front lines. They were put in prison, beat up, and worse. Murph's lucky he was born now. And

I'm never going to let you insult him, because he's stronger than you'll ever be."

"Jason," he says, "be reasonable."

"No. If being 'reasonable' is a code word for going along with how you think my life should be, I'm *not* going to be reasonable. I don't believe in being reasonable. I believe that love is love. I believe that the gender of the person I fall in love with doesn't matter. And it's him. I fell in love with him." I stand up, finally giving him some space. "You know what? I think you did me a favor throwing me out. Because now I'm free."

He opens his mouth to start saying something, but now I actually do hold up that index finger. "I don't know what I'm going to do for work, but I'm wondering why the hell I worked for you as long as I did. I don't like working here. I don't like being near you. I just feel pushed around when I'm with you."

Dad holds up his hands. "I only wanted the best for—"

"No. You wanted the best for you, not for me. If you wanted something for me, you would have asked me. You would have listened to me. You didn't. But now it's your loss, and I feel sorry for you. You don't have Mom. You don't have me. And I'm willing to bet you've lost Becky, too." I shake my head. "You need to update your attitudes to this century. Or you're going to wake up one day and realize you're all on your own."

Without waiting for him to say another word, I turn and stalk outside, my pulse pounding. When I breathe the fresh, cold air, my adrenaline is running so fast I almost heave a sob.

I feel the way I did when I figured out I like Murph. Like I can do anything.

But what?

I get in the car and start driving, because I need to think, and the car's a decent place to do it, along all these tree-lined roads, bare and ready for snow.

Road signs and towns pass me by, but I'm lost in thought.

I have a college degree. I know insurance.

And it hits me.

Those guys in my office who wanted to buy insurance for their partners. That's a niche that's been underserved and could be an opportunity. A big one.

Goose bumps erupt all over my body.

I wonder …

I pull out my phone and call Becky. "Hey," I say, "I need a realtor. Can you help?"

"Sure, big bro. Whatcha need?"

"Office space. I want to open my own business."

I explain my idea.

"Hallelujah," she says. "That's the best news I've ever heard. Let me see what I can do."

After driving for I don't know how long, I find myself at the Shipley farm. They've been clients forever. Griff Shipley's older than me, but we know each other reasonably well. He sees me pull up and walks over to me, a beast of a man in a big jacket, flannel shirt, and jeans. I get out of the car in my suit and shake his hand. He's got a very firm grip.

We start down the dirt driveway by the orchard. Our breath comes out in puffs. The apples have been picked, and the farm is bracing for winter. Normally when I come here, I'm inspecting the farm buildings, checking the roofs and outbuildings for any insurance issues. I'm sure my arrival without notice confuses him because we usually do inspections when we're changing the policy.

"Jason. Good to see you, man." He studies my face. "You okay?"

"Never better. Nice to see you, too. How're things?"

He strokes his beard and glances around the orchards. "I'm too superstitious to say much. But it's going well. Can't complain." He chuckles. "Actually, I can. Want me to?"

"If you like."

Griff gives me a wry grin. "It's constant maintenance. If something hasn't broken, it needs to be repainted. And so on. Let me show you." I follow him over to one of the cider-making buildings, and he explains what's new since the last time I was here. After a bit, he says, "You're a good listener. You should charge by the hour."

"Nah." I smile. "You're easy to talk to. And I like learning about your business."

That's the thing. If you ask questions and listen to the answers, people think you're something special.

"How's the insurance business?" he asks.

I wince. "I, well. Um."

He cocks his head.

I decide to tell him. "It's kind of personal, but I just came out to my dad. Told him I'm dating a guy."

Griff raises his eyebrows. "I had no idea you were gay. Or bisexual?"

"Yeah, that. Neither did I. Until him. The guy I'm seeing." The guy I *hope* I'm still seeing. "Anyway, my dad and I had a disagreement about that fact, and I was driving around. And somehow ended up here. Sorry to bug you."

"So this isn't a random insurance inspection?"

"No," I confess. "It isn't. Actually, while I was driving, I got this business idea. Opening up an agency that caters to queer people."

"That's not a bad idea. I'll send my cousin Kieran to you." He grins. "And it's not like you couldn't have straight clients, too."

"Correct."

"Well, when you get opened, ring me up. I'll stick with you wherever you go."

I nod and shake his hand, feeling lighter. "Thanks. Thanks much. I didn't intend to come out here to ask for that, but now that you offer, if it works out, I'll accept."

"Want some cider before you leave?"

"No, thanks. I've got a few more things to sort out today."

He walks me to my car, and I drive home. Once I'm there, instead of pacing around or staring at Murph's vacant room, I pull up my laptop, open a new document, and start taking notes.

What things do I like about my work?

I like the field trips to see clients' properties. Like I did on the spur of the moment today. I like helping people and listening to them. I like that my company helps take care of loved ones.

So that's it. I'm going to let my business become more than I'd let it be in the past. Instead of focusing on the things I don't like—death, pessimism, depression—I'm going to focus on the people I serve.

I'd thought being fired might mean I'd need to change my whole career, go back to school and become a therapist or something. But maybe I can do more good here, helping people to take care of each other.

I like that idea. A lot.

I start listing the things I need to do to create a business. Among them is a website. So I begin a separate document with a wish list for a certain web designer I know.

I write until it's time for my appointment with Becky. She's a genius at finding space fast.

And a few hours later, I've signed a lease. Impulsive? Maybe. But it feels right. It's *my* impulse.

I'll get the keys tomorrow. I stand in the empty office for a minute, thinking of what I could turn this place into. She gives me a hug and wishes me luck with Murph.

Now it's time for the next part of my plan.

With papers in hand, I knock on Reeve's door, hoping Murph's still there.

He opens the door and startles at me in my gray suit. He still looks like hell, but he's always utterly beautiful.

I want to draw him into my arms and never let him go.

"Can I talk with you?" I ask.

"I don't think that's such a good idea—"

I hand him one of the sheets of paper and blow on my hands, because it's turned freezing out here and I forgot my overcoat. He notices.

"Come in, come in."

I step inside and close the door behind me.

He furrows his brow. "What's this?"

"When I was in ninth grade, I played spin the bottle," I say. "And it ended up pointing to this guy, Toby Hansen. While we both kind of looked at each other and went, *Nah,* if he'd said yes, I would've kissed him."

Murph blinks at me.

"Read this," I order, pointing to my memories of the naked hockey players. And that time I got off while watching male underwear ads. And the awkward boner I got in class when we were studying Greek and Roman statues—ones that weren't missing any parts. "Murph, all these things add up. I just didn't have the self-awareness to realize I've been bisexual my whole life. You help me to be who I really am."

"Tell me more," he whispers, sinking into the couch. "I want to hear it all. Everything."

So I sit across from him and tell him every memory I have that now, looking on it, was a clue to my sexuality. I end with, "I watched Lady Gaga's halftime show on repeat. And sang along."

"Oh my goddess, that's so gay," Murph squeals. "I love it! I did that, too." Then he sobers. "You're telling me that you being into guys isn't a phase."

"No, honey. It isn't a phase at all. Or an experiment. In fact, the only phase I'm in now is not putting up with my own bullshit. I'm in the phase of loving who I want to love. Being who I want to be. And not letting anyone else tell me what to do. I'm in the phase of being my true, authentic self. And I have you to thank for being my inspiration." I laugh at the feeling of freedom the words and thoughts bring. "I haven't been straight this entire time. I just assumed I was, because I never thought I'd be anything else."

He starts laughing, too. "You mean you've been a queer boy your whole life and didn't know it?"

"I've always been bisexual. I'm a people pleaser, and I just kind of slid through life. It's easy if you like girls, too. No one confronted me with other parts of my sexuality—until you."

He places a hand on his heart, and we smile at each other from a few feet apart.

"My whole life I've been afraid to be myself," I continue. "I've been hiding. That's one of the reasons why you've made such an impression on me. Because you don't hide at all. In the past, I've missed out on parts of myself because I was listening to everyone else. You inspire me because you listen to *no one* else."

He opens his mouth to argue, but I hold up my hand to stop him and keep going.

"I appreciate so much about you. I appreciate the fact that you follow your own muse. You have your own goddess. You're one of a kind. You express yourself in whatever way you choose. You inspire me, Murph. You make me want to be a better man. To live more authentically."

Murph's crying now, fat tears tracing down his cheeks. He isn't wearing makeup today, and he's just as pretty as he is when he does. I like him both ways. All ways.

I hand him another piece of paper, still keeping my distance.

"What's this?" He sniffles. "More gay memories to make me cry?"

I shake my head. "No. This is a list of things I appreciate about you."

"Oh my goddess, I can't read it."

"Then I will." I take the sheet back and start reading. "I appreciate how much Murph supports me and encourages me to be my best self. He reminds me to make art. He lets me think it's okay to watch *Forged in Fire* for the weapons. Or not. He helps me to stay healthy. He willingly eats what I make."

"That's because it's tasty," he whispers.

I look up at him. "I might've been looking for someone to cook for my whole life. It goes on. Want me to continue?" I'm still not holding him, because I'm not going to do it until he tells me he's okay with it.

I get down on my knees before him.

"I choose you, Davey Murphy. My sister may have found you, but I'm the one who fell in love with you. And I trust this love because it's one of the first things in my entire life that I've decided on my own. Not because it was expected of me. Not because it was convenient. Not because you're super flirty or did anything to trick me. But because you have my whole heart. I trust the feeling I have for you, because it feels more right than anything I've ever experienced in my entire life."

He wipes tears rapidly with the back of his hand, and I can't stand it anymore.

"Can I hug you?"

He nods repeatedly and does this kind of leap into my arms. I catch him. I'll always catch him.

And then we're kissing like we're starved. He wraps his legs around me, and I move us onto the couch, where I sit down and he straddles me.

"This is where you belong," I whisper against his mouth. "And where I belong."

"With you?"

"With you."

MURPH

I'm overwhelmed with so much emotion, it's a wonder I haven't dissolved from my tears.

All I know is, the feelings I have for Jason? They're reciprocated.

And more? What he's telling me, I believe. Maybe I am worthy of love.

I snuffle into his suit and ruffle his Technicolor dream hair. "We're going to have to get this dry cleaned."

"Don't care."

"I don't want to move. But I want to go home so very badly."

Jason kisses me tenderly. "Then let's go home. You and me. What do you think of that decision?"

Which reminds me. "I forgot," I say.

He raises his eyebrows. "Forgot what?"

"Forgot to ask you whether a decision was yours or your father's. I told you I'd remind you. But I guess you figured it out."

His eyes wrinkle when he smiles. "I did. This decision was all mine. Just so you know, you're fucking mine."

I wrap my legs around him like I'm Saran Wrapped to him, and he struggles to stand. With one last kiss, he sets me down.

"I don't know if I've ever been anyone else's." I'm in complete disarray, but all I want to do is go home. "Let me get my things, and we can continue this conversation at our own house."

"Okay." Then he reaches out and takes my hand. "There's one more thing." He hands me yet another piece of paper.

"Is this going to make me cry more?"

He shrugs. "It's a proposal."

I stare at him.

"A *business* proposal," he amends.

"You almost gave me a heart attack."

"Sorry." He sticks his hands in his pockets and looks sheepish. "I have this idea. Well, I'm going to do it. So it's more than an idea. It's my next business venture. I'm creating an LGBTQ-friendly insurance agency that will be focused on using insurance to protect our rights."

I notice how he says "*our*" rights.

He starts telling me about how he was working with Harrison and Finn. And how he wants to make it so people like us have a comfortable place to take care of those needs.

I stare at the business plan.

The next page is a Request for Proposal for a website that advertises to the gay, lesbian, bisexual, transgender, and otherwise queer community on how they can take care of their loved ones.

At the bottom is a place for me to sign.

I fall in love with him some more.

I page through the documents he's handed me. "Are you serious?"

"As serious as I am about you. I've learned all sorts of truths on this journey with you, and it isn't only about how much I love you. It's also where my heart lies and how I can make a difference in this world. How I can do what I know how to do, but do it in my own way. Not repeating what someone else does, but creating my own path." He smiles.

I start nodding, the tears sliding down my face.

"Will you help me?"

And I know he's asking me if all is well between us.

"Oh, fuck yes," I say. And I launch myself into his arms again, papers scattering everywhere.

He staggers back under my weight but recovers quickly, his arms holding me close. "I missed you," he whispers into my hair. "I love you so much."

I look at him, my legs wrapped tightly around him as I snuggle into him. "I love you, too."

"I'm sorry things got so fucked up. I didn't mean them to," he says. "I just wanted to—"

"It wasn't your fault. I share the blame for my own hang-ups. I needed to work out a few things that were messed up in my head. I think I had some prejudices, too. Like if you were bi, you couldn't like me."

"But Murph, do you understand? I'll go anywhere with you and do anything. I want to spend the rest of my life with you."

"Holy shit," I breathe. "You do?"

"You don't?"

"I so much do." Goddess, that sounded like a vow. But it is. A vow to his heart. Because there's no one who fits into the broken places of my heart the way Jason does. He steadies me. He fills me up, and he lets me soar, and he anchors me. I've never met anyone like him.

And I think he's never met anyone like me, so we're even.

We're a good match.

I clutch his body even more, and he strokes my neck and shoulders and arms and suddenly we're kissing, and I'm somehow on my back on the floor and he's settling between my legs, and this is how I want to be for the rest of my life. In some similar position, taking breaks so he can cook and I can make him laugh. And he can have that lightness in his heart that I know I bring to him.

"You make me believe again," he says. "I'd given up on love. And on hope. I'd given up on ever finding someone who really got me down deep. And it's you."

The door opens, and Reeve and Oz walk in.

Jason and I sit up faster than you can say *uh-oh*.

Reeve smirks. "So I guess things are patched up between you two now?"

"We're all mended," I sing, waving a hand.

Jason glances up at Reeve. "Thanks for taking care of Murph for me."

"Anytime."

"But yeah, we're good," Jason says. He squeezes my hand. "Ready to go home?"

I nod, and we gather my things. I wave goodbye to Oz and give Reeve a hug and promise to text later. And thank him for dealing with my, uh, Murph-ness.

Friends are some of the most important people in my life.

When we step back into our home, I feel like I've come full circle. I arrived here believing I could never have my roommate as a partner. And now I know I'm never letting him go.

We set down my bags and look at each other.

While part of me wants to get him naked fast, the rest of me is exhausted from the emotions of the past few days. Jason senses this, because the first thing he asks is, "Have you eaten?"

"Reeve tried to feed me, but I wasn't hungry."

"Want to take a bath while I make you some food?"

"How did I ever get so lucky?"

He gives me a kiss and pinches my ass. "Go. Take a bubble bath. I'll fix us something."

I scamper off.

And he's right. Stepping into the warm water immediately soothes my tense body and battered heart.

Before I get too cozy, the door opens and Jason comes in to stand next to the tub, pulling off his tie. "Can I join you?"

I nod.

As a reward, I get my own striptease, complete with a man

who loves me. Jason unbuttons his shirt and puts it in the hamper, steps out of his pants, and strips off his underwear and socks. I scoot forward to give him room to step into the tub.

He settles in behind me. "Ahh, this is better. Dinner's in the oven. C'mere."

Trying not to splash too much—I live with the super—I crawl over and lie against him, my back to his chest, his knees on either side of my body.

For a while we just sit here, enjoying the warm water and the quiet. But after a moment, he asks me, "Is there anything else we need to figure out?"

I think about it.

"I'm sorry I thought you'd act like my ex. You're nothing like him. You've been nothing but kind to me and proud to be around me. You just had to figure out who you liked and why. With him, he knew, but he hated himself for it—and that made him cruel. There's a big difference."

Jason smiles against my wet hair. "So you'll take clueless over cruel?"

"Any day of the week."

"I know I have things to work on to earn your trust back—"

I splash when I turn farther and get in his handsome face. "You don't have to do a damned thing. You already *did* earn it. I just wasn't looking in the right place. If I would've paid attention, it was clear you didn't do anything to make me think you weren't into me. Other than telling me you were straight. And, um, since you're not, we're all good."

He laughs and drags me closer for a hug. I'm such a cuddle whore now, it's not even funny. You get yourself a warm man who lets you snuggle into him and then tell me you're not a cuddle whore. See?

"God, I love you," he mutters into my neck.

"I love you. And I'm never going to get sick of hearing you say it."

"I'll be as affectionate as you can take," Jason says. And I believe him. Because once he started touching me, he hasn't stopped. Hell, he even touched me before he knew he liked me. The way he threw his arm around me to protect me when we were near the bullies. When he hugged me in the glass studio. How he never shied away from my little touches. "And I think you knew I was bisexual before I did. You have some serious emotional intelligence."

"Gut reactions, yes. They tend to be right. Problem is, sometimes I override those because I think they can't be true. I assume things. That's when I get into trouble."

"Well, if we were perfect, we'd be insufferable."

"We only have to be perfect for each other."

He looks at me, and we both say, "Aww," at the same time. "We shall never utter that sentiment in public, because it was a little too saccharine," he decides.

"Can it be saccharine if it's true?"

"I don't know, and I don't care, because it's our truth."

"You make me feel like I deserve things," I say.

"That's because you do. All of it. Everything good. I don't mind spending the rest of my life proving to you just how lovable and worthy and strong you are. How much I love you. How much I've fallen so completely for you. All the love songs are true. I never thought I was the kind of person who'd have this epic love story. But that's what we have, Murph. An epic love story."

"I agree. With all of it."

He holds me, cradling me on his lap.

The buzzer dings on the oven.

"Kiss me, then let me feed you, then I want you to fuck me," he says.

As if that's a normal statement.

"Um, you do?"

He nods.

I scramble out of the tub, getting water everywhere, as he laughs. Then I extend a hand and help him out, handing him a clean purple towel.

JASON

We've had dinner. (Chicken parmesan.)

We've cleaned up.

We've made up.

We're in love.

After dinner we end up on the couch, wrestling, with him on top of me and me beneath him. Not entirely sure how that happens.

I gaze up at him. "I need you to fuck me, and I need it right now. I can't stand waiting any longer to know what it feels like to have you inside me."

Murph raises one eyebrow. "Next time be a little more direct, okay, my love?" Without further ado, he tugs at my shirt and pulls it over my head. Then he drags me to my feet, shoves me against the nearest wall—guess that's both of our thing—and kisses me hard.

I lose myself in his lips. In the feel of his body against mine. In the way he tastes.

He somehow frog-marches me to the bedroom—his bedroom. And my cock grows.

I had no idea I wanted him to be assertive like this. In bed, normally I'm the aggressive one.

He unbuckles my pants and helps me step out of my clothes.

"I'm gonna make love to you," he says, his eyes glittering, "but we're going to call it fucking, m'kay?"

I nod vehemently, not sure what I'm doing or what's going to happen, scared that it's going to hurt but wanting it so badly.

"Bend over," he orders. "And put your arms on the bed."

Before I know it, Murph's leaning over my back, kissing down my spine, making me tingle.

I love the way his hands rub my skin.

I love him.

He pauses, and I hear the click of a bottle. Then a cool, lubed hand starts jacking me, and it feels so *fucking* good.

With one hand reaching around me to stroke me, he traces his other hand, also lubed, down my crack to that spot where no man besides me—or a doctor—has gone before.

He presses against my hole very gently.

"I like it," I say. "Keep going."

He kisses my back. "Thanks for giving me the green light. We can still stop, though—"

"Quit it. Fuck, Murph, I want to feel you."

"Okay, bossy. Sheesh."

A finger slips inside me, and he knows what he's doing, gently stroking. And—

"Oh, god," I moan.

"Mmm, you like that, don't you?"

He shifts, and I realize he's added another finger. The fullness is getting intense now, and I'm apprehensive about what it will be like when his dick is inside me. But I want to know what he's feeling when I do this to him. I want everything with Murph.

After he teases me for a while, kissing my skin and murmuring encouragement, I start to relax. "There you go," he whispers. "That's what we want. Hang on."

His fingers withdraw from me, and I whimper. But he's shucking off his clothes, and I hear the rip of foil.

Then … nothing, for a moment. Just cool air against my back. I look over my shoulder, and Murph's studying me as if he can't believe he gets to do this. Or like he's evaluating a sculpture at a museum. Then he seems to come to a conclusion.

"Yes, we're doing it this way."

He stands behind me and moves my hips, adjusting my position and spreading my ass apart.

"I feel really exposed and vulnerable," I admit.

"And that's what makes you strong," he replies. "Some really smart guy told me that." After rolling on the condom, he lines up behind me. "Ready?"

I nod. I want this, even if it hurts.

Holding my hip with one hand and—I assume—his cock with the other, Murph presses inside me and *HOLY FUCKING HELL THIS IS INTENSE,* I want to scream, but I don't say anything or do anything but whisper, "Oh, god."

"Hang on, sugarplum," he croons. "Get used to me. Take your time."

The burning sensation eases, and I feel *him* inside me.

"Okay," I breathe out.

Murph kisses my back. "I'm gonna move."

He pushes me down harder on the bed and starts stroking in and out, and holy fuck, this is what it's about. His cock is grazing my prostate, and it's amazing, but it's more than that, too. It's *Murph.*

"This is incredible," I gasp. "*You're* incredible. Why didn't I know it would be like this? Why doesn't everyone want to feel this way?"

"Cool. I'm blowing your mind. I shall continue." Nonchalant words, but his sexy voice is strained.

Murph reaches around for my cock and gives it a few tight strokes, and it's almost enough to get me to come. In fact, I wonder if I could come without him touching me at all. Without touching my dick, I mean. Because this is everything.

The pressure builds up, and I'm dying, craving the release. I need it.

"Your ass is so gorgeous," he murmurs, his voice getting ragged. "I'm the luckiest man alive to be able to do this with you. I love you. I'm connected with you. I want to fuck you so hard you think of me all week."

"I think of you all day," I pant, "every day," pant, "anyway."

"Oh my, I found me a good boyfriend." He leans down and kisses me, and the angle sends me over the edge. I go spiraling into an *oh my god* orgasm where I almost pass out, shaking and making a mess on his bed.

Murph follows me, his thrusts getting wonky and uncoordinated as he gasps out his release.

I can feel his dick pumping into my ass in pulses. And I like it.

He collapses on top of me, wrapping his arms around my middle, until our breathing evens out, all the while leaving soft kisses on my back and murmuring his appreciation.

We stay that way until Murph starts to soften and slides out, and I miss him immediately. I want him back.

I turn around and grab him. "That was the best."

Murph's smile is full of love. "That's because it's you and me."

MURPH

The week that follows is the best of my entire life. Jason's busy setting up his own insurance office, but since so many of his clients have his cell phone number, they call him rather than him needing to reach out to them to announce what he's doing. And word gets around, I guess. Between that and the rainbow flag in the window, he attracts a whole bunch of new clients.

I spend my time when I'm not at work—or naked with Jason—designing him a kick-ass website and helping him decorate his new digs.

When I show him the site I made for his slump glass projects while I was moping around at Reeve's house, he yelps, then tackles me in a hug.

One night, Becky comes over for dinner and informs us that Marnie's starting to see a new guy, and both Jason and I heave sighs of relief. Marnie apologized to me two days ago, and I think it was genuine.

On Saturday night we're sitting on the couch after going for a run and showering, and I turn to Jason in delight. "I have an idea."

"Will I like this idea?" Jason asks.

"It involves getting naked afterward."

"Sold."

I laugh. "I think we should go to gay night at the bar."

He's been doing great, looking and sounding more and more comfortable the more he integrates with this new vision of himself. Going out dancing may take him outside his comfort zone a bit, but I think it's good to stretch and grow.

His face drains of color, and I rethink my approach for a minute. "Honey pie," I say in a soothing voice. "We don't have to—"

"No. We're going. It's a good idea," he says determinedly. Then his expression turns sheepish. "I'm just a terrible dancer."

"I'm not. I'll make you look good. Don't forget, Ginger gave Fred sex appeal and Fred gave Ginger class. I'm your Ginger. You're Fred."

He snorts. "Okay. But what do I wear?" His eyes dart all over the place like he's going to find the perfect outfit in the living room. "I don't—"

I put both of my hands over his mouth to shut him up. "I can see you starting to panic. No panicking at the disco." We both laugh. I look him up and down and like what I see. "Want me to dress you?"

He puts his face in his hands. "Yes. No. I don't know."

"Murph to the rescue. I'll get you so sexy everyone will be jealous of me because we have eyes only for each other, and it will be amazing!" I sing the last bit, then clap my hands and charge into his room to ransack his closet. He has to have something that will work.

He does. I dress him in form-fitting dark jeans and a dress shirt with the sleeves rolled up … under a thick jacket. I'm in a tight pink T-shirt with a sparkly unicorn on it and skinny jeans. Under a parka. Because Vermont.

Soon we're tumbling out of the Uber and into the bar. It's early, but that's okay. We're here to dance, not pick anyone up.

We hold hands without giving it a second thought as we take in the scene.

The place is loud and boisterous but not full yet, and we find a tall table to stand at. A couple of male go-go dancers are gyrating on the bar, and Jason observes them with a curious expression.

I think they're cute, but they don't hold a candle to my Jay.

I see Tai dancing with Emmett, and he waves vigorously at us. I wave back, and even Jason manages a friendly smile.

"We should invite them over for dinner sometime," Jason says, standing close so I can hear him. "That's your friend, right? And his partner?"

Given how my formerly clueless, formerly jealous, former just-roommate, now boyfriend thought everyone I hung out with was someone to growl at, this here is major progress.

I squeal and rock on my toes, already planning. "You would? We could? Oh my goddess, so much yes! I want to have everyone over. Only if you let me help you cook, though. I'm not going to make you do all the work."

"Deal. Hold that thought while I get you something to drink," he says, and five minutes later he sets down a glass of sangria in front of me.

I express my appreciation by eyeing him up and down and taking a swig. "You're the best, my little cabbage!" I shout.

He grins, and my heart thumps harder in my chest.

The music is too loud for us to talk much, so he moves closer and gives up any pretense of not hanging all over me. His large paw holds my shoulder, and his scruff tickles my cheek, and he smells so good and he's just so big and glorious and he's fucking mine and I want to kiss him and dance with him, but I'll give him some time to get comfy. I'm already in my element.

He seems to be on board with at least part of my plan. Before his beer is even done, he's got his tongue down my throat.

"Holy shit," I gasp when we come up for air. "What was that for? I mean, I'm not complaining, but *what*?"

"I didn't like the way a few guys were looking at you." He gives me a devilish smile, and my cock takes notice. It doesn't have much room in these pants. *Sorry, cock.*

"I *did* like the way this one guy's looking at me," I say, preening.

"Who?"

"You, silly." And I let him kiss me again. "C'mon. Let's dance."

I tug him onto the dance floor, which is getting busier, and hold him around his waist, chest to chest. He's stiff, I'll give him that. But I hold his hips and move toward him and back, and he smiles and loosens up, and actually, my man has some moves.

Oh, goddess, he has moves once he lets himself go.

I should have known. I've felt him inside me often enough.

"I thought you said you couldn't dance."

He shrugs. "I'm following your lead, Ginger."

Teasing him, I tug him close with a finger in his collar but refuse to kiss him, then turn around and swish my ass against his groin, and he groans.

And then we're laughing and all is well. The bodies around us become a sea of people moving and swaying, and while at first Jason was looking around, self-conscious, now he's only focused on me.

I've never had anyone pay attention to me this way, and I'm liking it a hell of a lot. I adore being the center of someone's world, and that thought makes me want to cry.

Fuck.

Dance, Murph.

His arms wrap around me, and we do this boogie where I'm wiggling into him and he's holding me and moving with me, and if I had to die anywhere, I think I'd choose right here, doing my favorite thing—or second favorite, after blow jobs—and being held by the guy who makes me feel the best I ever have in my life.

We get closer and closer. I cast a glance around, wondering if anyone has noticed that this is Jason Falkner, who used to be straight.

"I like this place." Jason nuzzles my ear, and I find myself being danced over to the bar, where he orders two more drinks and two glasses of water. Because he's thoughtful.

Goddess, he's thoughtful.

"I want to kiss you," I blurt. "Because you're you."

He leans down and makes that happen for so long that the bartender has got to have been standing there clearing his throat for a few minutes before we acknowledge that our drinks are ready. Jason tells him to add them to our tab, and I argue with him, and he kisses me again to shut me up.

After we take a few sips, Jason looks down to the end of the bar, then furrows his eyebrows and cocks his head.

I follow his gaze, but with so many people, I can't tell what's caught his attention. "What is it?"

His lips brush my ear as he speaks. "I know that guy."

"Who?"

He takes my hand and tugs me through the crowd. We walk up to a man with a short buzz cut who's talking to the bartender. The guy glances at Jason, then does a double-take, surprise and delight overtaking his face in turn. "Jason! Holy shit! How long has it been?"

"Too long." With a wide smile, Jason leans over and gives the guy a hug. When he pulls back, he holds my hand and drags me forward. "Brandon, you have to meet my boyfriend, Murph."

"*Boyfriend*?" Brandon looks between us, clearly interested in this piece of news.

Jason's nearly bouncing with excitement. He has to yell to be heard over the music, but he makes the effort. "Murph, this is Brandon. I went to high school with him. We used to do homework together."

"I was the only gay kid in school. At least I thought I was …"

I shake Brandon's hand. "Any friend of Jason's is a friend of mine."

Brandon's shaking his head. "If I'd have known in high school you were queer … *man*. All those study sessions would've been a lot more interesting."

"I'll bet." I'm not feeling jealous, but rather content that my man has more support and allies than he realized.

Brandon turns to me. "I always wished Jason would look at me twice, but he never did. Well, I'm happy for you, Murph. Jason's great."

"He is, isn't he?" I know I'm smug, but it's the truth.

We linger for a while for Jason to catch up, and eventually we all end up on the dance floor.

I finally figured out the answer to the equation: cute, not-so-straight Jason plus cute, gay me (plus dancing) equals *everything*.

Later that night, after dancing and getting *veh-wey* tipsy, Jason and I stumble outside into the cold night.

"Let's get something to eat before we call an Uber," he says.

"Okay, but I'm buying."

He catches my eyes and nods, and somehow it means more than if he'd said a million things.

We find our way to the diner and order fries and milkshakes because it's a fries-and-milkshakes kind of night. And we sit across from each other and talk and talk, and I know for sure that I'm forever in love with this man.

When we get home, we're all hands and kisses, skin to skin and lips to lips. Tugging off shirts and kicking shoes down the hall and hopping out of our pants, not wanting to break our connection.

It's funny. When we get to our rooms, we look back and forth, not sure which one to go to. "It doesn't matter," I say. "Just stay with me."

He nods rapidly and repeatedly, and it's so earnest that I grab his bearded cheeks with both hands and kiss him hard.

We've been kissing hard for a while, but this one feels special. More us. More in love.

We wrestle for the lead, but I give up after a moment and let him push me onto his bed. Then I scramble up and straddle him, my erect dick thumping my lower belly.

Jason lies below me, naked, hair disheveled. My fingernails trace his broad chest, and goose bumps rise. I'm sitting on his dick, pressing it into his groin and stomach.

"This is my happy place." I clasp my hands together and pose with them under my chin. "You're so fucking beautiful."

"I could say the same for you. God. I have no idea why you weren't snapped up already."

"I think maybe I was waiting for you," I confess. It makes my heart pound to say it, but once it's out, I know it's true. "I was always looking for you. Not someone like you. But *you*. You're open, and you dare me to expand and grow. You take care of me better than I can take care of myself. You're handsome as fuck, but not cocky. You're confident but willing to question yourself and others."

His eyes soften, and he doesn't say anything. He opens his mouth, but I put a palm over his lips.

"I love how you listen to me. How you feed me dinner and how you don't give a rat's patootie that I'm this weirdo—"

"You're not a weirdo." He sits up and holds me, one hand on each side of my waist. "Or, if you're a weirdo, you're my weirdo, and only because it's no fun to be normal. You're quite simply the light of my life. I know that's a cliché, but there it is. You bring me so much happiness, you have no idea."

"I have some idea," I say. "Because you do it to me."

"I know what I want to do to you," he mutters wickedly, and my heart starts revving into higher RPMs.

"Whatever you have in mind, yes, please."

He tugs me down so my narrower chest meets his broad one, and we make out lazily, as if we have all night.

Because we do.

40

JASON

I'm in my new office with its new paint—stylish colors chosen by me and Murph—and Becky walks in.

"Settling in?" She noses around, opening doors and straightening chairs like she can't help staging the place even though I'm already here. She's such a realtor.

I nod. "Owning my own business is a challenge, but it's dawning on me that I can do whatever I want, and I don't have to answer to anyone but my clients. Of whom there are many."

A broad smile stretches across her face. "I'm so happy for you. This is the best move you could have made. I'm so glad you're out from under Dad's thumb. Have you talked to him?"

"Not since I yelled at him. You?"

Becky scoffs. "Hell, no. After what he said?" Her voice lowers. "But I think he might crack. He called me twice, both times not leaving a message, which is so unlike him. And my neighbor said he stopped by."

I'm not sure what I think of that. "He hasn't tried calling me."

"Do you want to talk to him?"

I press my lips together. "Yeah, I think so."

"I'm pretty sure he'll come around."

And she's right. Not five days later, there's a buzz at the street-level door. Thankfully, both Murph and I are dressed, having just come home from work. I'm cooking, and he's setting the table.

When I find out who it is, I let him in, and in a few moments, open the apartment door to my dad.

He looks less powerful than I remember. More tired. Now that I've had some time away from him, some physical and emotional space, he doesn't seem as big or as scary as he used to. Kind of like when I visited my old elementary school years later and discovered how low the drinking fountains and how tiny the toilets were, while I remembered everything as huge and overwhelming.

I never noticed how his muscles have gotten smaller. His clothes are baggy on him. Basically, he doesn't scare me anymore. I feel sorry for him.

"Hey, Dad. What are you doing here?" My voice is carefully neutral.

He scrubs his face with his hands. "I wanted to talk with you. Can I come in?"

I turn around and ask Murph. "It okay with you if my dad comes in?"

"Sure," he says. I can tell he's holding his tongue so as not to say something cheeky. I almost wish he would, but Murph does have a sense of time and place.

I step aside and invite my father inside.

"This is my boyfriend, Dad," I say. "His name is Davey Murphy, but call him Murph."

To my dad's credit, he shakes Murph's hand, and he doesn't seem like he's giving him the grip of death.

"Nice to meet you," Murph says. He pulls me to the side while my dad stands with his hands shoved deep in his pockets. "Do you want me, you know, to get scarce for a while?"

"Absolutely not. There's nothing I'd say to him I wouldn't say in front of you. And if he's going to say something to me, he needs to have the balls to be able to say it in front of you. So no, don't leave. But I won't make you miserable by forcing you to hang with us, either."

"I'll take over cooking dinner," he decides.

I kiss him. "Thanks." It's a quick, almost platonic kiss, but my dad can see it. I'm serious about not hiding a damned thing from anyone. Especially in my own home. I don't look at my dad, so I don't know his reaction.

Rather than saying anything, my dad finds a place on our couch—the couch where Murph and I make out on the regular.

That thought makes me smile. "Want something to drink?"

He shakes his head. "No. I don't want to stay long."

I sit on the chair across from where my dad is looking distinctly uncomfortable. "It must have come as a shock that I'm dating a guy," I say. "But it's the real deal. I love him."

"That can't be true," he starts, but my expression shuts that right down.

"I know that this isn't what you expected for me, but I'm an adult now. You have to trust that I know what's right for me. Murph fits me in a way no other person on the planet ever has. I feel like I'm most myself when I'm with him."

My dad watches us warily, then clears his throat. "All right. I didn't come here to … debate how you feel. I wanted to let you know that while I'm not at all used to this, I am sorry for saying I didn't recognize you as my son. Even if I don't agree with your choices, you will always be my son. And I do want you to be happy. I haven't always gone about that in the best way. But it's the truth." He sighs. "I'm not comfortable with … all this modern sexual stuff, but I'm committed to figuring out how to make a relationship with you work. I want you in my life."

That's more than I thought he'd say. I nod.

"I'll think some more about this. And maybe have you and your friend—er, boyfriend—over for dinner sometime. But give me time to process."

"I can do that. I respect you, Dad. But this isn't about you, it's about me and it's about Murph, and we're right for each other. That's all there is to it."

He nods. "Again, I apologize for the way I treated you. I'm sorry you're not in business with me anymore, but I respect your decision to live your own life." He gets up and peers into the kitchen. "Bye, uh, Murph. Take care of my son."

Murph grins. "I will."

When the door closes, Murph comes running in and skids to a stop in front of me. "You," he accuses.

I look around. "What?"

"I'm gonna fucking marry you someday. Because you're the bravest motherfucker I know. And you are so getting laid after dinner."

That makes me laugh. "Sounds good to me. All of it."

His expression turns serious. "That could have gone in a way that made me feel like a second-class citizen. And it didn't."

"It could have gone that way for me, too," I admit. "He surprised me. Maybe losing me, Mom, *and* Becky was just too much for him."

"Losing the things you love can force you to make some important decisions."

"No kidding."

He hugs me. "You know you're my everything, right?"

"I do. Because that's what you are to me, too."

MURPH

We're back in Jason's glass-making shed, only this time he's pressed behind me while I work, completely ignoring his own project. He's nibbling on my neck and grinding into me while I clip pieces of glass.

"We're supposed to meet Becky at V and V later tonight. So we need to finish up," he murmurs against my skin.

"Okay." I continue arranging the glass while he does his best to distract me.

"And now that we're together, we should reevaluate our living situation."

"I'm still paying rent," I immediately reply.

"I'm agreeable to you sharing expenses. But let's look at them and figure them out together. Also, do we want to keep two bedrooms? Or turn one into an office for you? You might want one if you get that gig as an entertainment reporter for that new website."

I grin. "Yeah, I'm open to that. And I'll apply. Thanks for reminding me."

After I arrange a few more pieces of glass—with no help from the glass artisan—I bring up another topic. "I was thinking—"

"Good ..."

"You know how you secretly like musicals?"

He stills, and I can tell he's going to deny it out of old habit. But all he says is, "Yeah," his lips against my nape.

"And I do, too. Not secretly."

Jason nods.

"I often cast myself as the hero in my own musical. Like, I'm on stage and this isn't my real life."

"Okay." I can tell he doesn't know where I'm going with this.

"And you know how we both like swords and fantasy books and movies."

His hand wriggles down the front of my pants. "I do like swords."

I laugh and then moan. "I'll never finish this if you keep doing that."

"Okay."

"I guess I—or we—both have these fantasy-world escapes. Books. Movies. Places that don't exist. People we'll never know. And we want them to be real. We want those to be our lives, because it's so much more fun."

"Uh-huh."

"The thing is, I've learned that my real life is so much better than anything Hollywood or Broadway could come up with."

You could hear a pin drop. Then Jason extracts his hands, carefully helps me set down the glass I'm working on, takes off my gloves and glasses, and pins me up against an empty table, his tongue down my throat.

When we're both breathless, he presses his forehead into mine.

"Proving my point," I squeak.

"You're absolutely right. We're both the kind of people who like to think about the alternate realities in *Rick and Morty*. The epic battles of *Lord of the Rings*. But underneath it all, we really want to be the heroes in our own lives—at least for ourselves and the people we care most about."

"Exactly."

He kisses me. "Good point, my love. Now, if you don't mind, I would like to suck you off. Then you can continue making art."

My voice sounds tinny. "Okay. If, uh, you want."

Jason's on his knees, unzipping my jeans and drawing out my cock, and his capable mouth is on me.

And I don't know of any fantasy that could be better than this. I don't need a stage. I don't need costume design or lighting—although a girl can use some bling every now and then.

But find me the love of my life, and everything else is just details.

A few hours later, when we're at Vino and Veritas—as customers, I'm not working—we sit at a table with Becky while she waits for her friends to arrive. We're all sipping wine and enjoying Liam's guitar playing.

Offhandedly, Becky says, "I had a feeling that Murph was your type. That's why I chose him."

We both stare at her.

Jason recovers first. "You what now?"

"I thought that having Murph come live with you would force you out of the haze of denial you were in and make you figure out once and for all that you were into guys. And I thought he'd be great for you."

Jason stares at her.

I stare at her.

"You planned this?" I ask. "If so, I need to give you more credit."

"He's my brother. I know him. I knew how clueless he was. But also how caring. And I thought you might be just the person to spark life in him. The one he could come out of his shell for."

"You were right," I say.

Jason nods, still looking dazed. "You knew the whole time. And you were just playing me?"

She grins.

"I can't believe this," he says. "I don't know if I want to strangle you or hug you. Mostly hug."

"I only care about your heart, big bro. And I wanted you to know that you deserve love."

He reaches across the table and holds my hand. Then he gives me the best smile and bursts out laughing. "I can't believe it. I can't. Oh my god. Really?"

She smiles. "My plan worked."

"It did."

"See? You're so sweet, Jason. You just needed a little push."

"I did."

I'm gazing at my man.

That man in the gray flannel suit is one hell of a colorful guy once you get to know him. He even has moves.

If my life were a musical, this would be the ensemble scene. When the whole cast comes out on stage and dances with me.

There's Tai over there, dancing with his partner. And Reeve and Oz chatting. Harrison and Finn cuddling. Tanner and Jax laughing. But since we're in a wine bar, not on stage, it's low-key. We're just enjoying each other's company.

And I'm loving how many friends I have in this town. Real friends. What a huge community we are building, and how diverse it all is.

Soon enough, I think people might move here just so they can be welcomed and accepted. They can find their books at Vino and Veritas and they can get served wine by me. And maybe they can find a little bit of their true north.

As I look up into Jason's eyes, I know I have.

MURPH

One year later

Jason and I had friends over for dinner and D&D tonight, using dishes both of us made. I'm back to being dungeon master, and we all look forward to our weekly time to play.

And now it's quiet, and we're done cleaning up. We're on the couch deciding what to watch. I'm in that sleepy post-party state where all is right with the world.

Over the past year, his business has flourished, and he's the go-to guy in Vermont for insurance needs. Not just for the LGBTQ crowd, but for anyone who needs a listening ear and a gentle smile.

I've managed to leverage my *Rick and Morty* blog into a side gig writing review articles for a few online magazines. In the not-online world, while I still spend 90 percent of my time at the wine bar, that 10 percent filling in over at the bookshop makes my days delightful. And I do websites on the side for fun.

Snow is falling outside, and I think about the red scarf I bought for Jason and how he's going to look like a penguin in it. He'll be the cutest penguin I've ever met.

I'm about to say something along those lines when I notice he's turned the TV off and shifted to the floor in front of me. And is down on one knee.

Holding a box.

A very small one.

He licks his lips and gives me a silly grin. Then his jaw clenches, and I watch him close his eyes and take a deep, calming breath.

My hands cover my mouth, and my eyes sting. I get this weird sort of tunnel vision where all I see is him. While I'm trying to ground myself and not get light-headed, his voice makes it through the ringing in my ears.

"Davey Murphy," he says, and his voice cracks. He blinks a few times, clears his throat, and starts again. "You're the man I never knew I wanted, but the one I was waiting for. I want to live the rest of my life with you by my side. I can't imagine what it would be like to not wake up every morning to your handsome face, kiss your sassy lips, or look into your gorgeous blue eyes."

My heart appears to have moved up somewhere near my ears based on how loud it's beating. How hard and fast. A wave of heat comes over me, and if I wasn't sitting down, I'd need to right now.

Jason doesn't relent, though. He keeps going.

"You woke up parts of me that were slumbering, and you make me want to be a better person every day. Will you marry me? Spend the rest of your life with me?" He pulls out a ring carved in intricate detail. A ring fit for a fantasy world. He can't hide that his hand is shaking, and I watch the ring tremble in the air.

This overwhelming sense of euphoria overtakes me, and I'm hyperaware of my body. How close Jason is to me.

How much I adore this man.

I want to burst into tears. But I have to seal the deal first. "You know there's no way in hell I'll ever turn you down, wifey-poo."

His green eyes shine. "That's a yes?"

I beam, then squeal, taking the ring and putting it on my finger. "That's definitely a yes."

Jason presses his palms to his eyes and lets out a shaky laugh. "Thank fuck."

"No, thank Murph." I wink, but I'm trembling all over.

He laughs. "Yes, babe. Thank you."

And he leans in and kisses me, his tongue darting out to tangle with mine. The world goes soft and tilted, and I realize he's picked me up and is taking me to our bed.

Time slows down, and I'm noticing all the details of my boyfriend. Er—*fiancé*. The stubble on his jaw and the way I feel in his strong arms. The way he smells clean and how soft his clothes are.

How safe and whole I am with him.

He sets me down and proceeds to tear off my shoes, then rip off my socks, and I can't hold back a giddy laugh.

"So it's gonna be like that," I say saucily. "A caveman-style fuck?"

The look on his face is one of determination, brow furrowed and jaw set. Then he relaxes into the goofiest lovey-dovey face I've ever seen. His voice drops so I can barely hear it. "You bring out the best parts of me and the most basic needs. And you meet all of them."

"I *love* them."

His fingers fumble with my jeans, and they're off. Along with my shirt. Soon I'm wearing nothing but a lime-green jock.

Jason looms over me, shaking his head. "Jesus, Murph. When the hell did you get this?"

I pretend to think about it. "Last St. Patrick's Day."

He chuckles. "I don't know if it's horrible or if it's utterly amazing."

"Do you want to fuck me in it?" I ask, turning onto my side.

A long breath escapes him. "Do you have to ask?"

I give him a playful shove, then tug him closer. "Then let's go with you thinking it's utterly amazing."

"Sounds good to me."

His shirt somehow disappears, and he's naked and over me and I am so squirmy and happy. I want to rub myself all over him, and he knows it.

He kisses me again. "You're gonna be my husband. You good with that?"

"So good," I sing. "And I don't just mean what your hand is doing right now."

He chuckles. "Thank fuck."

"*Please* fuck." My body is tingling all over, and I'm not sorry to be begging. I can think of no better way to show him how I feel than to have him as close to me as he can get.

"Will do," he promises.

Jason reaches over for the lube, but I tilt up and show him the plug. "I'm ready for you."

He throws his head back to the ceiling and groans. "Fuck. You are perfect."

Sometimes when I get excited, I babble. And get impatient. "Lover, I know this. But it's time for you to show it, okay, big guy?"

"Absolutely."

He enters me swiftly, and I shudder with pleasure. "Don't wait," I say. "Keep pushing." He thrusts all the way in, and we pause, connected.

In love.

"I love you."

"I love you, too."

Jason's big body covers me. He holds me and caresses me, making me feel horny and loved, safe and dangerous, sated and insatiable.

"With you," I say, "I feel whole."

"Likewise."

"I'm so glad you figured out you weren't straight."

He throws back his head and laughs and fucks me, and all is well in my world.

THE
END

ACKNOWLEDGMENTS

Some authors base their books on classic stories like *Pride and Prejudice* or *Beauty and the Beast*. I chose a more modern fairytale: a viral Gay Star News article about a Redditor worried he was homophobic because he was a jerk to his gay roommate's dates. If you're familiar with the article, well, yes, that's the match that sparked the fire of this story. Thank you, anonymous Redditor, for being my inspiration and also to the author of the article for finding the romance.

Special extra gratitude to Sarina Bowen for taking a chance on me and for creating such a rich world for us to play in. You inspire me to step up my game. Thank you to Jane Bush Haertel for helping with the outline and being a cheerleader. I'm also so appreciative of the organized, efficient, and helpful support for the series from Jenn Gaffney and Natasha Leskiw.

I am surrounded by astonishingly good people who help me so much. Thank you to Mary Carr for stepping outside your comfort zone and giving me your spot-on insight. Kristy Lin Billuni—I can't thank you enough for your help with characters, story, and giving me permission to let Murph be OTT. Lex Martin, girl, I love you. Your tweaks made it better.

I had the luxury of working with the incredible editor Alicia Z.

Ramos (who has not seen these acknowledgments, so any grammar issues are mine). Simply stated, I could not have asked for a better editor for this project had I asked the Universe to custom-tailor one for me. You are amazing.

Thank you to my many beta readers who are fearless. Bottom line: the fact that you're unafraid to give me your honest opinions makes my work better. Thank you to Deb Markanton, Phala Theng, Julia Heudorf, Melissa Williams, and Michell Hall Casper. I'm also thanking Mary Carr again. Yes, she's in here twice.

Katy Cuthbertson deserves a special shoutout for her unwavering support and enthusiasm. Thank you so much for cheering me up on so many occasions as well as the scribbles from your electronic pen. Yes, Murph can be your best friend.

Jerica MacMillan always has my back. I'm extremely grateful for our friendship. And for your proofing.

Virginia Tesi Carey—thank you so much for your careful eye and giving me the confidence to turn it in.

Thank you to Heather Roberts for calming me down, picking me up, and packaging me. Much appreciation to Christine Frieseke-Miller for organizing me.

Thank you to all of the other True North authors, but especially Marley Valentine, Garrett Leigh, Jay Hogan, Annabeth Albert, Kim Hartfield, Kate Hawthorne, and Regina Kyle, who gave me feedback on early drafts and who were so generous with letting me use their characters.

Thank you to Cory Stierley and Joshua Alexander for taking a hot cover photo. Thank you to cover designer Christine Coffey for making it work.

Thank you to my long-suffering husband who only asked me two or three times, "When are you going to be done with this book so we can see you?" Given the deep dive I took for this book, that is remarkable restraint.

And all my love to my children. May you grow up to be exactly the people you wish to be.

Made in United States
North Haven, CT
03 September 2022